"Put your helmet on! Grit, grease, and fast-paced futuristic action, complete with hardbitten women throwing energy boomerangs while speeding on motorcycles, makes this a riveting ride."

    Cat Rambo, Nebula nominee and president of SFWA

"High octane and hard hitting. *Daughters of Forgotten Light* is exactly what I want from sci-fi: badass women getting it done… with unapologetic grindhouse glam."

    KC Alexander, author of Necrotech *and* Mass Effect: Andromeda: Nexus Uprising

"Grab your energy boomerang and get ready for a wild ride! Grigsby's latest book is a full-throttle nightmarish sci-fi *Mad Max: Fury Road*. It's violent, intense, and packed with passion as exiled women fight for their very right to exist."

    Beth Cato, Nebula nominee and author of Breath of Earth

"Another opportunity for Grigsby to deliver on a brilliant concept – in this case, a sci-fi thriller than blends the righteous anger of *Bitch Planet* with the crackerjack action thrills of *Escape from New York*."

    Barnes & Noble Sci-Fi & Fantasy Blog

"A fun, fast, foul-mouthed thrill ride with more than its share of real surprises and pathos."

    Spencer Ellsworth, author of A Red Peace

"An ingenious premise that Grigsby delivers on with intelligence and style. *Smoke Eaters* is a treat!"

    Jason M Hough, New York Times *Bestseller*

"I've been waiting for a book like this for years. Original, exciting, *Smoke Eaters* is a red-hot page-turner."

    Adam Christopher, author of Empire State *and* Made to Kill

"Sean Grigsby has conceived what promises to be a brilliant and harrowing series. Dragons have returned, bringing fire, revenant spirits and ash in their wake. Cole Brannigan, a grizzled no nonsense fire-fighter, is there to stand in their way. Profane and exhilarating, filled with unforgettable characters and scorching action, *Smoke Eaters* is an amazing mix of adventure, fantasy, and science-fiction. Grigsby is an electrifying new voice sounding out over the wraith-haunted land."

John Hornor Jacobs, award-winning author of Southern Gods *and* The Incorruptibles

"*Smoke Eaters* is a thrilling, exciting, funny and strangely heart-warming book, and Grigsby's experience as a firefighter shines through on every page, lending grit and realism to this rollicking ride of a tale in which firefighters become dragon-slayers. It's exactly as bonkers and as brilliant as you'd expect and I look forward to more from this author."

Anna Stephens, author of Godblind

"An exciting story that breathes new life into the urban fantasy genre."

Publishers Weekly, starred review

"This smoking debut is a shot of adrenaline to the urban fantasy genre. Grigsby's knowledge of firefighting combined with hot dragon action and blistering humor create an irresistible romp of a read."

Jaye Wells, USA Today *Bestselling author of the* Prospero's War series

"This red-hot debut will torch off all your skin and leave you in the burn ward. The skin grafts won't take, and you'll die of a massive infection after an agonizing month of pain unlike anything you can imagine. Also dragons."

Patrick S Tomlinson, author of Gatecrashers *and* Children of the Divide

"I love dragon stories in which the dragons are real monsters, laying waste to everything around them; and I love novels with protagonists who aren't callow young adults learning that they're chosen ones. *Smoke Eaters* has terrific dragons, and a hero with some miles and experience on him, plus great writing and a wicked sense of humor. I flew through it."

Alex Bledsoe, author of The Hum and the Shiver
and Burn Me Deadly

"Firefighters vs Dragons. If that doesn't immediately catch your attention or even just make you curious then we can't be friends."

Off the TBR

"This book had everything I never knew I wanted. It's action-packed and humorous, yet not afraid to slow down and be reflective every once in a while. *Smoke Eaters* by Sean Grigsby is a fantasy novel that does practically everything right. 5 stars from me."

The Fantasy Inn

"Read while listening to a thunderous thrash-metal playlist."

Financial Times

"A successful action thriller. By the time you've finished *Smoke Eaters* you'll be searching the ground and skies for potential hazards, and seeing political conspiracies around every corner."

Strange Alliances

"This book has so many elements that I love. You've got a cast of characters, with attitude and mild superpowers, who are up against ancient monsters, robots and a corrupt government. Seriously, what's not to enjoy?"

Purple Owl Reviews

By the same author

Smoke Eaters

SEAN GRIGSBY

DAUGHTERS *of* FORGOTTEN LIGHT

ANGRY
ROBOT

ANGRY ROBOT
An imprint of Watkins Media Ltd

20 Fletcher Gate,
Nottingham,
NG1 2FZ
UK

angryrobotbooks.com
twitter.com/angryrobotbooks
Unforgettable

An Angry Robot paperback original 2018

Cover by John Coulthart
Set in Meridien by Argh! Nottingham

Distributed in the United States by Penguin Random House, Inc., New York.

ISBN 978 0 85766 795 3
Ebook ISBN 978 0 85766 796 0

Printed in the United States of America

9 8 7 6 5 4 3 2 1

For Lisa,
if I forgot everything I knew,
you'd still be on my mind.

CHAPTER 1

That's one thing they never told Lena Horror about space –
how damn dark it is. Her gang sped down the glowing glass
streets of Oubliette, but it was only a tease of light, false and
too dim for comfort.

Their cyclone motorcycles didn't exactly have wheels,
even though Grindy had always called them that. They
were round like wheels, they spun like wheels, but the
bikes hovered on swirling circles of blazing light. Pretty as
Christmas in Hell and three times as hot.

No wind blew on Oubliette, but Lena wasn't about to let
that stop her. If she just went fast enough the illusion of
wind could be created. She adored feeling her hair *thwap*
against the back of her shoulders and tickle her ears, the
flapping brown strands a lot louder than the low hum of
two-wheeled death between her legs. But most of all, she
liked how the cyclones lit up the city, piercing the shadows
and letting everyone know, when they saw blue light
bouncing off the buildings, the Daughters of Forgotten
Light were coming.

Always traveling in a V formation, they rode five strong
now. Only a month before it had been six. Even missing a
rider, their bikes took up the street's width and anyone in

their path had better move or get run down. Riding like that, each Daughter was at another's side. If another gang shot at them from behind, they had more chance of seeing it coming, or at least one of the sheilas in the back could scream an alert before the rest of the Daughters got blasted.

There was a truce on, wasn't there? Truce or no, Lena wasn't about to drop her guard. Lena told herself a leader shouldn't question her own decisions, just like those under her shouldn't challenge them. Did they think paranoia had her all fucked up? This was still Oubliette, and trust had long gone extinct.

"The shipment just came through the Hole," Hurley Girly shouted from Lena's right. Her blond pigtails bounced as she whipped her head up, looking to where the box hurtled toward them like a meteor.

Shit. Lena could have spit if she didn't think one of her gang would have caught it in the face.

Beyond Oubliette's towering buildings, outside the city's green, fabricated atmosphere – the Veil – the quarterly shipment jetted from the space gate. The Veil made Oubliette a sprawling roach motel. Whatever came in never went out, and that included all the stale air, and all the sorry sheilas confined to the city.

Lena had watched every shipment entry over the last ten years. That made her – she always had to take a minute to remember – twenty-seven. The other Daughters were only a few years younger, except for Hurley Girly, who'd turned twenty the last quarter.

The shipment was the same metal box it always was, coming from Earth with the same fanfare. Emptiness and starlight filled the circle made by an oversized, ivory gate

– the Hole – and then *snap*, a new shipment came through with a couple thrusters to guide it. A million miles cut out of the trip, so the shipment could reach its eternity quicker. At least, that's how hyper drive was explained to them before they left Earth.

Faster, damn it!

Lena leaned into her cyclone, but she had her bike at full speed and all tapped out of patience. She just had to ride. The street curved round into a ramp that rose between the upper floors of two adjacent buildings then dipped into a steep drop. The downward slope helped, but the shipment neared and, fuck it all, they were late. It was the only disadvantage of claiming territory across the Sludge River and far away from the main thoroughfares, where trouble always waited.

Above the Daughters, the shipment broke through the Veil and green static sizzled around the descending metal, waves rippling outward toward the horizon like digital gelatin until the expanse settled again.

Two klicks still separated them from the receiving stage.

"They're not taking this from us," Lena shouted. "We've got first pick this time."

Someone was waiting for them at the bottom of the ramp, a dark shape against a dark canvas, save the minuscule lights scattered throughout the dwellers' buildings. Their unexpected guest had been leaning against her cyclone when the Daughters rounded the curve, but now she jumped onto her bike.

For a millisecond, a quiver in time, Lena considered slowing the gang behind her. But that would mean more seconds lost and the first choice of the delivery going to another gang. Worse, it would show weakness. Lena ground her teeth and let the false wind push her hair back. The bitch at the bottom of the ramp would have to make way or get flat.

The mystery woman lit up her cyclone – orange wheels. Amazon colors.

Those cheeky....

It wasn't enough that just a few quarters ago – before the truce – the Amazons had been hunting down dwellers under the Daughters' protection, butchering them in alleys and leaving behind the parts they didn't have a taste for. Now, they'd left one of their own behind to fuck with Lena and her gang.

This Amazon was the scrawny one, the one with the busted teeth Ava gave her for making cracks about her Down syndrome. Even in the low glow of the glass street, Lena could tell it was her. The Amazon didn't try to run. By the looks of it, she controlled her speed to stay at Lena's right side.

Lena gripped her cyclone's handles and smiled, wide and crazy. The rushing air dried the inside of her mouth. *Try it. I want you to. Raise your arm and give me a reason. Please.*

The rang gun on Lena's forearm pulsed to the same beat as her blood, begging to be discharged. When had she shot it last? Long ago enough to have flashing delusions she'd never fired it at all, like how aging hookers-turned-nuns could convince themselves they'd always been virgins.

Lena raised her left hand above her head, shaping it as straight as a shark fin, keeping her eyes bobbing from the street ahead, to the Amazon at her right, then back. The Daughters' wheels sparked and hummed in a slightly different octave. She didn't have to look. Her sheilas changed formation, gathering in a line behind her.

The Amazon's hair stood straight in a long mohawk. The streaks of purple and red staining the strands looked like a chemical fire in the glow of her cyclone's wheels. The colorful sludge the Amazons put in their hair was just one of the specialty items commissioned from Grindy – one of the reasons the Amazons didn't try to kill everyone and take over Oubliette. Lena thought the mohawk would make an excellent trophy when she cut it off at the scalp, brought it back to the ganghouse, and glued it to a wall.

But that damned truce. It ruined Lena's fantasies as quickly as they came. She knew it was for the best in the end. A means to create some form of order in the chaotic city. Still.

Do it, you twat.

The Amazon made no motion to raise her weaponed arm; only scrunched her face in a disdainful frown. A burn scar ran from her left cheek, down her neck, and then farther into the dark of her jacket. She was trying hard to keep her mouth squeezed shut, hiding the fucked-up grill.

Ahead, maybe a klick or less, the lights for the shipment receiving stage blasted on. The shipment, that big box of metal, hovered above the stage as if it had met the resistance of an invisible pillow. Slowly, it came down.

As much as Lena couldn't stand the mohawked Amazon's ugly mug, it became worse when she tilted her head and smirked. It was the eyes, twitching with secrets. *I know something you don't.* Lena's own grin faltered and she had to squeeze the cyclone handles to refrain from shooting her rang into the smug bitch's throat.

The Amazon zipped left, swerving into Lena's path, causing every Daughter to slow.

Angry shouts from her gang; Lena cut into the other side of the road. The Daughters followed in exact movement. Babies following mommy ducky. Lena regained her speed and cruised alongside the Amazon, whose frown had returned.

Lena laughed into the fake wind. So that was it. *Have one of your cannibal ass-plungers stay behind and slow us down, huh?*

"Put a rang in her ass, Lena!" Ava's voice could carry over any machine and always sounded clear and enunciated. Her tact was a different matter.

They neared the receiving stage. If the cyclones were more like motorcycles on Earth, the roar of the engines could have announced their impending arrival, but with the low hum of their bikes the Daughters had to rely on speed.

Lena raised her unarmed fist to the Amazon and extended a very direct middle finger. The cannibal widened her eyes and huffed from swelled cheeks. To make the insult dance at the edge of injury, Lena tapped the same finger against her bared, fully-intact teeth.

The Amazon snarled, giving Lena a fantastic view of what few teeth Ava had left inside the cannibal's mouth. The orange of her cyclone wheels only reflected against a tooth or three. The rest of her mouth was as dark and barren as the rest of Oubliette. The Amazon swerved again, this time not speeding ahead first. She zoomed straight for Lena.

A ramp came up on their right. Lena took it. Had to. The stage disappeared behind a black building and whatever ground they had gained now dwindled farther behind them.

The Amazon came along, staying close to Lena's left. The Daughters berated the Amazon with an unfiltered assault of four-letter words and shouts of, "Truce-breaker!" and "That counts! Let it fly!"

"You trying to get killed?" Lena asked the Amazon.

That counted. She attacked you with her cyclone. That's an offense. What other reason do you need?

The Amazon laughed in her own gruff, self-satisfied way. She'd done her job. And even if the Daughters of Forgotten Light were to stop and reverse course, they'd lost time. The Amazon would surely follow them, too, a mosquito in the ear. Not that Oubliette had any insects. It had enough pests already. Well, this bug ached for a squishing, and Lena wanted to give it another stretch of road, give the Amazon another chance to make an offense, something Lena couldn't argue away as a misdemeanor. What was another lost minute?

Draw your rang, Lena. Do it. Blast that glorious ball of light and send her off her bike.

Grindy's voice kept coming up to put a lid on the boiling pot of Lena's wrath. "The truce is the best thing to happen to this place since they started dropping every motherless child through the Veil," Lena could hear her say. "I'd do my damnedest to keep to it."

Damn it!

Lena raised her left fist. And the cavalcade slowed. They turned round, leaving the Amazon to hover off into the dark, and headed back toward Oubliette's center, the receiving stage.

"You should have done it," Hurley Girly said.

"We're late." Lena ground her teeth, wanting to scream.

She was about to signal them to return to the V formation, an ironic two-fingered peace sign, when a sparking noise rose from behind. Lena looked over her shoulder. The Amazon was back.

Yes!

No. They had no time for this distraction. They'd been short on supplies for weeks, not to mention the lack of a sixth Daughter. Lena would just have to ignore the Amazon and get to the drop. There'd be plenty of time for retribution later.

They came to the ramp that arched over the Sludge River, where Oubliette's fecal waste flowed, when the Amazon returned to Lena's side. With a sneer, she gave Lena a return on her universal "fuck you."

But the dumb bitch must have thought more about the "doing" than the way to do it. She'd used her *right* hand. The rang gun, strapped to the forearm, was pointed at Lena's head. Lena reacted. The pot had boiled over. Her body gave her no time to deduce what really happened, and it didn't matter. With her left hand, Lena snapped the handle back, killing the front wheel, and leaned forward with every ounce.

Aided by a lower gravity, Lena and the cyclone, both together in one kamikaze package, soared into the air in a somersault. She laughed rabidly as it happened, not just for the thrill of going airborne, but for the release, the removal of the truce's crushing formality.

The cyclone dropped on top of the Amazon. There may have been a blip of a scream but the rest of the noise was snapping and searing, bones breaking, flesh burning, and the cannibal's cyclone crumpling under the weight and heat of Lena's blue wheels. Lena almost flew off her bike as the cyclone buzzed and tottered over the wreckage, careening toward the edge of the bridge before she remembered to jolt the dead side of the wheels back to life.

Free of the debris, Lena spun in a circle. To the rest of the Daughters, it must have looked like a celebratory doughnut, but they didn't have much time to gander. The line of cyclones split, dodging the mess Lena had left in the street.

"Holy fuck!" Dipity, who, even though third in command, always insisted on riding caboose, hadn't seen what happened after Lena's short aerial journey. She swerved her cyclone to the right with dark-skinned, muscled arms. After avoiding the pile of metal and meat, she looked back to it every other second, as if trying to decipher what had happened.

The Daughters circled around Lena in an impromptu huddle.

Lena stared at the dead Amazon over Ava and Hurley Girly's shoulders and giggled. Then frowned. "Shit."

"Truce is broken," Dipity said.

Ava nodded. "She raised the rang."

"What was with the fucking flip?" Hurley Girly thumbed back to the wreck, putting her amusement on full display with a big grin.

Sterling, their fifth, hand-signed something so quick Lena couldn't catch it.

"Swallow your words, ladies," Lena said. "This didn't happen."

Ava began to object. "But–"

"Grindy's right about this truce," said Lena. "And that

pile back there can muck it all up."

They stared at Lena. The cyclones buzzed beneath them. Sweat beaded on Dipity's forehead.

"You wanna go back to before?" Lena asked. "One of us dying every week? Having to keep our supplies under lock and key? Getting dragged off and eaten by one of those shitheads," Lena nodded toward the Amazon, "if a straggler got cornered? No fucking thank you, ma'am. We got to keep things nice and orderly."

"But now we can have war, right?" Ava's peanut-brown hair hung over an eye.

"Maybe," Lena said. "But that's more chance to die. And I still plan on flying out of this dump."

The other Daughters traded glances. Sterling looked to the Veil above, probably fighting the urge to roll her eyes. Lena remembered when they used to laugh as she'd tell them of her escape plans. She'd let it slide since they went along with the many failed attempts to turn a shipment box into an escape ship. Now that Lena was leader of the gang, her pipe dream didn't seem to be so funny to them anymore.

"I've got it," Hurley Girly said. "I know why Lena got sent here. She was a serial killer."

Shaking her head, Dipity said, "Like she'd admit to that, even if it was true."

"This isn't the time for your stupid bet," Lena said. Then, after a silent moment had passed, "But no, goddamn it. That's not why."

Hurley Girly kicked the ground, mumbling a few swears. She'd have to put another manna loaf into the pot for guessing wrong.

Dipity cleared her throat. "So what do we do, Head Horror?"

Lena looked over the side of the overpass, down to the Sludge. It coursed through the glass river banks like rotten molasses. "Toss her over, whatever is left. It'll look like she crashed."

Ava shot her left hand into the air. "Not it."

"We all do this," Lena said.

They each grabbed a chunk of the Amazon. Ava and Lena shared the weight of what they guessed was a torso, while the others grabbed a severed arm or foot. The head must have flown over the side when Lena came down on her. It didn't even feel like pieces of a human being. They were just warm, squishy objects that smelled mildly like pork steaks sizzling on a grill. It had been a long time since Lena had eaten meat, and she was disgusted to find her mouth watering. She could almost sympathize with the cannibal mentality. Her stomach heaved, and she almost vomited the little bit of manna she'd swallowed before they left the ganghouse. She and Ava tossed the torso over, but the river lay too far down to hear a splash.

All five of them pushed the wrecked cyclone to the edge of the road, against the glass overpass where they'd ditched the Amazon's remains. From there, they sped toward the crowd gathering round the quarterly shipment, freshly sent from Earth, a place none of them were meant to see again.

Faster! Lena pressed.

They were late.

CHAPTER 2

Lena and her gang shut down their cyclones. The throbbing wheels faded and the chassis eased to the ground.

"I know we don't have clocks or watches here," Grindy said low, as she approached and rested against the front of Lena's cyclone, "but don't you think it's a little hard to miss a spaceship breaking through the Veil? Even some of these blind sheilas could *hear* it!"

An older dweller helped a cloudy-eyed sheila past, the blind one reaching out with her left hand.

Grindy flinched when she spotted them, widened her eyes. "No offense."

"She's right!" the blind dweller shouted, and moved deeper into the crowd.

Somewhere close to fifty, Grindy was older than the rest of them. Probably one of the oldest in Oubliette, which said something. She swung stocky hips on a short frame, but Lena would've never called her chunky. If anyone got fat in this city, they'd be blasted and accused of stealing food, in that order. Wrinkles and scars decorated Grindy's tough Latina face, but it'd been a long time since anyone could tell which was which.

She stood at the bottom of the receiving stage, in front

of the area designated for the Daughters of Forgotten Light. Dwellers shuffled at the sides of the waiting area, staring at the still-closed shipment or fighting for a better view. The streets Lena had left behind were a monastery compared to the bustling and shouting at the center of the city. Every damn dweller in Oubliette must have been there. Lena only knew a few of them outside those dwelling in her territory, and she'd never tried counting. It wasn't like the gangs took a census, and the Amazons were aggressive in hiding their numbers. But there had to be hundreds there at the stage, maybe a little over a thousand.

"Had some engine trouble." Lena swung a leg over the seat. *That's one way to put it.*

Grindy nodded. "Bring it by later. I'll take a look at it."

"I think we have her fixed," Lena said. "But I appreciate an extra eye."

"Anyway," Grindy flicked her hand, "I fought them to wait long enough for you to still get first pick."

"I owe you one," Lena said.

"Then that puts your tab at about a thousand you owe me." Grindy winked and stomped up the stairs to the stage.

Lena led the Daughters to the front of the multitude. Giant, black columns rising from the stage radiated a piercing blue light against the sides of the shipment. The box's jets hissed as they cooled, frothing steam at the back. It was just a big box. No pilot. No windows to see into, or out of.

The other gangs waited at either side of the Daughters in their respective areas. The Onyx Coalition stood to the left. An all-black gang, the OC had failed to charm Dipity over to their ranks. Lena had never asked if it was intentional that they were all the same race. Maybe it was just a coincidence, like how all the cannibals were white.

To the right, the Amazons waited. Farica Altstadt, their head, sat on the cold frame of her cyclone, cleaning the front of her teeth with a finger. Unlike the other Amazons, she refrained from the mohawk look, and opted instead for spiky mounds that resembled an inhabitable red planet on top of her head.

"We should have skipped your turn, Horowitz." Farica squinted one eye, aiming with fatal intent.

"Piss off," Lena said.

Farica's raised cheek twitched. She looked around the crowd and to the four Amazons behind her.

Missing someone? Lena pocketed her hands and choked down a laugh, staring at the glass below her feet.

Whispered words danced among the Amazons. One nodded and rode her cyclone out of the crowd, into the dark of the outlying streets. Farica turned back. She'd replaced the squinty eye with a leashed rage that weighed down the length of her cherubic face.

"I'm sorry, Horror," she said. "Fair is fair."

Lena really wanted to spit again.

"I feel like a damn broken record having to say all this every quarter," Grindy addressed the crowd. "But I know how you simpletons will forget everything I say as soon as the words leave my mouth, so here we go."

The dwellers looked on. They just wanted the box opened.

Shamika Caruthers, head of the Onyx Coalition, folded her arms and waited just like the rest. She reeked of attitude. The slight curl in her lips was all it took for anyone to know she gave the least amount of shit anyone in the prison city could. Lena envied it.

"The Daughters are down one," Grindy said. "That means they get first pick."

Groans from the Amazons. Silence from the OC.

Grindy continued. "After that, they'll pick which gang goes next. As if we don't already know who that's going to be."

Shamika nodded to Lena, who returned it.

"The last gang picks. We divide the food up. The Amazons have their business, and then we can all go home and get on with our lives until next quarter. Does anyone not understand this?"

A few hands shot up from the dwellers.

Grindy huffed and rolled her eyes, ignoring the raised hands. "Let's get on with it, then."

She dug out the shimmering card she kept on a necklace and shuffled over to the shipment, where she pulled out a small touchpad at the side. The glow from the touchpad's screen shone onto the crevices covering Grindy's face, reminding Lena of times around a camp fire, flashlight beaming under chin. Time for a scary story.

Grindy's card fit against the screen. A small chirp later and the door lowered like a ramp. Dwellers began to shove and grumble, an anthill kicked. Containers crammed the shipment, all gray and about the same size. The manna inside bore the same color as the boxes and was just as tasteless. But that wasn't really what everyone wanted to get a look at. In the center of the shipment container, more than a dozen girls stood huddled.

"Come on out," Grindy said to them when the door had

completely dropped. "No need to worry."

Lena sighed.

They looked like beaten puppies, even the ones who tried to pull off a "don't fuck with me" demeanor. In old films of concentration camps receiving new prisoners, or in more recent media of the illegal immigrant interstellar deportation, they'd all been weatherbeaten and dirty. But these girls were spotless, scrubbed free of any smudge – by force, from Lena's recollection – all wearing those ugly white shippee uniforms.

Has it really been ten years? Lena wondered.

"Line up, please." Grindy extended her left hand to the front of the stage. "As best as you can, anyway."

"Is the war over?" a dweller shouted.

"Who won the Super Bowl?" asked another.

"Please, God, tell me one of you brought some Tampax."

"Shut up!" Grindy said. "All of you. You can get your questions answered by going to your gang's right arm."

Lena had her own questions. *Is legislation moving to abolish Oubliette? When can we go home?*

The new arrivals shuffled into a crooked line. Each of them carried objects of varying size, single selected items to bring with them for their last days rotting in another galaxy. Here, a guitar in the hands of a thin shippee with wet eyes. There, a paralyzed girl in a wheelchair clutching a Bible, probably with the hope she'd find comfort in its pages. At the end of the line, a young woman cradled a bundle wrapped in black cloth like a baby.

"You're up." Grindy nodded to Lena.

The heft of Lena's boots thudded against the steps leading onto the receiving stage, then clanged when they reached the lowered metal shipment door. The shippees shivered under her gaze. Lena could never get used to that antiseptic smell they always brought with them, the kind of fumes you'd inhale when making out with your boyfriend in a janitor's closet or visiting grandma in hospice.

She appraised each of them. The Daughters couldn't use anyone too young – easily moldable, but too much to teach. They'd be too small to ride a cyclone anyway. Someone older, yes. Not one of the lot was over eighteen. None of them ever were, but Lena would try to get as close to that age as she could. Grindy once told Lena there used to be older shippees, all criminals, but that had stopped almost a quarter century ago. Oubliette was the best crime deterrent that had ever been invented.

Lena came to an Asian shippee with blue hair. This one didn't tremble – not her body anyway. You could always see it in the eyes, though, and hers, dark and coiled like a pressurized Slinky, were a textbook case. Still, she was trying.

"Shipper guards couldn't scrub out your hair dye?" Lena asked.

"It's a dope job."

"You injected yourself with that gene shit? Just for blue hair?"

Blue Hair swallowed, but didn't answer. She was smart, knew when not to talk.

Lena regarded her empty arms. "Didn't bring anything with you?"

"This," the shippee said. She raised her right hand – there was an automatic tremor of anxiety through the crowd behind – and flaunted brass knuckles.

Lena grinned. "Interesting." She eased Blue Hair's hand back down. Nodded. "The guards never let us keep weapons."

"They stole it from me at first. But it was the only thing I wanted to take. A guard slipped it to me before the launch. He had a crush on me."

"You give him a handy or something?"

She wrinkled her face in disgust. "Why would he have helped me if he'd already gotten what he wanted?"

Lena laughed.

Among Bibles and guitars, this one knew she'd be in for a fight. There'd be no comfort on Oubliette, only pain and, if you weren't wise and rough enough, death. She came prepared.

Lena moved to the next girl in line but stopped and turned back to the one with the brass knuckles and blue hair. "What's your name?"

"Sarah Pao."

Lena nodded again, committing it to memory.

Pow like a comic book punch. Looks like we have a frontrunner.

The next was probably ten years old. A pretty little girl, blonde-haired and soft-cheeked. She had her arms curled into her chest and chewed on her fingernails. When Lena smiled down at her as she passed her by, the girl began to scream, howling unformed words. She slapped herself repeatedly. Red marks appeared on her cheeks, across the bridge of her nose. Lena grabbed her arms. The little girl fought her at first, but soon calmed down into quiet moans.

"You going to let a toddler kick your ass, Horowitz?" Farica laughed, and her cannibals laughed with her.

"She's been doing that the whole way here," the one next

in line said, annoyed. The little girl tried to grab onto her neighbor's leg and cry into it, but the taller shippee kicked her away.

Lena scoffed through her nose and skipped over the rude older twat to the next in line. The slap-happy little girl was probably autistic, and her parents had decided they couldn't handle her. A shame. The older shippee dropped her mouth like she knew she'd fucked up in some way, but couldn't figure out how.

The next one looked the oldest, the one with the bundle wrapped in cloth. She wobbled from side to side as if she might faint. Her skin held little color, pale even by sunless Oubliette standards. Her eyes said, "What the hell have I come to?" She didn't realize that's exactly where she'd come.

"So what's your–"

The bundle cried.

At first Lena thought it might have been the mewling of a cat or even, God forbid, a ferret. But, no. It was distinctly human. A baby. Lena reached for the cloth. The girl pulled away from her, but that just pissed Lena off.

"Hey!" Lena kicked the girl's shin.

Pale Girl dropped to a knee, clutching the bundle as Lena opened the blanket. The baby inside had beautiful black skin and tiny, peachy palms that reached out as she stirred and croaked those whimpers of hunger Lena thought she'd never hear again. Not outside dreams. Nightmares. The baby girl couldn't have been more than two or three months old.

Like a distant radio message thrown across space, after a delay the crowd became aware of the bundle's contents. "A baby!" a dweller shouted. "They're sending anyone now," said another.

The pale girl brought the baby back to her chest. "Please, don't take her. I made a promise."

"She yours?"

Silence.

"Did you steal her?" Lena asked.

"No." Pale Girl shook her head, tears flicking off her cheeks. "Given."

Lena believed her. *Damn it.*

If the child wasn't hers, then whose? What terrible, soulless, donkey-fucking dishrag of a mother would send their infant to Oubliette?

Lena turned back to the crowd, her gang, the OC, the Amazons. Shamika fought quiet word battles with her left leg, her fourth-in-command. The subordinate looked like she'd been cheated out of a poker game and was ready to do some rang shooting. No doubt, Shamika had gotten a good look at the baby, and might have considered killing one of her own to open up a spot in the gang. It wasn't technically against the truce to kill your own gang members. At the other end of the stage, Farica licked her lips, squinting with both eyes now. Lena didn't like it. It meant the cannibal was thinking.

The Amazon envoy returned on her cyclone and whispered into Farica's ear. So, the time had come. Lena imagined what had crossed that mohawked mind when she'd come upon the wreckage above the Sludge River. Did she figure it had been a horrible accident? Just a bad day for one of their purple-haired people eaters?

If Lena was a betting woman, and she was, she'd venture

that Farica would find a way to seek vengeance on the Daughters whether they'd truly killed one of her Amazons or not. It just happened that this time she'd be guessing right.

Keep playing it off. When you bury something, you make sure it stays that way.

Farica's reaction chilled the back of Lena's neck. The head Amazon nodded at what her third-in-command told her, relaxed onto her cyclone, and smiled, staring at the pale girl rocking the cranky kid. Lena liked this even less. No, not one bit.

"Everybody needs to calm down," Grindy called out to the masses. "Granted, this is something we're not used to seeing."

Good. Grindy would see that the pale girl and the baby would be escorted away. No need in them staying around for this. For what came after. They could interrogate the girl and find out why in fuck the government would allow a baby to be sent up here.

"But it changes nothing," Grindy said.

Lena nearly choked. "What?"

Grindy held out her arms, as if in defense, as if she couldn't do anything about this. "The terms of the truce stand, Lena. Now pick a replacement for your gang or some other item in the box, and get off the damn stage."

Lena sensed a quiver in Grindy's mouth after she'd said it. It pained the older woman as well, but the truce was the truce, and she was determined to see it stand.

"Let me talk to my ladies." Lena stomped down the steps and waved her hand for the Daughters to huddle around her.

"Who are you thinking?" Dipity asked. "That one with the brass knuckles?"

"She's cute," Hurley Girly said with an impish smile. "I could use some blue hair between my legs."

They glared at her. Sterling shook her head.

"What?" Hurley Girly shrugged.

Lena dropped her head and sighed. "That baby."

The other Daughters groaned.

"I won't be able to live with myself if that baby dies," Lena said. "If one of those fuckers eats her."

I won't lose another one.

"They aren't *that* bad," Ava said.

Everyone stared at her until she nodded, knowing that wasn't true.

Dipity released a tight breath. She always saw these situations as purely business. Just another decisive act on the streets. Survival, nothing more. "We need someone who can ride."

"We don't have the shit we need to take care of a baby neither," said Hurley Girly. She opened her mouth to say something else, but, instead shook her head and looked outside their huddle.

Sterling placed a firm hand on Lena's shoulder. With her big nose shadowed in the blue stage lights, she looked like a gargoyle, ever watchful, ever silent. Lena didn't know what to make of her gesture, didn't want to sign to find out. She'd probably say the same thing. They couldn't take the baby.

Lena tore from their huddle and launched at her cyclone. She kicked, slamming her foot into the dark metal, screaming to high hell. "Goddamn it!"

Across from her, Farica laughed again.

"Hey, Horror!' Shamika waved her over.

Lena limped with her sore foot to where the OC stirred like bottled lightning. None of Shamika's gang looked too happy. They shook their heads, huffed, and made statements under their breath for no one but the Devil to hear.

"I've got a proposition for you," Shamika said.

"Yeah?"

Shamika tensed her brow, tightened her jaw. It must have been pretty painful for someone usually so brash to hold back for the sake of getting what she wanted. To her, the kid going to anyone besides the Onyx Coalition would be just as unholy as letting the Amazons gobble her up.

"A trade," Shamika said. The words could have been vomit the way she squirmed as they came out.

"What do I have that you want?" Lena knew what Shamika had in mind, but drawing out this torturous event might give her the half second she needed to come up with a valid solution.

Shamika rubbed her face, quick and hard. "Pick the baby. I'll trade you one of my gang."

One of the OC, the one with the big hair, spit and cursed. Lena knew how she felt. The spitter was the gang's ass, the lowest on the totem pole. So, Shamika would not only trade Lena the last in command, but one that clearly had a problem with leaving.

Not much of a deal.

"You gonna throw in some of your manna loaves, too?" Lena asked.

"Fuck you, Horror. A sheila for a sheila. Fair and square. You don't even know what to do with that baby. She needs to be with her own."

"In case you haven't noticed," Lena said, "we're all the same here. We're all forgotten."

"Our gangs have had an understanding out there on the streets, even since the beginning. I'd hate for something like this to ruin that."

A threat. Well, that just made things a whole lot more fun. Lena stood her ground, keeping her eyes on Shamika's. The OC leader thumbed her nose. Lena sucked her teeth.

Oubliette had been Lena's home for ten years and she'd been head of her gang for the last two. How could anyone forget Lena "Horror" Horowitz had one, unmistakable quality? Threatening her just made her dig in deeper.

"Grindy!" Farica hollered.

Lena and Shamika turned back.

Farica smiled from her cyclone. "Maybe I can move this along a little quicker."

"You know the rules," Grindy grumbled. "You have to wait your turn."

Farica shifted happily in her seat. "See, that's just the thing. You might see that I'm missing my ass."

"All you white girls are," one of Shamika's gang shouted.

The dwellers – all except the dirty, crazy-eyed ones under the Amazons' protection – exploded with laughter.

Farica laughed along with them, and that was worrisome. "Now if I'm not mistaken, the truce says whoever's lost a gang member most recently gets first pick."

Oh, shit. Now Lena really had to spit. But her mouth had gone suddenly dry.

Grindy folded her arms. "What happened?"

"Tula found my lowest sheila's cyclone on the bridge over the Sludge. Had a bad wreck, it looked like. Only thing left of her is a smear on the street."

"Just curious, why wasn't she with the rest of you?"

Farica smiled, then shrugged. "She forgot her knife and fork."

The rest of the cannibals giggled softly, looking around them as if they weren't sure it was right to do so. They'd just lost a sister, after all. On the receiving stage, the shippees shivered and looked over the crowd, probably wondering when they could just leave and find somewhere in the city to live out their sentence.

Grindy pointed from her place on the stage. "You better not be lying."

"I respect the truce as much as anyone." Farica winked at Lena.

"No," shouted Shamika. "Give her a turn, but after Horror's done. You can't interrupt a pick like that."

Grindy sighed. "I've got to stick to the truce, Shamie. Most recent loss goes first."

Shamika shoved at her cyclone. It didn't budge.

"Come on, Farica," Grindy said. "Hurry the fuck up."

"The baby," Farica said, grinning and showing her disgustingly perfect teeth.

The pale girl, up until this point trying to stay silent, screamed. "You can't take her! I made a promise."

Farica sent two of her Amazons to the stage.

No. Lena squeezed her fists, so much the knuckles felt like they'd shatter. *I've got to do something.*

But what? The Amazons reached for the baby. Pale Girl pulled away and one of them backhanded her, catching the baby as they both dropped. The other shippees in line skittered away. They could smell the death on the cannibal's jackets, no doubt. If the baby sensed anything, it didn't cry.

"Farica," Grindy said as an Amazon placed the child in Farica's arms. "I sure as hell hope you have good intentions for that bambino."

"Don't worry, Grindy." Farica made kissy noises at the kid. "I think I've developed a motherly instinct in my old age." She was only thirty-something, Lena knew. But on Oubliette that was an inch from the grave. Farica looked up and realized everyone was staring at her, appalled. "You all act like I'm some kind of monster. All we Amazons have done is make the most out of a bad situation. None of you like that manna shit anyway. Don't hate us 'cause we found an alternative. But you can cool your thrusters, my fellow scum. This kid is going to be treated like a princess."

Lena left Shamika to piss and moan amongst her gang. No words could quite encompass what she felt on her way back to the Daughters.

"Poor baby." Ava shook her head.

Those words seem to fit pretty well.

"Sarah Pao," Lena called. She kept her eyes on the Amazons cooing over the baby, something Norman Rockwell would have painted if he were schizophrenic and dropping acid.

The blue-haired shippee took a step, but stopped and turned to Grindy as if asking permission. The older woman nodded. Sarah Pao clomped down as fast as she could and stood in front of the Daughters with her arms held tight to her sides.

Lena didn't want to say anything to Sarah Pao, not yet. If Lena opened her mouth, she'd start screaming and wouldn't stop until she worked herself up enough to rip

Farica's throat out. Make a show of it. Let every skinny-assed sheila on Oubliette see that, indeed, the truce was over, baby. Welcome to the killing fields.

But she didn't.

"You can ride with me," Hurley Girly said to Sarah. "What's your name again?"

"Pao."

"Oh yeah?" Hurley Girly laughed and raised her left fist. She threw some playful punches. "Like *pow, pow*?"

Sarah crossed her arms and took a step back.

"Well, if you don't come with us, you can stay with those crazy bitches over there." Hurley Girly pointed to the Amazons.

Sarah glanced at the cannibals and quickly climbed onto the back of Hurley Girly's cyclone. Hurley Girly bobbed her eyebrows in victory to the other Daughters.

"You're so weird," Ava said.

Lena nodded to a dweller she'd put in charge of collecting the manna. The gang would retrieve their share after their dwellers divvied it up.

Riding her cyclone would be the only thing to take the edge off Lena's boiling brain, feel the fake wind in her face, hit the streets and get back to the ganghouse. She didn't want to spend another second in the quarterly circus.

Shamika finished with her pick of the shipment. She couldn't select any of the shippees, but she sure as shit would pick something nice and shiny to make up for losing the baby to the Amazons, something that would probably piss Grindy off to make it that much better.

The dwellers hurried away from the receiving stage as the Amazons moved in with greasy smiles.

"What about the other shippees?" Sarah Pao asked as the Daughters engaged their bikes.

"What others?" Dipity said.

The Daughters of Forgotten Light rode off, parting the crowd of dwellers. Behind them came the blast of rangshots that brought the final screams of newly arrived shippees that never really had a chance.

CHAPTER 3

I can't take this anymore.

Senator Linda Dolfuse guarded her lower abdomen, careful to make it look like she rested her hands in her lap. The pain had grown more annoying than abysmal, only turning up when she sat or moved a certain way, giving her instances where it disappeared and she thought, *Ah! Now I can get on with my life.* But it wasn't so. And the discomfort randomly appearing and subsiding was somehow worse than if it just came to stay. *That* she could get used to.

She leaned her head back against the wall and closed her eyes. Sharp shoes clicked down the hall, sounding like a deranged tap dancer shuffling off to eternity. No-No, the janitor, sped toward her with a big grin on his face. They all called him No-No because anytime you asked if he was doing all right, he would respond, "No, no." But he always kept his broad smile.

Dolfuse dug through her purse, finding a stick of gum. As No-No passed, the senator slipped it into his hand. They shared a smile, Dolfuse fighting the pain, and the janitor turned the corner.

Behind the door across from her, Vice President Martin's aides bustled in, gathering numbers, making phone calls to cash in on favors with some people and offer them up with others.

Well, I'm here for the same thing, aren't I? Dolfuse had known the vice president would come calling someday. She just didn't think it would be so soon. But it was better than being on Martin's bad list.

The chemicals of a newly waxed floor and the hint of coffee steaming from the office wafted under her nose as she waited for the ache in her gut to subside. The doctors had told her it would only hurt for a couple weeks at most. Nothing to worry about. It had all gone so well.

Yes, well, she'd paid them to say such things, and paid them even more to keep it all hush-hush. It had been three months since the operation, and she still felt miserable. A checkup the week before showed nothing wrong with her – not physically. Guilt, she determined. Guilt was slowly wrecking her insides.

Bobby, her husband, once had a short fad with spiritualism and had told her that the mind controlled the body. "Your thoughts are what make you sick, sugar bear. Change what you think about if you want to get rid of your pain."

She'd thought it crap at the time, but now that she was experiencing it firsthand, she wished he would have told her exactly *how* to change her thoughts.

The door to her right opened, dispensing amicable but insincere laughter.

"Give our boys my best, General." Vice President Martin said.

Linda couldn't see Martin. The bulking shoulders of a general blocked the doorway. He smiled back at the vice president and then looked down to Dolfuse as if she'd crashed a private party. His hair, even the eyebrows, had been doped a dark brown. If Dolfuse hadn't sat on various committees where General Rag, who stood over her now, had given reports of the war effort and had for the longest time been gray-haired and balding, she still would have spotted the awful charade atop his head with minimal effort.

For a second she had the compulsion to stand. Medals hanging above a breast pocket have a way of doing that to you. Instead, she fought the urge and remained sitting. She owed him nothing. Stirring up more pain in her gut, just to show him a little respect, wasn't worth it. And there was no love lost between them. Over the years, Dolfuse had hammered him on his alleged treatment of prisoners of war, and she had never let up.

General Rag secured his hat under an arm and took off down the hall.

Vice President Madeline Martin poked her head through the door. She and Dolfuse shared similar hairstyles, shoulder length with a little bounce, except Martin's was the color of hay colored by the sunset. It reminded Dolfuse of when she used to help her daddy roll up dead grass into big cinnamon rolls on their tiny Arkansas farm so many years ago. That's what she'd always called the hay bales – cinnamon rolls.

"Linda," Martin said. It was amazing how she could speak so well with her teeth bared between those thin, red-painted lips, like a veteran ventriloquist. But, Dolfuse guessed, that's how she became vice president. "Come in. I appreciate you coming to see me."

Better get this over with.

Martin disappeared into her office and, as she rose, Linda faked a cough to cover the groan of pain. The motion didn't hurt as bad as she'd predicted. A throbbing swell just above her unmentionable zone and she was back to normal. Of course, another chair waited inside Martin's office. A large, striped couch, in fact. To avoid it, Dolfuse would put on the role of proactive public servant, too busy to sit. *Yes, that might work. Don't think me rude, I've just got a lot of momentum and a constituency that won't let me rest.*

Martin cuddled up in the chair across from the couch and extended an arm. "Take a load off. Let's dish."

Dolfuse wanted to gag. She hated that term, and, frankly, never understood what it meant. It sounded even worse coming from someone she was indebted to, someone she'd never liked.

After shutting the door behind her, Dolfuse grabbed the back of the sofa like a podium. "Already used up my sitting quota for the day." She forced a smile. "I hope you don't mind."

"Not at all," Martin said. "I like it. You know I read somewhere that too much sitting can kill you?"

"I can believe it."

Dolfuse made her ceremonial appreciation of Martin's office. It had all the warmth of the desolate tundra Europe had become over the last few decades, but it was whispered knowledge the vice president liked her guests to gush over her workplace.

A small picture frame behind Martin's back showed President Griffin smiling, at the edge of tears it looked like, and squeezing Martin across the shoulders with a long arm. Dolfuse couldn't really understand it. She'd never been close to another woman like that. Never really had a female friend. Acquaintances, of course, people she snuggled up to in order to be where she was in the dog-eat-dog arena of Washington. But friends? Never. Maybe she could have changed that with her daughter. Well, that wasn't to be either. The little one was in a better place – she hoped.

"One of my favorite photographs," Martin said.

"You and her have always seemed so close."

"The president is a very affectionate woman. That was taken after we got the news we'd won the election."

Dolfuse nodded, continuing to look at the picture.

"You hide it well," Martin said.

Dolfuse snapped back to the present. "Pardon?"

Martin nodded toward Dolfuse's midsection. The senator hadn't realized she was clutching her stomach. The pain had come back and her mind had taken her somewhere else while her body still reacted to it.

"Guilt," Martin said. Her eyes blinked with concern, not judgment.

Dolfuse dropped her arm as the pain faded.

"It's only human, especially in our line of work. Anything you want to talk about?" Martin leaned against her chair, resting her head against her hand. Her silver bracelet jangled as she did.

The vice president wasn't the type of woman you went blabbing to, unless you wanted something in return. Dolfuse certainly didn't want to give Martin anything to hold over her head. Dolfuse had gone against the vice president before, when she'd still just been Senator Martin. The shipping contract with Australia was up for renewal, and Dolfuse had promised Martin a vote in favor of it. However, Dolfuse's conscience overcame her at the last second, and along with two other senators who'd promised Martin, she backed out and voted against shipping for the Aussies. The two other senators died six months later when their hover car crashed and dropped off a bridge. Dolfuse had been watching her back every day since. She'd considered running away to South America, being a teardrop in the flood of immigrants trying sneak past the Colombian Wall. But she'd been more afraid of that than her paranoid thoughts. Besides, Martin had never mentioned that voting incident since.

Dolfuse had been keeping her guilt fermenting for so long. Maybe talking about it would help.

"I was pregnant," Dolfuse said. "Not any more."

Martin smiled, pointing. "I thought you might have had one in the oven."

"It's been handled."

She'd given the baby to a family that had been waiting to adopt for five years. But she wasn't going to tell Martin *that* much.

"Hell, I remember considering keeping it, the first time I was pregnant," Martin said. It's what prevented me from getting rid of it sooner. Oh, the thought of filling out all those child request forms alone was enough to change my mind."

"Do you ever regret it?" Dolfuse linked her fingers, rubbing them together.

"Burning it out?"

"Not keeping the baby."

Martin breathed in slowly before she answered. "We have a country to run, Linda. Even if you were granted permission for a kid – which you could easily get, being who you are – you'd have no time for your career. Things like that should be thought out well in advance. You have nothing to feel guilty about. When you and Bobby are ready, you'll be great parents."

"I'm not telling him what I did. But it'll all work out. I'm getting better every day."

Martin stood and grabbed a thick file from the recesses of her desk. When she returned, she placed it on the couch by Dolfuse.

"What's this?"

"What do you know about what happens on Oubliette?"

"Oubliette? No one knows what goes on there." The room thickened, hot and wanting for air. Dolfuse flapped her collar and swallowed. "Not since the shippees destroyed all the cameras. That's not really an area I know much about. Conspiracy websites and the counterculture are the only ones who seem interested in it."

Martin tongued her gums. "Yes, we're supposed to forget them, huh? The shippees. Do you think they're surviving?"

"The whole of them could be dead for all I know. Every new shipment might arrive to a dead city. And the shippees may just as well strangle each other for the last piece of that gunk we give them to eat. What are you thinking?" Dolfuse eyed the file on the couch. It was thick and manila brown. Across its face, red blocky letters spelled out "CONFIDENTIAL".

"Have you ever considered the possibility we'd lose this war?"

"No," Dolfuse said.

Martin laughed, waving the senator's words away with a limp hand. "You can tone down the zealous patriot routine in here."

Just her saying it made Dolfuse regard the door, wondering

if guards waited outside, ready to send her to the prison city in another galaxy. This was the day Martin would get her revenge.

"Honestly." Martin stared deep into Dolfuse's eyes. "Is there a chance we could lose? Worse, could our enviroshields shut down and have us go the way of those poor bastards across the pond?"

"That's a lot of 'ifs,'" Dolfuse said. "And honestly? Anything is possible with the right variables in place."

Martin grinned, nodding.

"But I still doubt it," Dolfuse added.

"The EA feels just as confident about their chances, I'm sure."

The Eastern Axis will freeze to death if we hold them off long enough.

When Pakistan, India, and the rest of the Middle East had formed their alliance, the rest of the world laughed, thinking they'd argue and kill themselves out of the union they'd formed. The joke was on them when Russia and China joined the alliance and began pushing toward the inevitable – war on the United Continent of North America. The world was in the beginning of another ice age, and the EA wanted the Continent's enviroshield technology, and would kill every last North American to get it. Never mind every last North American was struggling to put food on their own tables, living in overpopulated, stack-on-stack metropolises, or struggling to grow food from an uncaring soil in the more rural areas.

Dolfuse hated the EA. Because of them, Bobby had to go halfway across the world just so the land of the free could keep its borders shielded from the coming cold.

But he'd been a soldier when she'd married him, one of the few to enlist on his own. That same patriotism had helped him rise above the ranks of those who'd been sold into service.

"The difference between us and the EA, though," Martin said, "is we have the option of a contingency plan."

"Contingency plan?"

Martin pointed to the file on the couch. "That's everything I have on Oubliette. Read it. It's all about the architecture and the original plan for the city."

"You mean before they made it a child's prison?"

Martin chuckled and wagged a finger. "I said tone down the patriotism, not completely remove it. Linda, I want to know more. I want to know what this interstellar city of glass has become. Use whatever resources you need."

"Why me?"

Martin placed a hand on Dolfuse's shoulder. It weighed virtually nothing but the discomfort it brought was immeasurable. "I know we've had our differences, but I know you're one of the few on the Hill who can get things done. And quietly. I'll help clear your schedule as best I can. Obviously you'll have to make your committee appearances and any public speeches you have lined up. Other than that, I need your full attention on getting us some intel."

"Does the president–"

"For now this is just between you and me. I'd rather have something to show Griffin before asking permission."

"Better to ask for forgiveness."

Martin leaned back into the chair, smiling still, but Dolfuse caught a flash of a sneer. "There's no such thing as forgiveness."

Dolfuse nodded, although she didn't understand what Martin meant.

The vice president glanced at the gold watch strapped to her wrist and bolted from her seat. "That's all we can talk about it for now, Linda. Just find a way to get us some information to work with and we'll meet again. Sooner the better."

Dolfuse's pain had disappeared. Her guilt had been replaced with purpose. Martin stood at the door and held it open. Clutching the Oubliette file to her chest, Dolfuse nodded to the vice president, who smiled graciously and shut the door as soon as the senator had passed through.

What the hell did I just get conned into?

That's all politics was – legal and encouraged bamboozlement. You could try to fight the current all you wanted, but you'd get dragged under and drown while everyone who played the game got to drink and dance on the riverboat. Dolfuse never claimed to be that great at cutting a rug, but she was always thirsty. That's how the world worked. She'd do what she was asked and use it to her own benefit.

As she clomped down the hallway, thinking of where to start, she found herself holding the confidential file in her arms just a little too tightly. The file was just a gathering of paper and ink, not a baby. But for some reason, right then and there, when she reached the steps in front of the Eisenhower Building, oh God, did she want it to be.

CHAPTER 4

Sarah Pao was in Hell. She was trying to think of how lucky she was to still be alive when the women, these criminals riding on wheels of light, brought her to their ganghouse. "House" was really the wrong word for it. The dark glass building stood tall amongst the ruin of former tall buildings, looking like a small skyscraper back on Earth, but much… stranger. All the buildings looked that way, as if she'd arrived on an alien world and not some unfinished dream of humans long dead. Unlike most cities on Earth, the lights here flickered dimly, and the glowing streets lay mostly silent.

The gang rode up a wide ramp and through the front doors after the big one opened them with a card key.

"Here we are," said the woman she rode with.

They got off the strange motorcycles in a large, circular room. At first she didn't know where they were, but lights buzzed on at their presence and she got a full view of her new home.

A lot of empty crates, the same ones she and the others had been shipped out with, just like the one they were told to eat from during the long trip to the space gate. God, she'd thought she'd only have to suffer eating that shit for the trip in. Now, she understood she'd better get used to eating it for the rest of her days. Manna, they called it. At least it only took a pinch of the loaf to get good and full.

The woman with Down syndrome jumped onto a couch made from an old shipment crate. Sarah's crueler schoolmates back on Earth would have called her all sorts of terrible things, but here, on the prison city, she seemed to be one of the more important inhabitants. "Sit down," she said.

Sarah looked around for a chair or at least another refurbished box couch. "Where?"

"Here on the floor." The gang member pointed just in front of her. "We've got to tell you about some things so you don't get yourself killed. Or wreck our bike. When you earn the right to ride it."

"And the bike is worth a whole lot more than you," the big, muscled one said. Her hair had been cut short with designs of stars and moons buzzed over her ears and around the back of her head.

The one who'd picked Sarah from the lineup – Horror, Sarah thought her name was – left them and disappeared behind another set of doors, up a long rise of black stairs.

"We just need you to understand what you're in for. My name's Rochelle Hurley." She grinned just a little too enthusiastically and sat on the floor beside Sarah, touching their knees together. Hurley was blonde and reminded Sarah of the Harley Quinn character from the Batman comics. She even wore some strange, streaky mascara to bring the comparison more strongly to mind.

"But we all call her Hurley Girly," the big one said. "She used to be the ass. Now that's you. I'm Serendipity Wales,

Dipity for short."

"Ass?" Sarah asked.

"Yeah," Dipity said. "You're at the end and take all the shit."

"We all have our place in this gang, like parts of a body," the one on the couch said. "I'm Ava Munoz. I'm the right arm. Dipity is the left arm. Sterling is the right leg..."

The quiet one leaned on a support beam with her arms crossed. She raised a thin, dark eyebrow, and nodded in greeting.

"...and you just heard what Hurley Girly used to be. Now she's the left leg."

Hurley Girly wrapped her arm around Sarah's shoulders. "And Lena's our head."

Lena. That's what it was. They'd called her all kinds of things at that horrible place when the shipment door came down. Lena. Horror. Horowitz.

"What happened to the other left leg?" Sarah asked.

They all looked at each other. Even Hurley Girly dropped her smile. Sarah's stomach tightened. She must have said something she shouldn't have.

"First rule." Ava put a finger in Sarah's face. "You don't ask questions. You take what we give you and you do what we tell you. Got it?"

Sarah nodded. Keep your mouth shut. Easier in theory, but she could keep to that simple task. She clasped her hands, focusing on squeezing them together.

Ava seemed satisfied with that. She pushed her brown hair from her eyes. "Rule two. You only speak when spoken to."

Sarah nodded again.

"So," Ava said. "I get first question. What did you do to get sent here?"

Sarah had expected she'd get asked this question when she got to Oubliette, if nothing else. She'd practiced her answer a thousand times on the trip to the space gate but now struggled to find the words she'd so carefully put together. "Nothing," was what came out.

They all laughed, except Sterling. She just smiled.

"All right, all right," Dipity said. "Let's have a little guessing game. You don't seem like a criminal. You don't look like you have anything wrong with you physically. You bipolar or something?"

"You a lesbian?" Hurley Girly smiled.

"Spying for the EA?" Ava suggested.

"Hey!" Hurley Girly said, "That's a good one. I might make that my next bet on Horror."

"None of that," Sarah said. "My family couldn't afford to keep me."

"So it's a poverty sentence you're serving," Dipity clapped her hands. "I should have guessed that. Most dwellers are here because their parents got caught having too many kids or they needed the money to survive."

"My father lost his job," Sarah said. "He had my mother sell Miko, my brother, to the military, but I guess it wasn't enough. And I was stupid, stole a dope syringe from a shop near my house." She waved a weak hand at her blue hair. "They tracked me down and made my father pay for it, since I'd already injected. That didn't help, so my parents decided it would be best to send me here instead of the military."

"But it was your mother who had to fill out the paperwork and make the final call." Hurley Girly made a *pfft* with her lips. "Your dad's an asshole."

"They prepared me before I came."

"Baby," Dipity leaned forward, "ain't nothing can prepare you for this place. I don't care if you were a Navy SEAL, a ninja, or a damn rocket scientist."

"Although that helps." Hurley Girly patted Sarah's knee.

"My turn," said Dipity. "Who won the election?"

"Who cares?" Ava said.

"Hey," Dipity slapped Ava's chest with the back of her hand – it seemed every woman here was left-handed. "You got your question. I can ask whatever I want."

Ava gave her the finger.

"You mean the president?" Sarah asked.

"Yeah," said Dipity. "I don't care about the other people."

"And we ain't got all night." Hurley Girly wiggled her tongue between two fingers.

Sarah shuffled an inch or so away. "Griffin won again."

All of them groaned.

"Lena's going to be pissed," Ava said.

"What do you expect?" Dipity shook her head. "Crime is probably so low and shit's probably cheaper to buy now, they'll keep voting in anyone who's pro-shipping."

Hurley Girly bobbed in agreement. "Yeah, they think they sent all the criminals out here. But they just ended up electing them instead."

In her mind, Sarah laughed. Even in the deepest reaches of space, people liked to get on their soap boxes and talk politics.

"OK," Dipity said. "It's Sterling's turn."

Sterling, the one against the beam, made a few motions and gestures with her hands. Seeing her sign was like watching a courtesan dance in an Arabian palace thousands of years before. The beautiful flow of the fingers, the elegance of her dark eyes to inflect the words. After she finished, Sterling leaned back again.

"The war is the same thing as always," Sarah answered.

Sterling grinned and the others were clearly surprised by Sarah's comprehension.

"Well, I'll be damned," Dipity said.

"We were going to have one of our dwellers teach you to sign," said Ava. "But I guess that's one less thing to worry about."

When Sarah had said the war was "the same thing as always," these women knew what she meant. The people on TV repeatedly informed the viewing public that the United Continent of North America remained strong, and their unwavering faith and patriotism inspired their men and women fighting on the front lines. Every report was of a victory. Sarah couldn't remember ever hearing of defeat on any scale. But if that were so, then why were they still fighting? Wars eventually ended – never mind that they were always resurrected in a different form.

"Sometimes I'm glad to be away from all that bullshit," Dipity said.

"My turn!" Hurley Girly bounced. She had to take a few breaths and collect herself into a more serious tone. "Are you into girls?"

Sarah had been expecting that one, but it still surprised her. "I…"

"You don't have to answer that," Ava said.

"Nuh uh!" Hurley Girly shouted. "She had to answer all your boring questions. So, Pao, what do you say?"

They all stared at her. Sarah wasn't sure if she understood the question. What did that have to do with anything? But Hurley Girly was sitting awfully close to her and had been overtly invading of her personal space. Sarah had just thought it a quirk of her personality.

"I..." Sarah's mouth moved but nothing came out. She didn't want to offend any of these women. Her mother had told her to find a group and fit in. Safety was in numbers. But she was who she was. "I'm not into anyone."

Hurley Girly crinkled her brow and Dipity almost fell over laughing.

"Satisfied?" Ava asked Hurley Girly.

"She'll have plenty of time to think about it out here." Hurley Girly leaned toward Sarah. "It's not like there are any boys to confuse you." With that, she rolled away and stood beside Sterling.

Sarah swallowed. Her parents hadn't prepared her for this.

"Some stuff you need to know," Ava said. "We've got this truce."

"Bullshit," Dipity said.

"Things are a lot calmer now, even though most of the shippees who come get eaten. Before the truce, we were all on the menu and had to fight for every shipment. To keep the peace, there are things you can't do. First thing, you can't raise your right hand to a member of another gang. Might as well practice being a lefty so you won't screw up on accident. We all wear these." Ava showed Sarah the top of her right forearm and pulled back the sleeve of her shiny black jacket. Attached to Ava's arm was a hunk of metal with lines of glowing blue light circulating inside. It looked like an oversized watch combined with an archer's bracer.

Sarah glanced at the others and saw they brandished their own arm accessories.

"Rangs," Hurley Girly said.

Sarah wanted to ask why they were called that but quickly remembered rule number one. She did blink in confusion and tilt her head.

"You flick your wrist down," Dipity demonstrated with her left arm, "and this ball of energy shoots out, blowing through just about anything. Bounces off the glass and comes back like a boomerang. We just shortened it to *rang*."

"Pretty cool, huh?" said Hurley Girly.

"But like I said," Ava returned her sleeve over the rang gun and the others did the same, "the truce guarantees you won't ever use it. And a lot of bitches here deserve to get shot."

Dipity hummed with approval. "Amen."

Sarah's words shot out before she could think. "Shouldn't I practice in case?"

So much for following a simple rule. Sarah could have kicked herself.

Ava grinned. "You manage not to piss us off before then, we'll take you to see Grindy and then practice anything you want."

"Yeah, anything you want," Hurley Girly said.

"I mean shooting and riding." Ava glared at Hurley Girly. "Grindy's still keeping Loveless's..." Ava cleared her throat. "Our other cyclone."

"That's those kickass motorcycles we rode here on," Hurley Girly said, ignoring Ava's visual reprimand. "In case you didn't pick that up."

"You lucked out, Pao," Ava said. "Don't shit on this

opportunity. Plenty of sheilas have tried to be one of us. If you can't hack it in the DOFL, you're out on the street. A dweller forever. And don't think they're are all kind-hearted. They'd sell you to the Amazons for half a manna loaf if they could."

Sarah's head began to ache, hollow and distant. What a strange place, with strange names for everything and the people just as appropriately odd. Her overflowing mind must have shown on her face.

Ava sniffed. "That's enough for right now, don't you sheilas think?"

"Sheila?" Sarah asked.

"Yeah," Hurley Girly said. "You know, like a rad chick, a ride-or-die sister. A sheila."

Sterling signed, *A lot of Australians were shipped here in the beginning.*

"We don't want to fry her brain before the big test next week," said Dipity.

Sarah widened her eyes and breathed in more sharply than she'd have liked. They all laughed, even Sterling, whose laughter sounded more like a television having its mute button turned on and off repeatedly.

"She's fucking with you," Ava said. "Welcome to the Daughters of Forgotten Light."

"There is one thing," Hurley Girly said. "Call it an initiation."

They all nodded, trying to hold back their smiles.

Sarah just wanted to go to sleep and wake up somewhere a little less dark, but took Hurley Girly's bait and asked, "What kind of initiation?"

CHAPTER 5

Lena Horror had the tenth floor all to herself. She didn't much care for heights, but the long window gave her a terrifically wide view of... well, not much besides the neighboring buildings, where a few dweller lights thrummed in the dark. But she'd be able to see any orange wheels headed their way if that's how it would play out.

How could she have let herself get so crazy out there on the streets? The stupid Amazon bitch hadn't even shot her rang. And now she was a dead stupid Amazon bitch.

Exactly, she told herself. You did something before she had a chance to blow your head off.

Lena had kicked her boots off to try to relax, but the hard glass floor chilled her feet like always. It would have been better to leave the boots on, but some habits die hard.

She'd begin to form a plan in her head, but it would turn to shit and she'd have to start all over.

There was a knock at the door behind her and Lena sighed. It was Sarah Pao. Lena knew before she even turned. None of the other Daughters would have bothered knocking, not even Sterling.

"I'm kind of busy right now, Pao." Lena continued to stare out at the city.

"They told me to come to you."

"Look, I really don't–"

Sarah stood in the doorway naked, not a scrap on her. She draped an arm across her breasts and stretched the other arm down to cover the rest. Sarah stared at the glass beneath her, shivering. To someone unused to it, the floor must have felt like ice.

"What are you doing?" Lena asked.

"I'm here to pay you." She looked like she was vomiting the words. "For saving my life."

Lena's laughter ripped through the tension in the room. Jolting, Sarah looked up with watery eyes.

"This is a new one," Lena said. "Which one of them put you up to this? I bet it was Hurley Girly."

Sarah nodded and dropped her head again. Lena guessed the only thing worse than the embarrassment of offering up your naked body was to have it turned down, a one-two punch of humiliation.

"Put your clothes back on," Lena said.

"They're downstairs."

"They made you walk up the stairs like this?" Lena didn't wait for an answer and laughed harder than before. Then, wiping tears from her eyes, "I'm sorry, I'm sorry."

Sarah didn't look up and Lena had no reason to make their new ass feel worse than she already did.

"Here." Lena walked to her bed and tossed Sarah the single glasscloth sheet she always kept crumpled on top. "Don't take their jokes personally. We don't get that many opportunities to fuck with people, and we're not here to punish you. You've already been sent to this damned place and that's punishment enough. It's just a little hazing."

Sarah covered herself with the sheet and wiped her eyes. "They asked me a lot of questions."

"We don't get much news or mail out here either, if you hadn't noticed. I've got my own questions, but I'll get to them later."

"Like what I did to get sent here?"

"I couldn't care less about that. You're here. Knowing the details isn't going to change that. Hell, none of them down there know why I got shipped."

"Why did you?"

Lena snorted. "Put your bet in with the rest of the sheilas downstairs. They drill you over the rules and the way things work here?"

"A little," Sarah said. "It's still hard to get used to."

"It's your first day. If you're lucky there'll be plenty more to come so you can learn everything. Just follow the ups."

Sarah's wrinkled brow urged Lena to explain.

"The ups. Shut up, listen up, hurry up. You do that, you'll be all right."

Sarah tightened the sheet around her. Lena was staring, made more awkward because the newbie was naked and clueless. Turning back to her window, Lena focused on a cluster of dweller lights.

Something still had to be done about the Amazons.

"You know, Pao," Lena said. "There's a way you can repay me without degrading yourself."

Lena waited for her to speak, but Sarah only cleared her throat to let Lena know she still stood there listening. Good. She was following the first up.

"Here's another *up* for you. You're going to back me up on everything. Any decision I make, whether you think it's a good idea or not, whether anyone else disagrees, you're going to side with me. That shouldn't be too hard, huh?"

"No," Sarah said. "That sounds easy enough."

Lena held up her left fist, a sign of finality. "Don't welsh on this deal."

"No, ma'am."

Ma'am?

Damn, did she look that old? Lena laughed again. It felt good to be genuinely amused, and not the psycho rage-cackling that riding a cyclone through the streets brought out of her. Pao would prove useful for entertainment at least. "Just call me Lena."

"Why did they kill them?" Sarah's question pulled Lena from the window. "Why did that other gang... *rang* the shippees?"

"The Amazons?" Lena sighed and gathered her answer. How to explain this to someone from outside their sandbox of terror? "It's part of the truce. The shipper port never sends enough manna and if you think the population is a problem on Earth, it's ten times worse here. The truce solves more than one problem at the same time. The cannibals get what they like to eat and the rest of us get enough manna to survive until the next shipment without having to fight over it.

"Each gang and their dwellers divvy up responsibilities so we all have to rely on each other. Our gang handles the mechanical and technical shit. That's why the Amazons don't try to wipe us all out. Not that they could. And I wouldn't feel too sore about those shippees you came here with. Some might argue they got the easy way out."

"Some of them were friends of mine." Sarah covered her

mouth for a moment, fighting something back, and then shook her head. "And that baby."

"Yeah, it sucks." Pao had been in the same box with that pale girl and the baby. She had to know who'd smuggled her out here. "How'd that baby get in your shipment?"

Sarah parted her lips. At first, nothing came out, but then she said, "I don't know." And it seemed to add questions to her own mind. "We were so scared and it happened so fast when our launch date came. Some of the shippees in our group ended up being moved to another part of the port, and we all swore they were being taken to be shot. Never saw them again. But that girl, the one who had the baby. When the guards lined us up and inspected what we were bringing with us, our one item, they marked down that she was bringing a doll and shoved her in the box."

"You saying the port guards couldn't tell the difference between a doll and a baby?"

"No. I'm saying she had a doll. Plastic skin, glass eyes. I know. I picked it up when she dropped it. But then, after the launch, she had that baby in her arms."

"Someone had already put the kid in the box."

"I guess. None of us said anything. We didn't know what to think. And honestly, it calmed us down a little. We took turns squeezing juice out of the manna for the baby to drink."

Lena ran fingers through her hair at each side of her head. It helped her think. "First time I've ever heard of someone Earthside fucking with the shipment."

And it meant one of many things. Either someone had used the shipment as their personal garbage chute, or the good ole UC of NA had started sending anybody, no matter the age. If things had gotten that bad, who's to say the government wouldn't abolish Oubliette altogether – and not in the way she'd been hoping for the last ten years.

"Is there always a shipment?" Sarah asked.

"I worry about that every damn day. Now get downstairs and get your clothes back on. Sometime soon we'll get you over to Grindy's and get you armed and ready to ride." Lena pointed at Sarah. "And I want my sheet back."

Sarah nodded and, most likely remembering the third up, hurried down the stairs. Lena turned back to the city hiding in the darkness outside the window. She looked toward the Amazons' headquarters, somewhere far off and blocked from view by another building used by the dwellers. That beautiful baby girl waited there, surrounded by those monstrous, crab-infested thundertwats.

What to do? Lena thought. *What to do?*

CHAPTER 6

"You that senator lady?" The engineer's voice surprised Dolfuse over the whining and buzzing.

"Linda Dolfuse."

"I'm Wickey." The grease-faced woman stepped forward and offered her hand.

Dolfuse regarded the hand as if it were a bomb set to explode as soon as she touched it. All that muck staining the palm. Still, diplomacy rode no high horse. She placed the tips of her fingers in Wickey's grip, minding to keep her thumb tight so their hands wouldn't officially link.

Wearing navy blue coveralls, Wickey had tied her blonde hair into a ponytail under a cap she wore backwards. Oil covered it all. Goodness, it was all over her.

Dolfuse afforded a smile. "Thanks for letting me come take a look."

"No problem. We're all in service to the continent, yeah?"

"Of course."

"Right this way." Wickey turned back to the tall, clean doors she'd come from. They were frosted white where only shadows flitted by every so often, a fog of glass. When Wickey opened the doors, a whining buzz escaped from the workshop.

Dolfuse plugged fingers in her ears.

"Oh, I almost forgot." Wickey closed the door and trudged over to a wall where an assortment of tools and knickknacks hung from hooks. She returned with a pair of headphones and a hardhat.

"What about you?" Dolfuse asked.

"Nah. I'm used to the sound."

Dolfuse secured her safety equipment and followed Wickey through the doors. Sparks flitted into the air at her left as an engineer welded on a large metal dome. The senator jumped and released a whimper.

"It's all right," Wickey shouted, smiling. "If we stay on the grating here, you shouldn't get hurt."

Shouldn't. An awful lot could be filled into "shouldn't."

Dolfuse followed the metal grating to a rust-covered guard rail that circled the entire circumference of the silo. It was nearly a half mile to the other side with nothing but air and flying lifts between there and where she stood.

She tried not to acknowledge the dark pit below, where firefly-sized red lights floated like scavenging sea creatures.

Levels upon levels of work floors rose to the top, engineers bustling endlessly on every single one. The lifts hovering from floor to floor were automated drones, carrying different items in their clawed arms. Hot exhaust warbled the air around their thrusters.

At ground level, Wickey and Dolfuse stood halfway between the silo's top and bottom. Dolfuse clutched the railing as she looked over and braved vertigo to survey the deep lower levels reaching into the Earth's recesses. She almost wished she'd brought a penny to see if it could be heard hitting the bottom. Ha! You couldn't hear anything in this mechanical circus.

"This way, senator," Wickey shouted. She extended her hand toward a set of stairs several yards away. "It's a few levels down."

"You all seem to keep busy," Dolfuse shouted back as they walked on.

"Yeah, the war sure helps with that. We've got recon drones aplenty. Amphibious drones, drones that can climb walls. Heck, I've even been working on a drone that can burrow underground."

"What about this one?"

They'd come to a black monstrosity – a flying ship of some kind that could carry at least a dozen women. Huge guns were mounted at each corner, and the glass covering the cockpit was blacked out. Dolfuse worried what the wrong person at the trigger could do with such a thing.

"Sweet Kiss," Wickey said.

"What?"

Wickey laughed. "That's what we call her. She's a prototype, hasn't seen much field action, but we show her off to the generals next month. Really versatile, since it can be manned like other fighter jets, but it can also be operated remotely, or set to blow away everything and everyone in the EA. This thing's packing four plasma cannons, a cluster bomb launcher loaded in the belly, and, my personal touch, a phase scanner that locates and tracks any enemy, human or machine. It's going to end the war."

Dolfuse believed it. A machine like that could swing the scales of the planet any way the operator saw fit. They moved on.

"Yeah, I love it here." Wickey stomped down the third

set of steps they'd come to. "When I was sixteen my mom told me I either had to find a job or get ready for Oubliette. Well, I bet you can guess I got my ass in gear and started searching for reasonable employment."

Dolfuse remembered waking up in the middle of the night when she was a little girl, screaming in terror from dreaming she'd awoken in that terrible city in the sky. Her mother had always comforted her with a glass of water and a back rub. "I'd never do that to you," she'd say.

Wickey's life story gave Dolfuse something to focus on besides the onslaught of cantankerous construction, and her own guilty criticism.

"Hell, I figured I love working with my hands and tinkering and stuff, and I sure ain't afraid to get dirty. About that time was when they were pushing for engineer recruits, and here I am."

"This drone I called you about," Dolfuse said. "Is it small enough to get into places, avoid detection?"

"Sure. It's only about the size of a big pigeon. Noiseless, too. If your op needs to be covert, it'll be just the thing. But here, see for yourself."

Wickey exited the steps, upping her pace, and Dolfuse struggled to keep up in her heels. The working noise lessened. No one was ratcheting bolts or burning cuts into metal here. All the drones on this floor were ready for sale and small enough to be displayed on a long table and under a square of glass.

"It's this one here I told you about." Wickey extended a hand to the third one from the right.

At Dolfuse's approach, a light brightened from below the drone display. Wickey had described the particular drone's size accurately. But its shape – it looked like a sperm, though Dolfuse fought hard to attach a less disturbing description to it. It really was just like one of Bobby's white swimmers, except the tail stuck out straight and a large camera lens sat in the large, round "head". The others on the display case were shaped like spheres or mechanical octopi.

"How's it controlled?"

Wickey picked up a small, white stick from a nearby cart. "This."

"Even *my* hands are too big for that."

Wickey chuckled. "It's not a remote controller, just a flash drive. You plug it into any computer. Software downloads immediately. The drone follows programmed variables: a certain area, large crowds, specific sounds, whatever."

Dolfuse looked at the other drones, the ones that looked less like sex cells. "What about those? Why is this one superior?"

"The one I'm suggesting is more maneuverable, for starters. The others are designed for more specific tasks – underwater operations, rough terrain. Plus, the other ones are crones, comparatively."

"How far away can it be operated?"

"Anywhere in the world. That Dropshot drone is the best."

Dolfuse stared at the sperm-shaped mechanism. Who cares what it looks like if it gets the job done, she thought. The space gate's relay would prevent a delay in the video feed, and Martin would know someone who could program it.

"You have any other questions about the drone?" Wickey bent her head a little, concerned.

"Yes," Dolfuse said, straightening her posture. "Does it come in black?"

CHAPTER 7

Sarah kept hearing the Daughters use terms like week, day, and quarter, but could never figure out how they told time here. It seemed just like one horrible, long night. No sun. No clocks or watches. Sleep would call to her every so often and she'd answer its summons after asking permission from Ava. Even then, she lost count of how many times she fell asleep. It still felt like the same day when she'd wake up.

When she got hungry, she would pinch off a moist bit of the manna she'd been rationed. Just like it had in the shipment box, the manna tasted like stale air, smelled like paint, and would release fluid as she chewed, keeping her hydrated, she assumed, and giving her the suitable amount of nutrients she needed to survive another span between sleeps.

Then one... day, she guessed, after coming down from the room they'd given her, Hurley Girly told her it had been about a week and a half since she'd stepped out of the shipment box.

"We're going to take you to Grindy. Get you supplied."

Oh, yeah. The rang gun and the cyclone. She'd almost forgotten. Her days had been spent moving boxes from one corner to the other or wiping down the shower room, futile exercises the Daughters had made her perform because they didn't know what else to do with her. At least, that's what she thought. It wasn't like there was much to clean. And even if there was, what did it really matter?

Lena came down from the black stairs. "I want to show her the Core, too."

"Damn," Dipity said. "Already?"

"Might be her only chance to see it," Hurley Girly said to Sarah with a wink. "Seeing how high the death rate is."

"Mortality rate," Ava corrected.

Hurley Girly rolled her eyes. "Whatever."

Sarah was just happy to go outside the building for once. Even though everyone kept mentioning how the streets were death for sure despite the truce, she'd risk it for a little taste of the night.

"Dipity, you let Pao ride with you," Lena said.

Dipity nodded, although she huffed an annoyed sigh, while Hurley Girly crossed her arms and frowned. Sarah hurried over to Dipity's cyclone and waited for the big woman to walk over and start the motorcycle.

"Just don't grope on me or anything." Dipity swung one of her thick legs over the seat and grabbed the handlebars.

It took barely a flick of the wrists to turn on the cyclone. The dazzling blue light that lived within the machine sprang forth, creating electric wheels that lifted Dipity up and filled the room with that low hum Sarah heard in her sleep, the noise she hadn't forgotten from that first night out of the shipment box. Thank God it was that she recalled and not the screams of her fellow shippees at the end.

"You coming?" Dipity asked.

Sarah nodded, keeping her eyes on the buzzing light. "I

still haven't gotten used to all this."

"Shit," Dipity said. "Neither have I. And I've been here a lot longer than you."

Sarah climbed on behind Dipity, grabbing the back of her jacket. She didn't want to wrap her hands around Dipity's waist. Hurley Girly opened the front doors, and just like that they were zipping after Lena and the others, out on the streets in a blink. God. No machine on Earth moved like the cyclones did.

The group made two lefts and rounded a curve that rose over a cluster of short buildings. The architecture here was some strange mix of roller coaster engineering and her brother's old Hot Wheels set. Sarah hoped there wouldn't be a loop-the-loop. Hurley Girly joined the procession after a moment and then the gang flew even faster.

Way better than a roller coaster, Sarah thought.

She kept expecting to see another gang through an alley or on the road ahead; maybe those mohawked women from the week before. The Daughters must have had some well-known path of travel that wouldn't have them cross paths with the other gangs, or they must have known when they'd have reign of the streets for themselves. Of course, it could have all been coincidence. The gang, Sarah's gang, didn't seem the type to avoid trouble. They were hungry for a good fight.

Dipity rode so fast most of the city whipped by in a blur, but from what Sarah did see several buildings stood crumbling if not completely demolished. A cluster of dwellers sat on a darkened stoop and cheered when the Daughters flew by. The street's glow painted their faces an eerie aquatic green. Hurley Girly had told Sarah that sometimes a building would "die" and quit working – no power, and sludge instead of water would seep from the showers. The dwellers living there would just move on and crowd another building. It was the Daughters' job to make sure the dwellers didn't kill each other in the process.

Sarah looked up to what she would have called the sky, had this been Earth. But no stars looked back at her, just the green haze stretched over the city like a mosquito net, and the fuzzy image of the space gate a little farther out.

"Where does the city end?" Sarah tapped Dipity's shoulder.

"Huh?"

"The city." Sarah raised her voice. "Where does it stop?"

"You ever seen a snowglobe?"

"No."

"How about a plate cover?"

Sarah shrugged, even though Dipity focused on the glowing street ahead. "I think I know what that is."

"Same concept. The city's flat, and the Veil covers it. Oubliette ends at the Veil."

"You guys ever try to go through?"

Dipity groaned. "Damn it, what did we tell you about asking questions?"

For the next few minutes Sarah stayed quiet and took in the rundown buildings and false wind caressing her cheeks, but the ride ended just as Sarah was wishing it would go on forever. They stopped outside a building as wide as the surrounding giants were tall. The shop didn't display a sign above the door, but Sarah figured they'd arrived at Grindy's.

Dipity turned off her cyclone and when the metal touched the street Sarah hopped off and waited on the curb for one of them to tell her what to do. Lena got to the door in two strides and went in without a word. Hurley Girly told Sarah to follow with a toss of her head, and once they were all inside Sarah let the door shut behind her with a high-pitched click.

Back on Earth her father would sometimes take her and her brother to the hardware store when he needed to replenish his laser cutter's battery or purchase a new tool for the next tobeunfinished project he had lined up in hopes of selling it. He always said places like that hardware store would be around for the next several centuries. "The tools may change," he had said, "but the need will always be there."

Grindy's looked just like that store. Of course, it was ten times bigger and had more people rushing here and there, working on strange machines that would make her father stammer and cry in appreciation. And it was awfully loud.

Lena waved to the older woman Sarah recognized from the receiving stage. Grindy. She was griping at one of her workers while they traced a laser on a flat piece of glass that looked like it had come from one of Oubliette's buildings. In fact, everything looked like it was just a recycled piece of the city.

Stopping in the middle of her lecture, Grindy smiled at Lena. The two of them hugged and shared some words Sarah couldn't hear. She'd stopped walking, watching all the gadgets being built, and the rest of the Daughters waited way ahead of her.

Grindy waved Sarah over. "How you getting along?"

"I'm still alive," Sarah said.

The older woman grinned in an agreeable way. "Well,"

she wiped her brow with the back of her hand, "let's get somewhere we can talk without risking laryngitis." She pointed to Sarah and Lena. "Just these two, though. I don't want the rest of you crowding my office."

It *was* an office, in a way. Empty shelves lined the walls, but it wasn't clear if they'd always been there or if Grindy had put them in herself. A desk made of empty manna boxes stood in front of a black glass chair that resembled the melted remains of a statue Sarah would have seen in a city's business district.

"Where you from originally?" Grindy said, as she took her seat in the melted chair.

There were no other places to sit, so Lena and Sarah both remained standing.

"Scranton," Sarah said. "Well, Blakely. I always say Scranton because no one ever knows where the other is."

"You're right," Grindy said. She raised a questioning hand to Lena. "She always this fidgety?"

Lena smirked. "I think you make her nervous."

Fidgety? Sarah thought she was doing a good job, being the quiet, confident new Daughter they expected her to be. It made her wonder what a mess she'd been the first night she got here.

"Mexico City, myself," said Grindy. "We bring the places we left behind with us, yeah? Thing you got to understand is, you have to take what you can use and let the rest fall back through the Veil."

"What's the Veil anyway?" Sarah asked. "I keep hearing about it."

Grindy cocked an eye to Lena. "You haven't been telling her what she needs to know?"

"Ava was supposed to be handling it." Lena sighed. "I've had other stuff on my mind. I'll make sure it gets taken care of."

"They told me not to ask questions," Sarah said. "So I didn't."

"You're smart," Grindy said. "The Veil is what keeps the air we breathe from flowing out into space. It also ensures we never leave either. You and the others in the shipment came through because our dear friends back home in the UCNA install a device in the shipments that allows them through the Veil. Soon as that happens, though, *pfft.*" She snapped her fingers. "Thing gets fried so we can never make use of it. Got to hand it to those *culos.* They know what they're doing."

"So, that's why no one has ever tried to escape."

Grindy bunched her lips and looked at Lena as she said, "Oh, several have *tried.* But like I said, without one of those devices, no one can get through the Veil. But then what? I can build just about anything for the street. Space…"

"Grindy knows more about engineering and machines than anybody on Earth or Oubliette combined," Lena said.

Grindy beamed. "You're just trying to get free repairs from flattery."

"Is it working?"

"Hell, no!" Grindy laughed. "But don't let me stop you from trying."

Lena dropped her smile and her amicable vibe. It scared Sarah how her gang's head could do it so quickly. "Pao says they're nowhere close to bringing us back home."

"What's forgotten is easy to stay that way." Grindy nodded. "Hell, Lena, I'm sorry. But you should have guessed as much."

The room went quiet. Sarah didn't even want to swallow and interrupt whatever unsavory moment she'd gotten wrapped up in.

"Your rang gun!" Grindy raised a finger and bent down behind the manna box desk.

When she came back up, she held the same device that the other Daughters had strapped to their right arms. It looked so glossy, it reflected the yellow glow of the room's dim light.

"OK," Grindy said, beckoning Sarah over with a finger. "When I strap this on and power it up... you know about the truce and keeping your right arm down?"

Sarah nodded, feeling strangely proud. She was becoming a part of something, the lowest on the tier, but still important. The first few days, the thought of dropping out and hiding away as a dweller crossed her mind several times. The desire to leave had grown hot when Hurley Girly and Dipity would dump water on her from the top of the stairwell, or when Ava would pop out of nowhere, scaring the crap out of her. She wondered if she wanted to be involved with these cruel women, to be a Daughter. But it seemed on Oubliette there could be no greater honor. It must have been what girl scouts felt like when they received their first gun, police cadets when given their badge.

"Now, you don't get as old as me being a fool, at least not in this city." Grindy strapped the rang onto Sarah.

It felt like her arm had always been missing something until that point. The rang completed her. Martial arts had been the only thing her father supported as an extracurricular activity, being that he could teach her and her brother himself, and had friends who would let them join one of their classes at no charge.

But Sarah had always felt underwhelmed. It came too easily to her. She was better than her brother and anyone else in the free classes. It had gotten to where she'd go to the library for advanced books on different styles of fighting, and would use one of the study rooms to practice.

This strange new weapon, the rang, was a game changer.

"I'm not going to let you shoot up the place, trying to figure out how to aim the damned thing. Lena will turn off your safety when you get back to your ganghouse to practice. But…" Grindy pressed a switch on the side and the rang lit up with blue light. The dullest of hums vibrated through Sarah's arm, just like the cyclones, but on a smaller scale.

"Wow," Sarah whispered.

"It gets better," Lena said. "Wait till you get to shoot it."

"Practicing." Grindy raised her eyebrows at Lena like a mother ensuring her kids stayed in the backyard while they played.

Lena only grinned. "Can you get Taylor to set her up with Loveless's old cyclone? I need to talk to you about some stuff." She glanced at Sarah. "In private."

Grindy nodded. "Sure, sure. Pao, was it? Go out there and get one of the Daughters to take you to Taylor. Sure hope that crazy blue hair of yours means you can ride. If not, you're sure fucked."

Sarah breathed heavier. She'd never even driven a car, gotten shipped before she ever had a chance to take a driver's test. She wondered if some of the former gang recruits never made it past the riding lessons. An image came to mind of her face bloody and squished on the smooth glass of an Oubliette street, but she quickly shook the thought away.

"Taylor. Ride. Got it." Sarah made for the door. The two other women watched her leave, and without shame or any sense of sentiment, Sarah prayed it wouldn't be the last time she'd see them.

CHAPTER 8

After Sarah left, Lena turned back to Grindy. "There's some bad shit you need to know about, but it can't leave this room."

"With you there's no other kind of shit."

"I've been doing a lot of thinking–"

"Ain't much else to do around here if you don't like pussy."

"Will you shut the fuck up and listen?"

Grindy put her hands behind her head and leaned back in her glass throne, smirking. The old sheila always liked to rib Lena. "There's something bugging you," Grindy said. "Spill it."

"The truce is broken."

That got her attention. The eyes, always the eyes. But Grindy didn't jump up from her relaxed position just yet. "First I've heard of it. Did one of the Amazons blast an Onyx? My damn dwellers are slacking in getting me information."

"No one besides us and the Daughters know. It happened when this last shipment came in."

"Shit fire." Grindy sat up at that. "Farica's last in command. You took her out."

"She drew on me. It was a legit kill, but I figured Farica

wouldn't see it that way and since we were the only witnesses, it makes it look shady. Plus... the truce."

"Would be down the drain and swimming the Sludge by now. Another war. Blood in the streets and all that jazz. You hid it to keep the truce."

"It's what I figured you would have done."

The sound that came from Grindy's throat could be called a groan, if a lion's roar could be called a cough. Grindy would have thrown something if the office had anything left to grab.

"I'm not mad at you." Grindy lowered her face to her hands and rubbed at it for what felt like hours before she sat up again.

Lena chewed on her lip, drummed her fingers against the side of her leg.

"I know you can get a little psycho out there," Grindy said, "but I know you always think things through. If you say it couldn't be helped, it couldn't be helped."

"Have you heard anything about the Amazons?"

"Like what? If they know what really happened? Shit, Horror. None of this would be such news to me if I'd caught any wind of something like that."

Lena breathed and paced to the other side of Grindy's office. This next part would have to be done right. Grindy could smell bullshit a klick away. "No. That's not what I mean. I've been wondering about the baby."

Grindy wrinkled her eyebrows.

Shit. She always did that when she thought Lena had something up her sleeve or boiling in her brain.

"She's still alive, last I heard. Farica's become a regular mother of the year. Even getting her dwellers to trade for some manna so she can squeeze juice out for the kid. It would be the strangest thing I've seen on Oubliette, but maybe this baby can change Farica for the better."

"Who says monsters can't change? That stupid twat doesn't ride around with the baby does she?"

"How would I know? I'm sure she leaves her with one of the dwellers or something. What's up with you?" Grindy said. "Why are you so interested? You usually move on pretty quickly after a shipment."

Lena clamped her teeth. She'd pushed the issue a little too hard. *Back off before she gets wise.* "Look, no one under ten years – much less ten months – has ever stepped out of the box. I just feel a little raw there's someone that careless and stupid to send a baby out here."

"No more careless than your mother or mine. I hate she'll grow up a fucking cannibal, but at least the girl will have some kind of life."

"There is no life here," Lena whispered, looking at her boots.

Grindy squinted her eyes, like it would help her hear better. "What?"

"I said let's get your old ass out to wherever Taylor is showing my new sheila her cyclone. We don't want to miss this."

CHAPTER 9

Sarah was wringing her hands as Lena and Grindy walked outside in time for Taylor to bring the cyclone from the back. Taylor was a dweller, grandfathered in from before the truce, when freshly arrived shippees weren't the only ones who had to worry about getting slaughtered by the Amazons.

Taylor hadn't said anything, not when the other Daughters had brought Sarah out back to find her, or even after Sarah told her what she was there for. At first, Sarah thought she might have been deaf or mute like Sterling, but she didn't respond to any of Sarah's hand signs either.

Sarah's bike glided over the glass, low hum flowing from the gorgeous blue wheels, the black curves of its body shimmering. Sarah wasn't sure if she liked it more than the other cyclones because it would be hers, or if it really was that spectacular.

"Dents are all knocked out," Taylor said from the bike. "Handlebars rewired and taken in a bit for better steering. Loveless had asked us to do that and I didn't see a reason not to honor her wish even after–"

"That'll be fine," Grindy said. "Shut her down and show Pao how to start it up."

Taylor sucked on her teeth and pulled back on the handlebars. The wheels dimmed and the cyclone lowered as if it was on a deflating air cushion. "Come on over."

"Don't push the wrong button," Ava shouted as Sarah stepped toward her new ride. "You might blow yourself up."

"You better not make us pick up all your gory pieces," Hurley Girly joined in.

There was a heavy *whack*.

"Ow!" Hurley Girly cried. "Shit, Sterling, what did I do?"

Sarah didn't turn back to see if Sterling signed. Besides, her eyes were glued to the waiting cyclone.

Taylor crossed her arms. "You ever ride a motorcycle?"

Sarah shook her head.

"Have you at least ridden a bicycle?"

"Yeah, mountain bike."

"I'm not going to pretend it's the same thing but, hop on."

Sarah grabbed a handlebar.

Taylor shouted a strange gargle. "Not like that," she said. "You don't want this thing flying off without you. If you're going to grab something to get on, use that spot just in front of the seat."

Sarah tried again and eased onto the cyclone. The seat cupped her rear like a dream while leaving enough room to move, especially without having to share it with someone else.

"Nice seat," Sarah said.

"Glass leather. Maybe I'll show you how it's made sometime. It's the Daughters' specialty. None of the other gangs know how to burn down the glass just right. But first let's make sure you don't kill yourself on this machine."

Sarah agreed with a nod of her head, eyes blinking from nerves.

"It's all in the handlebars," Taylor said. "They don't just help you steer, they turn it on, shut it off, speed it up. You can also lock them in place if you need to take your hands off while riding."

"Like to shoot something?"

"Or someone. But there's a truce on. Didn't anybody tell you? Go ahead and grab both handlebars and roll them forward. Just a little! You're just trying to engage it."

Sarah took a quivering breath and grabbed both handlebars. They were covered with the same material as her seat. She rolled her hands forward, centimeters at a time, until the cyclone began to rise.

"That's it," Taylor said. "Your cyclone is ready to ride."

Dear god, it was! The blue light rose from below and coursed through the bike like nuclear blood through the veins of a speed-crazed automaton. It hummed and buzzed and ached for street. The light could have been flowing into her own body for all she knew. She could think of no other way to describe it – she and the cyclone were one.

"You think we can let her ride a bit?" Taylor called back to Grindy.

"No other reason we're out here," the older woman said. "We'll stay back, make room for her."

"Show time," Taylor said low, thinning her eyes as if to say, "Don't make me look stupid!"

The Daughters of Forgotten Light, along with Grindy and Taylor, backed off toward Grindy's shop, leaving an empty square for Sarah to wreck all she wanted – which was not at all, but at least she wouldn't kill anyone else if she ended up crashing and burning under the blazing wheels.

With a light push of her wrists, Sarah eased the handlebars to roll forward. The cyclone responded and she had to fight for balance before instinct decided to take over. It was just like riding a bike. A big, outer space, light-infused bike.

Sarah laughed. "I'm doing it!"

"You're also going slower than ass sweat," Taylor said. "Up the speed."

Confidence fueled Sarah now. Speed? Damn right, she could up the speed. Sarah flicked her wrists forward and the cyclone bolted faster than she'd anticipated. Her back snapped, her body like a ragdoll taped to a rocket, no control. She was heading toward the gathered women and the back of Grindy's warehouse.

"Holy shit!" Dipity screamed, and threw Ava and Sterling out of the way. Hurley Girly and Lena jumped in the opposite direction.

Grindy simply sidestepped and shouted, "Flick back the handles!"

Sarah flinched to obey, snapping the handlebars back as hard and as quickly as she could. The cyclone sank and slowed, screeching against the glass floor until it came to a stop by lightly bumping Grindy's building.

"I'm sorry!" Sarah huffed from her nostrils and lowered her head, embarrassed. She could have killed them all, the only people who would have any use for her in this godforsaken place. And she'd wrecked it all.

Someone laughed. Then the rest of them joined in.

Sarah looked up. Lena was bent over in her hilarity. Sterling smiled and brushed off nonexistent dust from her knees and shoulders. Hurly Girly and the rest laughed in a huddle.

"Grindy barely even fucking moved," Dipity said.

The older woman shrugged. "I've seen the same shit before. Worse even."

"You're not mad?" Sarah asked. Had they been expecting her to screw up?

"Hell yeah, I'm mad!" Ava said through her chuckles. "But for your first time, it wasn't too bad."

"You should have seen Lena's first ride after I picked her from the box," Grindy said. "I bet a walrus could have driven it better."

"You picked Lena?"

"Who do you think started this gang in the first place?" Grindy said, cupping Sarah's face in her hands. She wiped away one of Sarah's tears. "Now quit all this crying shit, chica. You don't have time for it."

Sarah cleared the rest of the wet from her cheeks and eyes. She moved to get off the bike but Lena held a hand up for her to stay put.

"Stay on," Lena said. "We're going to the Core."

"Hell, I'll get my cyclone and come with you," said Grindy. "I have to top off a few of my energy reserves anyway."

"Sounds good," Lena said. "We'll have to go slow until Pao gets a better feel for it. You riding along might discourage anybody from fucking with us."

"Well," Grindy winked at Lena, "it's a good thing there's a truce. Ain't there?"

CHAPTER 10

Dolfuse lugged a metal case up the steps of the shipper port as a drizzle began to fall and wet her green blazer and matching skirt.

Why couldn't the enviroshields block out all the other godforsaken weather? Yes, flowers needed water, and grass was needed to accent those fine buildings downtown. But if they could put women on a floating square, light years away, surely they could find a way to do without disgusting, cold precipitation. Despite what detergent companies sold as "spring rain scent," it always smelled like a wet dog.

Shaped like a white cube, the shipper port stood bigger than any monument in Washington. Dolfuse had often thought some former Disney World architect had a hand in its design. She'd never gotten used to its size and color, gaudy and yet so plain. What would shippees brought here be thinking as they approached the massive square? Probably what Dolfuse had thought as she rode the monorail from the entrance gate. Those girls – shippees – would be going for a ride, no doubt, but there was no illusion it was a theme park.

Dolfuse shook the droplets of rain from her clothes and let a twosome of armed guards open the door for her. The men nodded without smiling and she returned the same. Nothing gave her goose bumps like that curt masculinity Bobby made so attractive. And hell's bells if she didn't find herself missing her husband for the millionth time that day.

Immediately through the door stood the scanner. One would think a UCNA senator would have immunity from such things, but the space port was a different world and the shippers working within its walls were a different breed, loyal to their leader, a woman named Beckles. Dolfuse had planned her script for the anticipated scrutiny of the metal case in her arms. She just had to keep calm and follow her plan.

"Senator Dolfuse," said a chubby woman from behind the control panel. Her rash-red cheeks glimmered under the lights. "I've only seen you on TV. You're shorter than I thought. What are you doing here?"

Screw you, too.

Dolfuse conjured a smile. "Just a small favor to ask of Spangler."

"Put your case on the track and step through the gate, please." The guard's politeness dripped with insincerity.

Dolfuse did as she was asked, and the alarm remained silent when she stepped through. Now she had to wait for the case to clear its own scan.

"I'm wondering if I can ask you something," the guard said.

"Yes?"

"I hear they might be trying to amend the Interstellar Relocation Act. Make it to where anyone over sixty-five can get sent up by their adult kids. That gonna happen?"

"I've only heard a few mentions of the idea. There's no official proposal."

"I'd love to see the look on my mother's face when I tell her she's on a one-way trip to the O. She tried to send me to Oubliette back when I was younger. My dad begged her not to. Never forgot that. Hey, what is this thing?"

Dolfuse's throat tightened. She wished she could throw out a quick answer, or at least swallow. The guard's eyes squinted at a screen showing what lay inside Dolfuse's box: a dark, shadowy, giant sperm.

"What are you bringing in here?"

"Model ship." Dolfuse cleared her throat. "Spangler is good with fixing them. My niece, she broke it, and I thought he could take a look."

"We really have enough to do around here without worrying with this kind of junk. Him especially."

"I understand." Dolfuse stood a little straighter, propping up what confidence she could. "It'll only take a minute."

The guard rolled her eyes and handed Dolfuse the case. "OK." Dolfuse tried to pull the case away but the guard didn't release. "Let me know when I can give Mom the good news."

"I'll be sure to keep you up to date."

The guard let go and turned back, talking to herself. "Just you wait, Mom. I'm going to push the launch button myself."

Spangler oversaw port control five stories up and had a full view of the launch room. He had assistants every now and then, but sending a few girls, manna, and whatever church donations the guards decided they didn't want for themselves was an easy enough job for one man, especially after five years.

"Hey, babycakes!" Spangler said when Dolfuse walked in.

A single lamp lit the gloomy space, casting computers and monitors as shadowy corpses. It didn't get exciting around the shipper port until the quarterly launch day, with the next one scheduled for the following month. The launch room, on the other side of a long, curved window, lay dark as well. Leaning over a cluster of buttons, Spangler had been poking them with a single finger.

Spangler hadn't cut his hair since he and Dolfuse were in high school and now it neared his elbows. He wore glasses rimmed with wild colors and always found a way to work the old United States flag design into his wardrobe – a response to the nickname he'd gotten when they were kids: "Star Spangler Banger." It made absolutely no sense and seemed to irritate Dolfuse more than it did Spangler. At least, until the day she told him it was some roundabout way of insulting him for being gay. The other kids whispered he'd be sent to Oubliette because he was too much of a lady to be sent to the army. That's when he got worried.

Dolfuse had no problem lying to Spangler's parents, saying she was his girlfriend. She would even throw in the occasional smooch to solidify the charade. Apparently, his parents were agreeable to an interracial relationship. Dolfuse had no doubt the senior Spanglers, deep down, knew the truth about their son. According to Spangler, if he ever came out they'd throw him on the first ship to basic training. No son of theirs! And all of that.

"I just have to keep pretending a little while longer," Spangler would say. "Eighteen seems so far away."

"I'll help you get there," Dolfuse had told him, on more than one occasion. "Any way I can."

And he'd made it. They both had.

"You must be here to worship my beautiful face," he said now in the control room.

"I've got it bad for you." Dolfuse set the case on a control desk. She'd wait for him to point it out.

They hugged.

"Caught me at a busy time."

"I can see that." Dolfuse waved a hand toward the empty room.

"What's in the box?" he asked.

"Open it and see."

Spangler hopped up from the control panel and stretched, pressing his hands to his lower back. A few clicks from the latches and he had the case's lid up. "Bobby sending you his oversized seed from overseas now? But it's black, must have died on the way over."

Dolfuse would have normally laughed. She would have. But it was much too soon. She turned away.

"Oh, Lindy, I'm sorry. You know my mouth is always a mile ahead of the rest of me. Here, hold on." He got up and went somewhere behind her, and came back with a tissue in his outstretched hand. "He'll be back soon. The war can't last forever."

"It's not that," Dolfuse said. "I'm still thinking about the baby."

"I see. So why are you here? With that thing in the box?"

"The vice president," Dolfuse said. "She's given me a job."

"I thought you worked for Arkansas, not the West Wing."

"You know how things work in Washington. When they say jump…"

"You strap on a rocket. Yeah, I get it. But I don't like what

I'm piecing together."

"Martin's wanting to know what happens on Oubliette," Dolfuse said.

Spangler's eyes darted from side to side. He always did that when he began to worry and his mind became garbled like one of his terrible abstract paintings. Hurrying to the door, he locked it, peeking out the glass inset. When he turned back to Dolfuse, his sympathetic disposition had vanished. His nostrils flared, his eyes wild. When he next spoke, he was much quieter. "So you want *me* to smuggle a package in the next shipment?"

"Not inside. I don't want the drone getting spotted. It needs to be placed on the exterior."

"Well this just keeps getting better and better. How the hell am I supposed to do that?"

Dolfuse looked down and glided her tongue over her top teeth. "I don't know."

"Lindy, we go way back. I'd be God knows where if it weren't for you. But this... I'm paid up. We've been even for a while."

"I know. This would be a huge favor. To me and Martin. For the continent."

"If they even *thought* I would mess around with the launches, let alone smuggle something, I'd be out on my ass, if not on the front lines in Pakistan."

"Let's not pretend we both don't want to keep this quiet. My career would be over, same as yours."

"Y'all won't be able to save me if I get found out. You wouldn't be here all secret agentlike if Martin had gone through the right channels. This is back room, under-the-table type stuff."

"I guess it is. Look, see if you can find a way. If you can't, you can't, and I'll understand. Fair enough?"

Spangler stared at her, not speaking for a while. Then he said, "You always get me with that 'fair enough' line. Like I'm the one getting the deal." With a sigh, Spangler threw his hands in the air. "I'll try."

"I appreciate it." Dolfuse smiled. "More than I have time to say right now. I promise I'll find a way to make it up to you."

Spangler nodded and picked up the drone. He held it in front of his face, turning it over.

"I have to go," Dolfuse said. She saw his attention was now completely focused on the drone.

"Yeah," Spangler said, as if he hadn't heard a word.

Dolfuse stepped back into the hall with a hollow feeling, like she was a smoking crater left by a bomb. The pristine white tiles in front of her went on forever and she just kept walking, looking for any mark or scuff. But none ever came. She'd never left Spangler with so few words, or so harsh a vibe between them. She was so focused on replaying their brief meeting in her head, she didn't notice she'd lost her way and stood in a part of the shipper port she'd never seen before.

The halls became more maze-like and unending, but she finally found an elevator. This wasn't the one she'd taken up to see Spangler. She wouldn't have even noticed it if she hadn't been focused on the slick white walls to her right and spotted the small lift button set to its side.

The inside of the elevator only had one button to press, so Dolfuse pressed it. Maybe it was a quick way for personnel to reach the lobby.

But she didn't step out into the lobby. Here, there was

only more antiseptic white – except for the clear glass wall ahead. On the other side, guards marched young women under the threat of sticks buzzing with electricity. The shipper guards wore blue and the brim of their hats hid their eyes. Heads down, the prisoners marched on.

Outcasts. Unwanteds. Shippees.

There had to be at least a dozen in the group. They wore white jumpsuits and if their hair was long they'd pulled it back with a white band. The shippees were all races, shapes, and sizes, a veritable representation of all of Earth's womenfolk, not to belong to Earth for much longer. Some walked with crutches or shook their heads uncontrollably as they went, others didn't show any physical reason their mothers gave them up.

A girl stumbled and fell to the floor. A guard lifted a stun stick and marched toward her, but one of the other shippees reached the fallen girl before the guard did. She placed the girl's arm around her shoulder and moved back into alignment. The guard stopped, lowered the weapon, and the group continued on.

Dolfuse moved closer to the glass after they'd gone, thinking the hallway on the other side would be empty. But another group trotted past only a minute after the others had left. Same number of girls. Same number of guards. None of them gave recognition of her standing there. They kept moving and Dolfuse looked beyond them, to the huge room they stomped toward.

It stretched below ground, like an upside-down tower. Hundreds of shippees either marched around or let the guards drag them out of tiny cells with glass doors and white walls.

Hundreds.

Dolfuse and most others on the Hill were under the impression the port launched the girls soon after arriving. But what she'd stumbled on, what she saw on the other side of that glass told her the Warden, Beckles, was stockpiling shippees, probably holding back a few from every shipment, building their numbers slowly at a time. For what?

"Senator Dolfuse." The voice jolted her.

When she turned, two guards stood shoulder to shoulder, dressed in the same blue uniform as those leading the shippees through the subterranean prison.

"Yes," Dolfuse said.

"Come with us." The one on the right spoke.

"I was just leaving."

"No ma'am. Warden Beckles instructed us to bring you straight to her. Now."

CHAPTER 11

The Daughters of Forgotten Light tore through the streets of Oubliette. In a way, Sarah found it easy being the ass of the gang. All she had to do was follow where the others led. On the other hand, a few times on the way to the Core she'd become freaked out about how fast they were going and slowed down, having to go even faster to catch up.

Hurley Girly had to stop once to fetch her. "We can't take it slow out here just for you. Slow is dead. Got it?"

Sarah said she'd try, and that was good enough for Hurley Girly.

Lena let Grindy have her old spot at the head of the V. No words had to be said. Lena just waited for Grindy to rip onto the street and the rest followed as usual. The Daughters respected the old woman a whole lot, and it showed in their voices, in how they held themselves. Reverence had to be earned on Oubliette, Sarah realized, but it held for life.

"Slow up, Pao!" Hurley Girly screamed from in front of her.

Sarah slowed and veered clumsily out of the V.

"We're coming up on the Core."

A few heaved breaths and Sarah got back into formation. They rounded the next curve and a hundred feet or so ahead, dropping into unknown darkness, waited the gaping mouth of a large tunnel entrance.

"My favorite part!" Dipity shouted.

The tunnel swallowed them, the blaze of Daughter cyclone wheels their only light, as the bikes dropped faster and faster. Sarah's gut tightened. But she wouldn't have traded the feeling for all the manna in Oubliette.

She held on tight, always staying behind Hurley Girly, the only thing she had to worry about. The gang turned suddenly left. Sarah shook with nerves, but turned with them. Light came from somewhere below, and as the gang stayed tight in the turn it showed they were rounding a spiral path that led down to something very large and bright. The Daughters raised their left arms with a fist, whooping and yelling like it was their last hoorah.

Sarah tipped her head toward the side of the spiral. At the bottom spun a massive ball of energy between two columns, one column hanging above and the other sticking out of the floor. Turning like a small sun, the Core was blinding. When the gang reached the bottom, they slowed and had to split to each side of the lower column. The other Daughters shut down their cyclones, but it took Sarah a minute to remember she needed to pull the handles all the way back.

"This is the Core," Grindy said. "Everything that moves or lights up in this suck hole derives its power from this. The Veil, the engines that recycle our air, everything."

The orb changed color, from blue to green.

"Look at that," Hurley Girly said. "It likes you."

"What?" Sarah caught her breath. Was this thing alive?

The Daughters laughed, even Grindy.

"Hurley, you're so stupid," Ava said.

"This thing isn't sentient." Grindy swatted the hair from Ava's eyes. "It changes color from the reactions of the different elements inside it. These poles," Grindy pointed to the one above and the one below, "are what keep it from causing a nuclear explosion and sending us all to a worse Hell."

Sarah watched it for a few seconds in silence, until buzzing hums and howls came from above the Daughters. An orange glow filled the dark of the spiraling track, getting brighter as it sped closer, the laughter and swearwords getting louder. Trouble was coming.

"Fuck me," Ava said.

The Amazons hovered off the bottom of the ramp, stopping to block the only exit. Each of their faces dropped its celebration, turning into scowls when they saw Sarah and the other Daughters. The Amazon at the back even spit at the ground.

The baby was there, too. The woman who'd spit carried her in a sack strapped around her chest. It didn't make sense, though, for this Amazon to be at the rear. At the receiving stage Sarah assumed the redhead had been the head of her gang.

"You get demoted, Farica?" Lena asked. "I hope so. Ass suits you."

"Watch your mouth about our dearly departed," Farica said with a frown that quickly flipped to a grin. "Wanted to show Rory the beauty of a cyclone parade through the city. Don't want to go too fast with her, you know."

The baby cooed in her sleep.

"You shouldn't be riding with the kid like that," Grindy said.

"Thanks for the advice, old woman. But I think I can call my own shots without your input." Farica got off her bike and the others did the same. "Well, well, seems your own pretty little birdie hasn't died yet." She stomped over to Sarah with hands on hips. "You want to take one for the team, little girl? See if you can rang me before I break your teeth."

The verbal attack came so suddenly, Sarah had to fight the urge to back away like some coward. She wasn't ready for a fight.

"She knows about the truce," Grindy said. "Just like you."

Farica got in Sarah's face, no longer talking. Her breath smelled like a boiling pot of dog droppings and wet rat. Pieces of whatever she'd last eaten hung in her teeth. Feeling for the brass knuckles in her pants pocket, Sarah hoped she wouldn't have to use them. The rang gun might have been useless to her then, but the knuckles had no safety switch. Sarah kept her gaze locked on the crazy woman's own shaky eyes.

Just a little more wiggling and the knuckles would be on Sarah's hand. And then she'd swing.

Farica backed away and laughed. "I'm just messing with you, China Doll. Jesus, you sheilas are so serious sometimes."

"What the fuck are you doing here?" Lena said, stepping around and putting a tight hand on Sarah's throwing arm. She must have known what Sarah was planning.

Farica waved one of the baby's limp hands. "Like I said. Showing Rory the Core."

"Looks like we were here first." Lena's head twitched, just for a second, like she'd been zapped by a shipper guard's electric rod. Clenching her fists, she shook it off, like she'd only been mildly annoyed by this rival gang. But Sarah had seen the monster trying to come out.

Farica pointed to her gang behind her. "Yeah, well, there's the exit."

"I'll show you an exit!" Lena shouted.

"OK," said Grindy. "Let's all ease off. Farica, do you think your sheilas could give us a minute. I just need to refill some canisters."

"Nowhere in the truce does it say we can't be in the same place at the same time."

"I'm asking as a favor," Grindy sighed. "It'll be easier that way."

"I don't owe you shit, old woman." Farica raised the baby's hand again and danced it in the air. Instinct made the kid wrap its pudgy digits around Farica's index finger. Had to be instinct. Sarah couldn't see any living creature choosing to show Farica a shred of affection.

"Fine," Grindy said, as she hobbled to her cyclone. "I'll come back later."

"You don't have to take this shit," Lena said. "Tell them to go."

"Can't we all just get along?" said Farica.

The other Daughters stayed silent, caught between loyalties. Sarah remembered her promise to support Lena. No matter what. And besides, she already had the brass knuckles in place.

Grindy got on her bike and stared at Lena with tired eyes. In the ever-changing glow of the Core, they looked dark and foreboding. "Let it go, Lena."

Lena's arm twitched, probably aching to shoot her rang.

But after a moment she got on her cyclone, as did the rest of the Daughters. The tension reaching its peak must have woken the baby. Her cries echoed from the Core as the Daughters rode back out to the city. No one said anything the rest of the way home.

Sarah sat on her bed, staring at nothing through the window when Sterling knocked at her door. The sound jolted her from thought, and the only thought she seemed to have when she found the time to be alone was whether this was really happening.

She smiled and nodded at Sterling. The woman came over and sat at the end of the crate bed. Her face was long and tanner than the others, but still watery from the lack of sunlight.

You're fitting in well, Sterling signed.

"It's hard to tell. I feel like I'm a constant screw up."

That just shows you care. I'd be worried if you were apathetic.

Sarah smiled and laughed softly.

Where did you learn to sign?

Sarah shrugged. "My father traded free plumbing jobs to the lady down the street who taught it. He thought it would help me make money later on. And I was never good at learning other spoken languages. What about you? I guess you learned early."

My father thought it was a blessing for me not to have a voice. My mother secretly took me to a mosque where they taught ASL. I went every day during the week. Until my father found out.

"Is that why you got sent here?"

Sterling tilted her head a little and the dweller lights from outside caught in her eyes. Sarah wondered what she'd have to do to get eyes like that.

Nothing so simple, Sterling signed.

"Can I ask you something?"

Sterling nodded. A strand of her dark hair fell across her face.

"I don't mean to be rude," Sarah said, "but doesn't it make things harder that you don't have a voice? In the gang, I mean."

Shrugging, Sterling signed, *Most of Lena's commands on the road are hand signals. And it doesn't take words to ride or shoot. We've made it work. And with all the spare time we have here, everyone learned to sign so they could bitch to me about something I'd rather have ignored.*

"I really wanted to hit that woman today. Farica. I've never wanted to do anything more in my life. Lena stopped me before I could."

Horror sees everything, Sterling signed.

"Could I have done it? Would that be allowed by the truce, if I used my left hand?"

I'm not your mother. You don't have to ask me for permission. As long it's your left hand, I'll have your back.

"Why is the truce so important?"

Sterling took a deep breath and sat there a moment. *The truce gives the ones already here a chance. Things were tougher before you came.*

"That's hard to imagine."

It was every woman for herself. The gangs provided protection to the dwellers who swore loyalty to them, but we could only do so much. When you hear an expression like "the streets ran red with blood," I've actually seen it. Guts don't clean off glass streets so easily.

Sarah latched onto something to change the subject. "Why didn't Lena pick a dweller, someone already here to replace Loveless?"

You saying she made the wrong decision?

"No!"

Sterling laughed, breathy with no weight behind it. *It's the rules. If you don't get picked from the box, you're a dweller forever. Most dwellers are just glad not to be on the Amazons' menu.*

"What happened to her? Loveless, I mean."

Sterling looked away. *It's not my place to say.*

Sarah ached to see Sterling's eyes again, especially since she'd clearly said something to upset the mute Daughter, but, after a while, not being able to come up with anything to say, Sarah stared through the window again, into the night where the streets twisted in steep curves.

A horrible feeling gripped her from inside. She didn't know where it had come from, but it was like a premonition without any hint of what it meant. But it was coming, whatever *it* was.

"Is there any way the truce could end?" Sarah said, turning back to Sterling.

Sterling cleared her throat – strange, since she never used her voice. *Grindy wouldn't let that happen,* Sterling signed. *Neither would Lena. They know what it would cost.* She put a hand on Sarah's own, smiling gently, as if she'd never tried to be happy before.

The smile didn't last.

But Lena has been losing her mind for a while. When Loveless died, it just made it worse. Horror needs a break. Leading this gang has worn her out. I don't want it. But I know it shouldn't be Lena. Not anymore.

Sarah shook her head. "I'd hoped the worst was behind me, in that space port they kept us all in. But… I've got this feeling… something I can't shake. I'm beginning to think the worst is just around the corner."

CHAPTER 12

"What are you doing in my port?"

Warden Cynthia Beckles was a wall of a woman, both in her large, imposing build and in the way she transacted business – at least, from what Dolfuse had heard. Sitting there in Beckles' office was the first time she'd had the misfortune to meet the warden. Beckles wore her gray hair in a tight ponytail that ended in the middle of her back, and she stood tall enough that Dolfuse would have had to jump to grab the end.

On the wall to Dolfuse's left, thousands of ID tags on silver chains meshed together in a pile, hanging in a glassless frame. A spotlight hung from above to showcase the "art".

A monorail zipped toward the port as Beckles looked out to the courtyard four stories below. From this position, with her back to Dolfuse, the warden had asked her question. Between them, on a large white desk, a steak lay half-eaten and neglected.

"I came to see Spangler," Dolfuse said. "A personal matter."

Beckles turned, fingers red from squeezing her arms. Her eyes bulged like some junkie on a high. "Do you think this is some kind of laidback office where you can drop in whenever you like and have a chat?"

"No. But–"

"In case that scanner you went through didn't give you a clue, or the guards marching around here, this port isn't some visitors' center. You came in through the public entrance. How would you like a tour of the back way in, like all the shippees?"

Was that some kind of threat?

Beckles shifted her jaw. An underbite, Dolfuse swore she had a touch of one. All the warden needed now was a large club and green skin to finish off the ogre look.

"I did get a glimpse of some of the young women to be launched," said Dolfuse.

"That was nothing, senator. Those are shippees who were held back for extra… correction. It takes a while to break them, you see. These girls, these outcasts, aren't fit for the military or society for that matter. I love each and every one of them, but they're still animals. And Oubliette is their ark."

"I didn't take you as religious, warden."

Beckles smiled and shrugged. She walked over to the desk and Dolfuse instinctively tensed. The warden bent down and retrieved a metal bowl that sang with clinking contents as she stomped over to the silver tag cluster hanging on the wall. "You see these?"

Dolfuse nodded, swallowing.

"They're identification tags. Every girl gets one when they come to me." She appreciated them as if she'd earned them in some hard-fought contest. "I give them a hug and wish them well before I take the tags back. You're looking at a piece of every shippee that's been through here. Even before I took this position. Thousands of them."

The joy dripping from the warden's words turned Dolfuse's stomach, making her squirm in her seat. With a toss of the bowl, Beckles threw a new cluster of tags and chains into the air. They flew into the rest of the colorless collage by an invisible force. A few metallic clicks and they were stuck there for good.

"Magnets," Dolfuse said.

"The strongest."

"I apologize for any inconvenience I've been." Dolfuse cleared her throat. "I'm sure you've heard of my continued support of your funding."

Maybe that'll get her off my rear end.

Beckles harrumphed. "Then you should know we don't need any of you snooping around here like a bunch of bloodhounds. I treat these girls as if they were my own daughters, temporarily. We may not be the military, but this port has always been granted autonomy. It works better that way. For all."

"Agreed."

Dolfuse just wanted to get on the fastest monorail out of there. Tossing Beckles a few agreeable tokens was just the price of the ticket. It didn't hurt her pride to do so. After all, Dolfuse was a politician.

"What did you discuss with my chief engineer?"

"Just seeing if he could look at a toy rocket for my niece. He's good with that sort of thing."

"I know." Beckles put a thick hand on the back of her chair and dragged it from the desk. The chair didn't have wheels, so Dolfuse endured every screeching second of metal-on-floor scraping.

"I need him to focus on those *sorts of things* for this port.

I don't want to see you in here again. Not without my permission."

"If that's what you'd prefer."

"It's what I command. In here, I am God. You've walked into my universe."

Dolfuse stood. "Then, perhaps I should leave you to your flood. Oubliette being an ark and all."

She clomped to the door.

Beckles waved a limp hand. "And tell all of your smarmy friends on the Hill to stay out of my hair. I've got enough to worry about, sending out their trash." Her voice echoed off the walls. The warden said something else but Dolfuse was already on the other side of the door.

"Smarmy?" Vice President Martin nodded her thanks as the waiter set down a martini. "She used that actual word?"

"I didn't wait around for her to call us all bloodsucking et cetera, et cetera." Dolfuse stared at the drops of condensation trickling down the sides of her glass of water. Being in Martin's presence ground her gears as much as Beckles, just in a different way.

"She sounds just as bitchy as I used to think she was. People don't change, do they, Linda?"

"Only the good ones."

The Terrace was Martin's favorite restaurant. Even if Dolfuse's staff hadn't provided that information, Martin herself had made it known at least six times before they'd even received their basket of rolls. It was a politician's haven most citizens couldn't afford, and one of the only places serving real food.

Sharp laughter from the back of the restaurant caused

Dolfuse to jump, lifting her head to see where the noise had come from. The light here hurt her eyes, given off by dozens of bulbs the size of sea shells, hanging from chandeliers or sconces.

"She really put you on edge." Martin sipped her drink.

"That place," Dolfuse said, "is awful."

Martin eyed Dolfuse for a moment and chewed on a piece of roll. "How are you doing? Dealing with all of this?"

"Like a professional."

"Emotionally?"

"I don't have time to consider my emotions at present, Madam Vice President. You've given me an important task."

"Is that thing today with Beckles going to interfere?"

"Not unless she gives my guy a hard time. My main concern is this ansible thing I spoke to you about."

Martin finished off her drink and nodded approvingly. "That chip I gave you, did you put it inside the drone?"

"Yes, but–"

"I have someone. Lundgate is his name. He's an excellent programmer and drone pilot."

"Are you sure it will work?"

"I don't think we have a choice, Linda."

She was right. Dolfuse couldn't ask Spangler to risk his job again if it failed. This would be the only shot.

"Of course," Dolfuse said.

"Another month or so?"

"Next shipment is five weeks from tomorrow."

"Goddamn, that drink packs a punch." Martin sighed and sat back in her chair.

The waiter arrived with their food: a big bowl of chicken alfredo pasta for Martin, only a Cobb salad for the senator.

Dolfuse stared at the boiled egg slices and cubes of ham. She only ate like this when she was out with bigwigs, like Martin, and she always felt guilty. The people in her state, in the whole damn continent, had to live off rationed, heavily preserved, and fabricated junk.

"You've done good work so far, Linda." Martin swirled noodles onto her fork. "I knew you were the one to get things done. And keep it quiet."

"Of course."

"We're finally going to see what's been going on up there."

CHAPTER 13

"Come on, you big pussy, hit me like a girl!" Hurley Girly spit blood and motioned for Dipity to come at her again.

Dipity heaved and wiped sweat from her eyes, keeping the other hand in a fist. Another ill effect from the truce was that aggression became bottled up. Without other gangs to whale on without good reason, the Daughters of Forgotten Light had no one besides themselves to release a little tension.

Dipity swung again, but this time Hurley Girly ducked and landed a hit in Dipity's stomach. The air left the big woman with an *oof*, and Hurley Girly hopped in a semicircle, giggling.

Lena watched from atop a manna box in the corner, scratching a fingernail into the glass wall. Scratching, scratching. She could sit there and do it for another decade and never make a blemish – a benefit of Oubliette glass.

That shit stain, Farica, she thought. *I should have let Pao knock her out. Took the baby and ran.*

Rory. What kind of name was that anyway?

But she'd just stood there and let Grindy grovel to the truce, to those murderous savages. Grindy had weakened them in that moment. Lena remembered the old days, when Grindy was ruthless and didn't put up with a damned thing. Then one day she'd given it all up, fell in love with that dweller, Taylor, and decided to put her rang-shooting days to bed. She made Lena head of the Daughters and it wasn't long before Grindy concocted the truce.

Had it been Taylor's idea? Some suggestion whispered in Grindy's ear while she lay in bed with the dweller's arms wrapped around her? Dangerous ideas were planted in positions like that. Women liked to think they weren't susceptible to pillow promises or swayed by swinging hips, but weakness to lust and other four-letter words was a fault that knew no gender. It's why Lena had sworn it all off before she ever left her shipment box.

Fuck the truce.

Lena waited for the voice of reason, the one hiding in the back of her head that always shouted against her craving for blood. But it didn't come. The voice had disappeared or, more likely, harmonized with the urge for war.

Well, I'm one less person to convince, Lena thought. *Five more to go.*

Hurley Girly and Dipity had their arms grappled and stumbled around the ganghouse like a pair of locked-up crabs.

"Call it a match, sheilas," Lena said.

They dropped their arms and turned to her, breathing hard. Sterling and Sarah looked up from where they sat, but Ava still slept.

"Wake her up," Lena said.

Sarah gingerly put a hand on Ava's shoulder and shook it. The gang's right arm woke with a frown. "What the fuck?"

"I want your attention," Lena boomed.

"I was asleep."

"And I don't give a shit!"

Ava snapped to her feet and walked toward the others.

Lena stayed on the manna box. "Are you all as tired as I am?"

"I was trying to fix that with a nap," Ava said.

"I mean tired of playing nice. Did you see the smirk on those Amazons' faces? They were laughing at us. Kicking us out of the Core like they owned the fucking thing. Is that who we've become?"

"Hell, no," Dipity said.

"Apparently it is. This truce has done nothing but weaken us since the day it started. I'm tired of it. I'm tired of always second-guessing myself, telling you sheilas one thing while believing another. I feel like two fucking people wrestling inside the same skin. I feel like I'm losing my mind."

None of them spoke. They looked to the floor or a wall, except Sterling. She kept her eyes on Lena, listening.

"Well?" Lena sat straighter.

Sterling signed, *You're two people? Which one should we listen to?*

"Don't be a wiseass," Lena said. "I thought we could keep the peace, like Grindy wants. But it's not going to happen while those dick nuggets are still around."

"The Amazons?" Dipity asked. "Or everybody?"

Lena rubbed her eyes. Tired. So tired. "I'm not looking to dominate the city. And I'm not worried about the OC."

"But if we break the truce, we're all fair game. You said that yourself not too long ago." Hurley Girly bit her lip and shook her head. "Sterling's right. I don't know which one of you is the real Lena."

"It was a fucking *metaphor!*" Lena jumped off the manna box.

"What do you want us to do?" Sarah's voice cracked. The others turned back to her like they'd forgotten she was there.

Lena grinned. Pao would side with her. She'd given her word and that was a rare commodity, on Oubliette or anywhere else. "We need to give them a reason to come looking for us. And when they do, we'll be ready."

"Like an ambush?" Ava asked. "What could we do to piss them off?"

"Take the baby," Lena said.

Dipity whistled.

"Holy shit," said Hurly Girly.

"What about the OC?" Ava asked. "They'll come for the kid, too."

"We'll worry about one gang at a time," Lena said.

Ava scoffed. "Not if they tag team us."

"You know what I think," Dipity said. "I think you need to cool down a little, Horror. You aren't thinking this through."

"I've been thinking it through since we tossed that Amazon bitch over the bridge. Now who's with me on this?" Lena looked over the group, but none of them raised their arms or spoke up. She stopped and stared at Sarah Pao, waiting for her to do what she promised.

Sarah shied from Lena's glare and looked at Sterling. The mute tightened her crossed arms and sniffed. Sterling had obviously made up her mind, but Sarah stirred and, with glances from Lena to Sterling and finally the floor, she raised her hand.

"I'm with you," Sarah said.

"You just earned your jacket," Lena said. "Is she the only one?"

Ava stepped forward and shrugged. "Fuck it, I've got nothing better to do."

"Sorry, Lena," Dipity said. "I don't think it's a good call."

"Me neither," said Hurley Girly.

"Well," Lena said. "I'm sorry you all think this is a fucking democracy."

Groans croaked under breath and they all stirred on their feet. It was something every leader had to do sometimes: tighten the belt so they didn't get too big for their breeches.

"We're going to do this," Lena said. "But I'm going to make it a fair deal. Any of you feeling froggy and want to challenge my authority, come get some. You knock me on my ass, you can lead the gang."

Dipity and Hurley Girly stepped back and harmonized in saying, "It's your gang."

Sterling stepped forward and took off her jacket. She threw it to Sarah and signed, *Hold on to that for me.*

Sterling, huh? Lena never thought it would be her. Ava maybe. Sterling was always a rock, consistent, loyal. But even rocks could be crushed. Lena left her jacket on. She fought better that way, and it took some of the sting from any body shots. "You sure?" she asked Sterling.

Sterling nodded and immediately swung for Lena's face. Lena flinched backwards, bringing her hands up. The punch had almost taken her out.

Never trust the quiet ones.

Lena let loose, a flurry of punches, although Sterling quickly blocked them with her forearms. Lena weaved and ducked, aiming for the body when she couldn't see an opening for the head. Sterling met her fists with a block each time.

Lena roared and stomped into Sterling's kneecap. When Sterling dropped, Lena went in for an ending blow, but Sterling lashed out and socked Lena in the gut. Both women fell to their knees, wrestling for a hold of each other. Hair was pulled, screaming and spit huffed through gritted teeth. Lena's swelling rage bubbled up, the one she kept deep down in the dark. It wanted out.

So she let it out.

Sterling's nose appeared through a gap between their arms and Lena thrust her head forward. The crunching cartilage against Lena's forehead felt exquisite, like autumn leaves under a new pair of boots. Sterling fell back and Lena spun around to catch the mute's head and locked her arms around Sterling's neck.

Squeeze. Squeeze the fucking thing off!

Lena vaguely heard shouting behind her, and then pats that became punches in her back and side. Sterling stared up at her with bloodshot eyes, red face, blue lips. Blood filled her nostrils but never dripped from them. Lena had wanted something like this for a long time. It felt amazing. But it wasn't the face she wanted. It wasn't Farica.

Jesus!

Lena released her grip and scrambled back with hands and heels. Squatting over her, Sarah rubbed Sterling's back as she hacked and spit. Sterling's color slowly returned to normal.

"What the fuck is wrong with you?" Sarah screamed, keeping her teary eyes on Sterling.

For a split instant, Lena wanted to apologize, to comfort Sterling along with Sarah and the others. But that would be too easy. It was a fair fight, one Sterling had willingly gone into. Hell, she wasn't even dead. They needed this sort of thing every now and then. Remind them that they could die at any moment.

"You OK?" Dipity helped Sterling up by the forearms.

Sterling nodded and hid her face from Lena.

"Get yourselves together," Lena said. "We're taking that baby and we're wiping out the Amazons for good."

Lena hurried toward the black stairs, toward her room, to cool down. The dark would envelop her with peace and silence, just the thing to let her mind settle and think of a good plan for what was to come. She'd do it alone if she had to. Let the others chew on what had just happened.

In Lena's wake, among Sterling's coughs and the soft assurances of the others, Ava said, "And that, Pao, is why we call her Horror."

CHAPTER 14

Four weeks after meeting with Martin, Senator Dolfuse curled up on her couch to watch the replay of the State of the Union with a Coke and a bag of Skittles. Her and Bobby's anniversary had been the week before, and she'd had to buy herself the regular gift of candy and soda – an annual treat that cost more than the clothes she wore.

She'd been studying the packet again; the one Martin had given her, the one with everything they knew about Oubliette, which wasn't much more than what Dolfuse was already wise to.

Oubliette had started as an experiment in interstellar living, initially funded by a small group of investors who were rich enough they hadn't invented an -illionaire to describe their combined wealth. They'd planned it to be their own private island in space – or rather, for their children's children, seeing how long it took just to send builders out to construct the space gate. It took over a century and their combined estates as endowment.

But it wouldn't belong to any of them.

It was only after the space gate was functioning, with the city nearly finished, that the Earth decided it would bring about another ice age. That's when the United Continent of North America stepped in. The continent's best minds quickly constructed the enviroshields to block out the cold, while the UCNA seized Oubliette in response to the encroaching disaster. Thus, the issue arose of what to do with the blasted city.

With a flick of her wrist, Dolfuse tossed the packet to the other side of the couch and hit play on the State of the Union recording.

Of course, she'd been there to hear the address in person. From where she sat, she could have counted President Griffin's wrinkles without squinting. But she never seemed to be able to concentrate during those kinds of things since it was so loud and electrified by partisan bias, and the entire continent's eyes were on them all. Dolfuse had practiced being good at faking it, but every time without fail, she found herself drifting on thoughts of other things while the president spoke.

Tonight had been one specific thought, on one specific person. Two, if she counted Bobby's occasional cameos.

"There are still those," President Griffin said on Dolfuse's television screen, "that claim we are needlessly controlling the population and that we have no cause to be in the east.

"I stand before you tonight to proclaim there is only so much food and room to go around. It's a hard fact that we have to face. We are not callous, we are supporters of choice. We do not murder, we give second chances to those given up. Oubliette and the Interstellar Relocation Act are still working. Crime is nonexistent. North Americans are living better since this cataclysm affected our planet. The Eastern Axis is dwindling to nothing. My fellow citizens, the state of our continent is strong, and will continue to be, so long as I am its president."

A standing ovation from the congressional floor followed. Dolfuse popped a few Skittles into her mouth and spotted herself in the crowd – a toothy smile and enthusiastic clapping.

I should have been an actress.

She surfed through television channels bloated with advertisements for new hovercars or public access poetry slams speculating what had become of shippees long forgotten. There wasn't much on at this time of night. Against her better judgment, she decided to see what the crazies were discussing on the Vox Network.

"…and tonight we're discussing Oubliette. What happens there? Is it working after all these years? Or should we bring these women home?" The host, John Fillmore, sported his usual greased-back hair and scowling face, a UCNA flag pin ever-present on his lapel.

"My guests are Tom Scott, editorialist for the *Boston Commuter*, and Trax, a member of underground anti-Oubliette group, No Ship, who's asked us not to reveal his real identity."

The TV showed a middle-aged white man on the left and a shadowed figure backlit with red light on the right. Dolfuse guessed watching this trash wouldn't aid in her mission to discover Oubliette's secrets, but it wouldn't hurt.

"I don't know if it's Mister or Miss Trax, but let's start with you," Fillmore said. "Why hide in the dark? Why the secret?"

"Well first, John, this government, and this administration in particular, doesn't make it very safe or welcoming to publicly protest shipping. Second, it's no secret what we stand for, and that's the complete shutdown of Oubliette and the return of all women who've been sent there."

The white guy to the left shook his head.

Fillmore responded. "But supporters of shipping say it's not like the government is forcing mothers to send their children away; they're given the choice. And most continental citizens say they aren't even pro-shipping, they're just in support of the mother having authority over their children's lives and if their family can afford them."

"That's where these confused individuals are mistaken," Trax said. "I fully believe in mothers choosing how they raise their children. However, I don't know about you, but I've made plenty of bad choices in my life. And what about a shippee's choice? People don't consider that mothers could be coerced by an abusive spouse or family member. Hell, even the government preys on the impoverished by offering them money in exchange for their children. When this administration uses the word 'choice' they're incentivizing the choice *they* want to be made."

Fillmore smirked and nodded.

"I was the only girl, with three brothers and a single mother," Trax said. "Never once did she consider sending us away to the military or Oubliette. What the government has done is hide a population control agenda within the guise of maternal choice. This whole thing is hypocritical. Our continent doesn't want to be labeled murderers, but that's just what we are when we send our children to die in an unwinnable war, or our 'noncompliant' females to some city in space. We spend millions of dollars shipping them and sending them food every quarter. This government feels guilty but is too big of a pussy to just kill all of them like they'd really want."

"OK, you can't say–"

Dolfuse laughed.

"And that's why we want it shut down," Trax finished.

Fillmore huffed from inflated cheeks. "Tom Scott, what do you have to say about all this?"

"John, one thing myself and the lady behind the curtain," he laughed, "have in common, is that I believe how we're proceeding right now with Oubliette is totally wasteful. However, I would never want to infringe on shipping or military acquisition."

"So, you're saying–"

"John, I'm saying we keep shipping without all the hubbub of feeding them, too."

Trax lifted frustrated, shadowy arms. "Did you just suggest genocide on continental television?"

"That's not what I'm saying–"

"No," Trax said. "That's exactly what you're suggesting. At the very least it would be the worst case of neglect and abandonment. John, this is exactly what I'm talking about. This kind of attitude…"

An email notification appeared in the bottom corner of the TV. Bobby had sent it.

Dolfuse gasped and nearly choked on her candy. By God, it was like hearing from someone long dead. Bobby, he was alive. She ran to the TV screen and touched the notification. The broadcast paused and the email appeared.

L,

They finally let me up for air. I'm coming home in a few months. I miss you a hell of a lot. I don't have much clearance for a long letter, but I wanted to let you know the

good news. I also have a surprise for you. How would you
like to start a family?
  Love you terribly,
    B

Oh god, it hurt. The joy and the despair together like
some mismatched lump of fire and ice lodged in her chest.
Her eyes stung and then the tears came. She lay on the
couch so as not to wet the carpet, placing her hands to her
face.

We'll be happy, she told herself. He'll be back soon and
everything will be like before he left. He won't find out. He
can't.

She wished she was as good at lying to herself as she was
the rest of Congress.

CHAPTER 15

"The baby," Lena said as she stepped into the main room of the ganghouse. "We'll take her the night the shipment comes in."

"Don't you think it'll be pretty obvious we're not there?" Ava was cleaning off her jacket. They all wanted to look sharp for the night's ceremony.

"That's the point," Lena said. "We want them to come looking for us."

"And if they bring the baby with them to the stage?"

"They'll leave her with the dwellers," Lena smiled. "I have it on good authority."

What she had was a good mole in the Amazons' dweller population, a psychotic who'd choke herself with her own hair mid-conversation. But the information she traded for manna made it worth dealing with her crazy ass. It was Lena's little secret and she wasn't a bit ashamed of keeping it to herself.

Hurley Girly and Dipity entered next, they had their jackets zipped up to their chests and their hair finger-combed out – what accounted for "dressing up" on Oubliette.

"Let's talk about it later," Lena told Ava. There'd be time enough for a quick rundown of what she had in mind. It was going to be spectacular.

Sterling brought in Sarah, linked onto her arm. Hurley Girly frowned and hunted for something else to look for in the room. Sterling's nose swelled purple and yellow.

Shit, Lena thought. *I feel like shit.* But she didn't show it.

Ava handed over Loveless's jacket. It had been cleaned off, ready for a new owner.

"I always feel like there should be music," Dipity said.

Hurley Girly shrugged. "We could hum."

"Shut up, you guys!" Ava snapped.

Lena stood in the middle of the room, hands on her hips. Sterling led Sarah over and then took her place with the other Daughters.

"Kneel," Lena said.

Sarah did.

"This jacket is made from pieces of this city, boiled down and made into something new. You're a part of this city now. Do you want to be made new?"

"Yes," Sarah said, following the script Ava had coached her through.

Ava stepped forward. "Are you willing to kill for your sisters?"

"With everything I have."

"Will you ride into death if you have to?" asked Dipity.

"I will."

Lena glared at Sterling, who focused on Sarah and the ceremony. Lena hoped she heard that last question well enough, remembered that she'd taken the same oath not too long ago. How easy it is to forget, she thought, even when you have nothing to do but ride or die.

Sterling signed, *Will you care for the dwellers under you?*

"They will be like my family, their pain is my own."

Hurley Girly breathed in slowly, holding back laughter. She stared at Sarah, probably having forgotten her lines. Finally, she said, "Are you forgotten?"

"Long forgotten," Sarah said.

"Then stand up and be forgotten with the rest of us," Lena said.

Sarah stood and Lena helped her ease into the jacket. The rest of the Daughters whooped and patted Sarah hard on the back. The thin glass leather looked good on her if not a little big. Her short blue hair above the collar brought it all together. She fit in, and Lena didn't just mean the jacket. Despite all recent and questionable decisions, Lena had made an excellent pick from this last shipment, she knew that much. The smile on Sarah's face brought Lena back to the night she'd received her own jacket from Grindy. She'd been exactly where Sarah stood. When her arms had slid into the sleeves – damn, there was no other feeling like it. She remembered sleeping with her jacket on, never taking it off until the following quarter. Grindy had forced her to take a shower, saying the other Daughters complained she smelled like the Sludge River.

"How's it feel?" Hurley Girly asked Sarah.

"It feels…" Sarah's eyes watered, still smiling. She was trying hard not to cry. When she hid her face in the crook of her newly jacketed arm, the other Daughters slapped her shoulders, a little harder than before.

Dipity laughed, and Hurley slid her arm around Sarah. Sterling mussed Sarah's hair.

"This is the last time you get away with crying in front of us," Ava said, but even she smiled like a proud big sister.

"Thank you, guys," Sarah said. "I'll try not to screw this up."

"OK, enough of all this sentimental shit," Lena said. "Pao, you've got your first order of business as an official Daughter. Our dwellers will be here soon. Eat some manna, and piss if you have to. This is going to take you a while."

Hurley Girly and the others left Lena and Sarah in the middle of the ganghouse, laughing and scrambling up the black stairs, eager as hell to get away from what was to come.

"Dwellers?" Sarah said. "What do I have to do with them?"

"Just because I'm blind doesn't make me stupid!" The scrawny dweller pointed her cane at Sarah, most likely the sole item she'd brought with her from Earth.

"I'm... I'm not saying you're stupid," Sarah stammered.

"You don't think I can count? I know how many manna loaves I have in my apartment. I count them every day. You're new here, so you probably still don't understand that food has to last until the next shipment. If people go around stealing it from under your nose, it means you could die. And I know she took it!" The blind dweller swung her cane toward the accused to her right, a big-boned woman whose crossed eyes darted from floor to wall like a skittish chameleon.

Back on Earth, Sarah had seen courtroom television shows when she'd stayed home sick from school. She'd always thought if she sat in the judge's position she could tell who was right and wrong and would throw down her hammer of justice without blinking an eye. But now she *was* the judge and mediator for the dwellers who'd come for reprisal and absolution. Now she knew why the other Daughters had fled to their rooms.

Lena had only stayed long enough to tell her what she was expected to do, and where to sit when the dwellers started floating in. Sarah, now officially the gang's ass, had to handle all dweller disputes. Mostly, it had been simple acts of thievery and spats between neighbors that she sorted out easily due to quick confessions or the involved parties coming to agreements without her even having to make a decision. For a while, Sarah thought that most of the dwellers were used to how things went and could figure it out on their own. All of this was just for show, and respect for the Daughters of Forgotten Light. Then the blind woman had come.

"I knew she'd been in my apartment when I walked in. I could smell she'd been there."

The cross-eyed woman mumbled something.

"Speak up, please," Sarah said, trying to show at least a little authority.

"I said I don't even smell!" the woman shouted.

"The hell she doesn't," the blind dweller said. "Even if all my remaining senses weren't so sharp, a pig with a cold could smell her dirty ass!"

"OK," Sarah said. "Let's just–"

"I wouldn't touch your manna if it was covered in chocolate sprinkles and sang me to sleep," the cross-eyed one said.

"I hope you choke on it, you trashy piece of–"

"Shut up!" Sarah stood. She wanted to hit something. These dwellers were driving her crazy. Why couldn't people ever get along? It didn't matter if it was on Earth or in the deepest reaches of space, people would complain about anything and squabble over the dumbest things. They couldn't set aside their petty, selfish ways and understand the bigger picture. She could almost see why their mothers had given them up to Oubliette.

Sarah sat back down and breathed slowly as she rubbed against an approaching headache. "Do you have any proof besides a smell and a few missing loaves?"

"Well…" the blind dweller leaned against her cane "… not really."

"And you," Sarah pointed to the accused, "did you steal her manna?"

"No. I didn't."

"Then it looks like we're at an impasse. If you find any evidence that's worth bringing back, we'll look at this again. Make your manna last as long as you can. If you get to a place where you're going to starve, then we'll see what we can do." Sarah tried to sound confident and like a Daughter who'd been surviving Oubliette for more than a decade, not the newbie who hadn't even shot her rang gun yet.

The two dwellers in front of her stared back in silence. The cross-eyed one looked satisfied, and even though the blind dweller soured her face and looked to spit, she nodded and turned back to the front doors.

As they walked away, keeping distance from one another, Sarah smiled a little to herself. She could do this, was good at it. The dwellers just needed someone to bitch to and, if need be, to be given a tiny nudge in the right direction. As she saw it, she'd put in a hard night's work, but as soon as the last two dwellers passed through the doors, a mob entered.

Sarah leapt to her feet, taken by surprise at the angry group stomping toward her. At the head, a shirtless Asian woman with a terrible attempt at a crew cut led a bony dweller forward. Crew Cut bared her flabby breasts with no modesty or care for where the huge things swung, and her missing shirt tied the prisoner's hands behind her back. A cut under the bound woman's right eye bled.

The horde of dwellers stood eerily silent as their prisoner cursed them all to Hell and back. A few dwellers in the rear carried some kind of bundle, but Sarah couldn't see much past the huddled shoulders in front.

"What's going on?" Sarah said. She'd wished she hadn't sounded so nervous, but who could blame her.

"Murder," the shirtless woman said.

Oh, great, Sarah thought. Now I have to deal with a lynch mob.

"Don't listen to these psycho bitches." The prisoner hacked, almost gagging. "They've got the wrong sheila!" Her curly black hair fell over her face as the shirtless woman shook her to be quiet.

"We found Dandelion here hunched over my girlfriend..." the shirtless woman swallowed and blinked away tears that began to fill her eyes. "...with her hands around her throat. We were too late to save my Susan, but we were able to grab this piece of shit."

The other dwellers murmured their agreement.

"We wanted to do this right," the shirtless one said. "Even though I wanted to beat her face in when we found her. We brought her to the Daughters for judgment."

Sarah couldn't find her voice. Whatever confidence she'd begun to build off the last few dweller disputes had flown away. She was saved a few moments' embarrassment when the dwellers in the back came forward with the mysterious bundle. Laying it down the way they did, it revealed a corpse's eyes that begged for a reckoning. It was the dead woman, Susan.

"I was checking her fucking pulse!" Dandelion said.

"With two hands?"

"You were seeing things. I would never have killed her." Dandelion turned to Sarah. "I would never kill anybody."

"We have all these witnesses who can confirm it," the shirtless woman said. The other dwellers nodded or affirmed with, "Yep!"

"Half these whores weren't even there." Dandelion became red in the face and she squirmed against her bonds. However they'd tied that shirt it must have been pretty snug.

"Um," Sarah said. It had come out as her mind raced for something, anything to say. But the dead woman's eyes kept staring and the blue of her lips matched Sarah's hair, and this was all so far over Sarah's head she couldn't think straight. "I'll be right back."

She hustled for the black stairs, ignoring the grunts of confusion from the dwellers thirsting for blood and a swift judgment.

Sarah knocked and entered Lena's room in a flurry. "I really, really need your help."

"It can't be that bad." Lena lay on her bed, hands cradling the back of her head. She didn't open her eyes when she answered Sarah. "Just tell them to get along and share their manna. They're like five year-olds."

"Well these five year-olds formed a lynch mob and want justice for a murdered dweller."

Lena bolted up. "Ah, shit."

Sarah explained the matter to Lena as best she could while they flew down the stairs. When they came to the ground floor, the dweller mob's yelling filled the ganghouse. The rest of the Daughters, except Ava, stood there listening to incoherent complaints and fruitlessly trying to calm several red-faced dwellers. The front door was smashed open and scratches ran along the wall beside it. The Asian woman with the crew cut was yelling and pointing wildly. She still hadn't put on her shirt, even though it now lay tattered in front of her. Dandelion was gone.

"Everybody quiet!" Lena yelled, speeding ahead of Sarah. "What's going on?"

"I'm not entirely sure," Dipity said. "We just got down here after hearing all the commotion. But they're pissed."

"You're damn right we're pissed," the shirtless woman said. "Your new recruit ran off, and the bitch that killed my Susan broke free and took off on one of your motorcycles!"

All the Daughters stopped and turned to the Asian woman.

"What did you say?" Hurley Girly asked.

Before the woman could repeat herself, Lena broke in. "Whose bike is missing?"

Dipity quickly scanned over the cyclones parked against the wall. Her expression went from annoyed to oh-shit-fearful. "Ava's."

"Who the fuck took my bike?" Ava stood at the entrance to the stairwell. She might have just walked in, but she was in time for things to get worse.

CHAPTER 16

Lena trotted away from the crowd, toward her second-in-command. She raised her hand to hold back Ava's rage, but that was like making love to a bear trap – never a good idea in the best of circumstances. Helpless, Hurley Girly and Dipity looked at each other. Sterling shook her head.

"No!" Ava shouted. "I want to know the name of the low-down, rotten-assed sack of shit I'm going to be killing tonight for stealing my cyclone."

"Her name is Dandelion," the shirtless woman offered.

A short black sheila entered and circled around the crowd. The mob continued to roar as she snuck by. She wasn't a part of the bloodlust crowd.

The short woman walked up to Sterling, the closest Daughter. "I need to talk to Horror," she whispered.

Sterling and the new arrival looked to Lena.

Shit just got even more serious. "Wait for me over by the stairs," Lena told the newly arrived dweller, and she obeyed.

Ava grumbled half-words as Lena led her over to the other Daughters. Instinctually, they made a huddle.

"Go get Ava's bike," Lena said. "Pao, let Ava drive yours while you ride bitch. When you sheilas find this Dandelion, you know what to do."

Sterling, Hurley Girly, and Dipity nodded. Staring at the floor, Ava gritted her teeth and pounded a fist into her palm.

Lena turned to the Asian woman. "Where does this Dandelion sheila live?"

"In the Right Twin tower, just south of the Sludge."

"Would she be dumb enough to go back to her place? Pick up manna and stuff?"

The Asian woman shrugged. "She always seemed like a dumbass to me. Are you going to–"

"Might as well start there," Lena told the Daughters.

The shirtless woman continued griping and the rest of the dwellers started in again with angry shouts.

"You not coming, Horror?" Ava asked.

"No," Lena looked quickly to the woman by the stairs. "I've got something important to deal with here, and I'll keep these heathens appeased until you get back."

CHAPTER 17

Sarah had no idea what the Daughters would do when, and if, they retrieved Ava's bike. It was another time to be thankful for her position in the gang. The ass just followed.

Dipity led the way as the Daughters hustled to their bikes. After she climbed onto her cyclone, Sarah scooted back to leave room for Ava, but the gang's right arm was stomping toward the shirtless woman.

"My girlfriend, my love, my Susan is dead!"

In one smooth motion, Ava swung a right hook, connected with the woman's jaw and turned back to Sarah's cyclone. The shirtless woman hit the ground with a dead smack. Her flab quaked and her bare breasts flopped lopsided toward her face.

"Someone had to shut her up," Ava said.

The Daughters shot through the open door, headed into the dark heart of Oubliette. Dandelion may or may not have been a murderer, but she was definitely a thief. Sarah wondered if the punishment for it was any less severe.

CHAPTER 18

Ava had made it easier on Lena. After she KO'd the shirtless woman, the dwellers who'd stormed in with her became silent and disoriented, like bees whose big-mouthed queen got squished. Lena told the dwellers to wait in the ganghouse until the other Daughters got back. Then they'd get the justice they were after, but no sooner. She excused herself and led Jessica, the lone dweller who'd come in during all the uproar, up to her room.

"I have to say," Lena said, as she entered her room and headed for a manna loaf she'd left on her bed, "you being here worries me."

"You said to let you know if I had anything worth your time."

"That's what's worrisome. But let's have it."

Lena offered Jessica a pinch of manna but she refused.

"Shamika is planning on stealing that baby the night the shipment comes."

"Mother. Fucker."

Lena threw away her piece of manna and darted for the big window overlooking the city. What did she think she was going to see? The Onyx Coalition riding by and flipping her the bird in defiance? Lena had to admit she'd only gotten up to hide her silent scream from Jessica.

"You did good," Lena finally said, getting a tiny shred of composure back. "How'd you find out?"

"They had some of us come help put up barricades and fortify their ganghouse. That's what got me suspicious to begin with. They said it was because Shamika had always wanted more security. But then I heard Shakes asking Brenda if she'd ever taken care of a baby before."

"Which one is Shakes again?" Lena asked. She was familiar with Brenda, Shamika's right arm.

"She's their left leg. The one who's always jittery. Anyway, Brenda told her to shut her mouth and they walked away before I heard anything else. Their ass kept telling us to hurry up, that we had to come back tomorrow and finish before the next shipment. A lot of them think we're stupid, but it wasn't hard to figure out."

For fuck's sake, Lena didn't need this. There had to be a way to use this to her advantage, capitalize on it, but she couldn't see how. Her whole plan had been to take the baby the night of the shipment, secretively and quickly enough to where her and the Daughters could get back to their ganghouse to fight off the oncoming retribution.

Shamika had been smart in building up her defenses. Lena wished she'd thought if it. Maybe it was too late to fortify the ganghouse without making it obvious they were planning the same thing. Besides, the Daughters' dwellers were in such an uproar over the murder it would be impossible to get them to do anything until after they were appeased.

"OK." Lena walked over to Jessica and patted her shoulder. "I need time to think this through."

"Wait," Jessica said, halting against Lena's guiding hand. "I can't go back there."

"Why would they think you know anything? You said yourself, they don't consider you guys to be that smart."

"Me being here is enough. A lot of your dwellers saw me, and the OC will know I came to you, if not now, then after the shipment. Just give me somewhere to stay. I think I've earned it."

Lena sighed. Jessica was right. She'd risked her life in bringing bad news, and with all the things sheilas on Oubliette could say about Lena Horror, being unfair wasn't one of them. "You got it. Wait with the others downstairs and I'll have Hurley Girly find you somewhere to stay when she gets back."

Tears that she'd, now clearly, been holding back poured from Jessica's eyes and she wrapped her arms around Lena's neck. "Thanks, Horror!"

Lena froze, her arms extended in surprise, and an instinctive desire to shoot her rang came over her as the dweller hung like a heavy necklace. But after a few seconds of feeling Jessica cry into her shoulder, Lena brought her arms around and patted the dweller on the back. She was now under the protection of the Daughters of Forgotten Light.

CHAPTER 19

It hadn't been but a few minutes when Sarah saw the flash of cyclone wheels whipping around the corner a few blocks ahead.

"Don't shoot until she's off the bike!" Ava shouted.

Sarah tapped Ava on the shoulder. "We're not taking her alive?"

Ava ignored her.

They whipped around the same corner Dandelion had taken, and Sarah had to squeeze Ava's waist tighter so she wouldn't fall off. Ahead, right in front of a building, Ava's cyclone lay on its side, slowly spinning from the energy buzzing off the still-engaged wheels.

"No respect," Ava grumbled to herself. "*Fuckfuckfuck fuckfuck!* I'm going to rip her eyeballs out…" She continued in her murderous oaths, but it got to where Sarah couldn't understand them.

They pulled up behind the overturned bike, and all the Daughters turned off their wheels. After jumping off Sarah's cyclone, Ava began an attempt to lift her own.

"Come help me with this!" Ava blurted in the midst of her effort.

"Girl, shut it off and leave it there for now," Dipity said.

"I thought you wanted to nab this dweller."

Ava let go of the bike and stood straight, as if she only just remembered the dweller who'd stolen her bike. She turned off her overturned cyclone's wheels and gave the bike a cursory onceover before leaping over it and running toward the tower's entrance.

"We better hurry," Hurley Girly said. "Ava's gonna have all the fun without us."

Sterling waved for Sarah to follow, and they all jogged after Ava.

Climbing the stairs put a hurt on Sarah's legs as she started huffing after the first couple flights. It was the most exercise she'd done since leaving the space port. She hadn't done much *real* training at all, come to think of it. "We're not going to shoot her, right? I haven't gotten a chance to practice with my rang gun yet."

Dipity stopped at the top of a flight. "Hold it," she said. "Get up here, Pao."

Sarah obeyed and pushed past Hurley Girly.

"If your rang goes off," Dipity said, "I sure as hell ain't going to be the one standing in front of you."

Dipity disengaged the safety with the press of a button, and Sarah's rang hummed a bit more angrily. Sarah took a deep breath and led the way as they continued their climb.

"You're about to get some shooting practice… when we catch that dweller," Hurley Girly called from below, just as winded as Sarah.

Whatever happened to innocent before guilty? Sarah wondered. If the dweller attacked them it would be one thing. But if she gave up willingly, they would have to take Dandelion alive.

Wouldn't they?

"She's going out on the roof," Ava shouted from a few flights up.

"That dweller's a dumbass," Dipity said.

Sarah surged up the stairs with renewed energy, and the others behind her did the same. The thought of Ava nearing the roof and beating them to the punch – more like several punches – must have done it. Sarah caught the door to the roof as it swung back in the wake of Ava's charge, and The Daughters poured onto the top of the tower.

Ava slowed her gait, steady and prematurely victorious. Dandelion stood in a defensive crouch looking for a way to escape, but only one other path led back to the street – over the edge and twenty stories down, quick and final.

"And they used to call me retarded," Ava said. Laughter seasoned those words, and it was horrifying.

"I didn't kill anybody!" Tears dripped from Dandelion's swollen eyes.

Ava raised her rang, aiming it at the dweller's chest. "I wouldn't give a shit if you slaughtered every last dweller in your building. You fucked up when you stole my bike."

"Apology! Apology!" Dandelion raised her hands in defense. Sarah doubted it would block whatever came out of the rang. "I had to. They were going to kill me."

Ava didn't say anything. She must have been done with conversation. Her rang spoke, though, silently. It was the tiniest of sounds, but Sarah was sure she heard it, like the rising energy of a dying star. It was as if the rang *wanted* to be shot.

The tension was too much. It wasn't right. None of this was–

"Wait, Ava," Sarah blurted.

At first Ava didn't respond, her head only twitched enough to make her hair fall to one side. But then, slowly, she lowered her arm and turned to Sarah. She was not amused. Her squinting, glaring eyes could just as well have been another weapon in her arsenal.

"I just..." Sarah gulped and tried to steady her breath "... they want justice. The dwellers. We should take her back and have a trial."

Hurley Girly laughed behind her. Dandelion backed away.

"She's dead anyway," Ava said. "What difference does it make? I kill her, everyone's happy."

"I'm not happy," Sarah said.

"Don't think because you're a Daughter now, it gives you the right to go against me. You're still the ass."

"I just want to help you make the right decision. I know you're pissed–"

"You don't know shit!"

Sterling clapped her hands. It got everyone's attention. *She's right,* she signed. *It would look better if we brought her back alive. This is a dweller thing.*

"It *was* a dweller thing," Ava said. "Now we have to make a show of force. Unless you want every dweller out there to think it's cool to rip us off. Hell, let's start a cyclone rental business."

"Maybe we can show force and be fair at the same time," Dipity spoke up.

Ava groaned. "Not you, too."

"I'm not going back there," Dandelion made the mistake of reminding Ava of her presence.

"Don't you worry!" Ava pointed a finger at the dweller, who cowered at the edge of the roof. "I'll make sure you don't."

"I don't give a shit one way or the other," said Hurley Girly. "Just kill her so we can get back and mingle with some hot dwellers."

"The majority says we should bring her back," Sarah said.

Ava took slow steps and put her nose to the tip of Sarah's. "Don't talk to me about the majority. The *majority* sent all of us out here to die."

Sarah stood taller than Ava, and she was surprised to realize it now. Ava's demeanor and commanding presence had always made her seem ten feet tall. But her lack of height didn't mean a lack of violence and psychotic rage. Oubliette seemed to breed that in every woman who stepped foot on the city's glass. But Sarah would fight the crazy in herself. She had to. Everything had changed. But this, this moment here was one thing she knew she was right in. This would be the first step in keeping herself sane.

"Keeping her alive will give you plenty of time to think of ways to torture her." Dipity was trying to help, but damn it, she was doing a terrible job.

"You daddyfuckers stay the hell away from me," Dandelion said.

Ava scratched the side of her face. Her toxic frown morphed into a satisfied sneer. "All right, then. Pao, since you're so wet to arrest her, you go get her before she decides to jump."

Ava joined the other Daughters and they all stepped back a few paces, always eager for a new form of entertainment.

Hurley Girly made shooing motions with her hands. "Go get her, Pao!"

Well, Sarah thought, now she'd done it. Shame on her for expecting help in apprehending Dandelion all neat and tidy. The dweller clung to the edge of the roof, fidgeting and eyeing Sarah as she took each step with care. Surely, Dandelion had to realize Sarah just saved her thieving dweller ass. Sarah didn't expect a thank you. She just wanted no trouble in Dandelion coming back to the ganghouse. No fuss. That was all.

"You're not touching me!" Dandelion snarled like a rabid dog. "I'm not going to let those hags put me on trial. They've hated me since I came to this shithole."

Sarah pocketed her hands in her new jacket, trying to make herself seem a little less threatening – if anyone could have ever called her that. She felt her brass knuckles and began to roll it around in her palm to keep her focused, calming the nerves.

"Dandelion," Sarah said. "I believe you. But if you don't come with us it'll look bad. If you did nothing wrong, you have nothing to worry about. Running is for..." Sarah paused for a second, embarrassed about what she was about to say, "...pussies. Do you really think you can hide in this city?"

"I'll go to the Amazons," Dandelion said, so matter-of-factly that it looked like she could float down from the top of that building if not walk past all the Daughters without any resistance.

"Oh, hell no!" Ava shouted.

"It's O –" Sarah reached out a hand, hoping Dandelion would take it, but instead the dweller threw a punch. It was a sloppy throw, and the months of training Sarah's parents had run her through kicked in like a reflex. Sarah blocked Dandelion's punch and in the same moment removed her right fist from the jacket, brass knuckles in place.

Sarah never landed that punch, even though it was as sure as sin. It never landed because Dandelion's face was blown off before Sarah's knuckles could find it.

A blue ball of light had blasted from the top of her forearm – the rang. It had gone off and did what it was designed to do: destroy whatever was in its path. Dandelion's head shredded into bits of blood and bone that shimmered against the glow of Sarah's rang ball. The dweller's lifeless body fell backwards. Sarah gasped and reached to grab it, but wasn't fast enough. The body toppled over the edge.

"No!" Sarah could do nothing but fill the space where Dandelion had been, and watch the dweller's body plummet through the air, slamming into the street with a sudden squish. Sarah's stomach lurched. She wanted to vomit, but a steady diet of manna left her heaving unproductively.

A buzzing ricochet filled the air. The ball of light from Sarah's rang kept flying in the direction she'd accidentally fired, toward the twin tower across the street. When the light ball hit the building's glass it buzzed and popped, reversing its course and speeding back to where Sarah stood on the roof.

Her fighting instinct was only good against a human opponent. She had no maneuver to battle the oncoming orb. She should have run or ducked, but her legs were glued and her whole body shook from what she'd seen that rang shot do, what it was about to do to her. Sarah screamed and crossed her arms in front of her face, squeezing her eyes shut and hoping it wouldn't hurt.

Another buzzing pop racked her forearm. She waited, for pain or the light at the end of the tunnel, or the blackness of nothing. None of that came. She opened her eyes and dropped her arms. The city returned to quiet. The other Daughters didn't laugh or make any noise whatsoever.

"Holy shit," Hurley Girly said.

Sterling stood with her mouth agape.

"There goes that plan," said Dipity. "Glad I wasn't in front of you coming up the stairs, Pao. Fucking A." She looked at Ava, whose stone face made the hollow pain in Sarah's gut throb even greater. "I knew we should have had her practice before now."

Ava stalked over to the edge of the roof and peered down to the bloody mess on the street. Sarah dropped to her knees and clung to the glass next to her, no longer caring about showing a tough exterior or being the Daughter she thought they all wanted her to be. She'd killed someone, unintentionally or not, and if she had a soul it felt like she'd bathed it in sulfuric acid. And the thing that scared her more than what she'd just done, was that it'd be easier to do again. The next time could be on purpose, and maybe she wouldn't feel... anything.

"Where'd you learn those moves?" Hurley Girly asked.

Sarah ignored her. They were just words, noises, they had no meaning when they reached her ears.

"It was like some kung fu shit," Hurley Girly said.

Sarah looked up at Ava, who rested on stiff arms against the roof's edge. The thought couldn't be helped, even among the other voices racing in Sarah's mind – if she'd just let Ava do what she was going to do, Sarah wouldn't have blood on her hands. She would still be one of the sane, just a guest in this house of horrors.

"It was an accident," Sarah whispered.

"I know," Ava said.

"The truce..."

"Is only for gangs. Don't worry. You're in the right on this."

"No." Sarah closed her eyes and cried.

Ava grabbed Sarah's chin. It wasn't a caring gesture, more like grabbing a dog that wouldn't obey. "Whatever moral standard you're still living by – drop it. This isn't Earth, if you can't tell. We have our own rules. That dweller was going to die one way or another, it was her destiny. I just hope her death will mean something if it gets you to dry your eyes and act like a Daughter for fuck's sake."

Ava stomped away. Her words echoed in Sarah's mind, at first as a whisper, but then growing in volume. It was enough to get her on her feet. Then all she had to do was put one boot in front of the other, following Hurley Girly and the others down the stairs and back to their cyclones. She'd dry her eyes and grit her teeth to hold back guilty tears. But she wouldn't forget. Until she found a way to make herself whole again and be rid of the dark cloud around her, she'd fake it.

CHAPTER 20

Lena had seen the blue light of Daughter cyclone wheels from her window. She took her time going down to the main room of the ganghouse and sat in her favorite spot against the wall.

The shirtless Asian woman walked over. "Are we going to stay here all damn night?"

"My gang just got back," Lena said. "We're going to need your help fixing our door."

"That wasn't our fault. If your newbie hadn't left us here by ourselves–"

"You're also going to help us with adding some other stuff inside the ganghouse. Now go back over there with the other dwellers before I lose my patience."

The dweller huffed and turned away.

"And put a shirt on."

The low hum of the cyclones grew closer and soon the Daughters rode in through the open door. Ava didn't look as righteously happy as Lena expected. All the Daughters, besides Hurley Girly, looked despondent as if they'd lost one of the gang. But Lena counted all of them present with Ava's stolen motorcycle returned with them. Sarah looked the worst, but Lena could tell she was trying to be tough.

Dipity got off her cyclone with a blood-soaked body over her shoulder. She hurried to the gathered dwellers and dropped it on the floor. The dwellers jumped back when they saw what was left of Dandelion's corpse. It was like Ava had punched her through the nose and just kept going. The body lay open like a busted, gory piñata. It was fucked up, even for Ava. She must've really been pissed.

"Are you satisfied?" Lena asked the Asian dweller who'd paused in pulling on her shirt to gawk at Dandelion's remains.

"No one's ever going to steal a cyclone again," the dweller said. "Not after seeing that."

Lena swallowed, fighting the urge to puke. *You got that right.*

"Two of you go to Grindy's with Sterling and Hurley Girly," Lena said. "I need you to get some tools and other stuff. I'll get you a list. And get these fucking dead people out of here. I'm surrounded by stiffs."

Nodding, the dweller finished putting on her shirt.

Lena walked over to Ava, who was inspecting her bike and running her hand over its curves. "Did you have to be so fucking thorough? I'm pretty sure that dweller was dead after you shot her face off."

"Wasn't me," Ava said, not looking up from her cyclone. "Pao did some ninja shit when the dweller threw a punch. The rang went off."

"No kidding?"

"Yeah, then the body fell off the roof. You might want to teach her how to shoot."

"Hurley Girly can teach her. She's next in line."

"Sure. But I think you need to talk to Pao, too."

"What's wrong?"

"Nothing. Well, not if you talk to her."

Lena sighed. *What the fuck now?*

Ava got up from babying her bike. "I think she's having some morality issues or some shit. I tried telling her that kind of stuff doesn't matter here. Maybe you can get her thinking right."

"Oh, great."

"I'm taking a shower," Dipity said, and headed for the black stairs. No one would have been stupid enough to stop her. She tossed her jacket to Sarah. "Wash that for me."

Sarah caught it and nodded, staring at the floor.

"Hurley," Lena said. "I need you to find a place for a new dweller to stay."

"New dweller?" She perked up at that. Hurley Girly always liked fresh meat.

"I need you to keep it professional."

Hurley Girly brushed it away with a *pfft*, and a wave of her hand. "I'm always professional. Is she hot?"

"Just get it done. Today."

"No probs. Wait. Is it that dweller from the OC?"

Sometimes Lena hated how small a world Oubliette was. You couldn't take a piss without someone knowing about it. "Yeah."

"Whoa. Why is she coming over here? Ain't that going to cause some trouble? Does she have any good dirt on them? What did she say to you while we were gone?"

"Will you relax?"

"Sorry," Hurley Girly said with a big smile and buzzing energy that never quit.

"Yeah, what was so important with that dweller?" Ava asked.

Here was another crossroads, another time the two competing sides of Lena's brain would argue over which path to take. She could tell them what Jessica had told her. She could warn them the Onyx Coalition was going to put a major wrench in their operation. They'd argue that it was a sign that they should stay out of it, remain neutral. The OC and the Amazons could kill each other and the Daughters of Forgotten Light could reign as the last gang left standing. But like last time, when she came to this place of decision, the voice of caution and reason was gone.

"She wanted to come where there was a more diverse choice of women." Lena shrugged. "And ones that wouldn't eat her."

Hurley Girly, mind always in the gutter, grinned.

CHAPTER 21

Just hold on. Hold on. You're almost there. Holding both hands to her mouth, Sarah clomped down the hallway, toward the shower room.

She refused to let the other Daughters see her cry anymore. On the roof, Ava had looked at her like she was such a pitiful thing, not cut out to ride in their gang. If Sarah could just get to the showers she could cry and let the water mix with her tears and no one, not even herself, would be the wiser.

When her boots clacked against tile instead of glass, she dropped one hand, letting a whimper slip out. Sticky moisture filled the air with the funk of mold, and as she rounded the corner she bumped into a wet, naked body.

"My bad, Pao." Dipity grabbed Sarah's shoulder to keep her from falling. Her enormous arm tensed, her muscles bulging from her dark, slick skin.

Sarah quickly looked away, listening to the *pat, pat, pat* of water dropping off the big woman's body. There were no towels, and unless she wanted to use her glass cloth bedsheet Sarah would have to do like Dipity and let her body air dry.

"I saved you some hot water." Dipity laughed.

If it was a joke, Sarah didn't get it. They'd told her the Core provided an unlimited amount of hot water as it recycled the Sludge and what dripped down the drain. Besides, Sarah wasn't in the mood for jokes, especially from someone dripping wet and missing their clothes.

"You did good tonight," Dipity said. She patted Sarah's arm.

This got Sarah to look up, dodging her third-in-command's massive breasts and settling on her eyes. With a smile and a nod, Dipity left the shower room, whistling a familiar song Sarah couldn't place. A few minutes later, Dipity's slapping steps faded, and after a few more minutes Sarah pulled off her clothes.

The water burned as it left the faucet, and Sarah had to turn it down to make it comfortable, but the initial pain set her to wailing under the spray, sobbing until the air left her lungs, breathing in deep and wheezy as if she'd crawled from below a dark ocean. When she opened her eyes and put her head against the wall in front of her, blood and bits of dark flesh flowed off her head, circling the drain. She hadn't noticed that pieces of Dandelion's face had splattered over her blue hair, staining it red, like one of the Amazons.

If I look like this on the outside, I wonder what the inside looks like.

A hand caressed her back. Sarah started and turned, and there was Sterling. The mute Daughter kissed Sarah's lips, and instead of being freaked out like she was around Hurley Girly, Sarah welcomed the kiss, glad to have something to comfort her, something else to think about besides the face of…

Pulling out of the kiss, Sterling smiled, signing, *Do you*

want to come to my room?

Oh. Sarah hadn't thought of that being the next step, she was just appreciating a friendly gesture. "You're beautiful," Sarah said. "I'm just... I'm not attracted to you... in that way. I've never been into boys *or* girls. Even when all my friends... oh God, what's wrong with me?" Sarah buried her face in Sterling's bare shoulder, crying even harder.

With gentle hands, Sterling moved Sarah in front of her. *Nothing is wrong with you.*

Sarah lowered her head. She didn't do what she'd done with Dipity, averting her eyes from Sterling's naked body. She wanted to see. But she didn't expect Sterling to have boy parts, hanging there, right between her legs.

Catching her gaze, Sterling gave a small smile. *I was born in a body that didn't match my soul.*

Sarah started to speak, but couldn't find any words. She stood there staring at all of Sterling, trying to figure out if she could have ever guessed... no, she would never have known. Not until that moment. "How did you get sent to Oubliette? Wouldn't you have gone to the military?"

My father walked in on me one day, Sterling signed. *Caught me wearing one of my mother's dresses. By the time my mother found me, I'd lost consciousness. I guess it must have been after the twelfth punch my father gave me. I woke up later in my mother's car. She was driving us somewhere and had a black eye. I never found out what happened to my father, but my mom emptied their account and paid for me to have surgery on this beautiful face you're looking at.* Sterling smiled and touched the backs of her fingers under her chin.

"But she shipped you?" Sarah wiped shower water from her eyes.

She saved my life. She knew my father would have found us eventually, even if we had a restraining order or something. She didn't want me going to the military. In her eyes, I was who I am. So Oubliette it was.

"The shipper guards. When they hose you down–"

Tucking it between my legs seemed to work OK. Sterling shrugged. *And if they saw it, they didn't care. I was just another body to process, another shippee to ship.*

"Do the other Daughters know?"

Of course.

As Sarah stared at those dark, wonderful eyes, she felt her own swell with heat and tears. "I killed that woman tonight!"

Sterling held her, stroking Sarah's head. They stayed that way for a long time. And Sarah didn't feel ashamed to cry, despite the whole reason she'd come to the showers in the first place. This was different. This was Sterling.

CHAPTER 22

Sarah wanted nothing more than to lie down in her bed and never get back up. When Lena had come in and told her to meet her on the sixth floor for rang-shooting practice, the desire to sleep tripled. Why did it matter if she practiced? She'd never shoot her rang again, not after she'd seen what it could do. She didn't want to be the reason someone else died, especially like that. She'd asked Lena if they could save it for another night. If she was slippery enough, she could put it off forever, holding back when they went to take the baby, letting the others shoot... kill. She could fake being sick or something.

"We've put it off for too long," Lena said, "and I don't want you accidentally killing one of us." She must have seen the pain in Sarah's face, because then she added, "No offense."

Sarah climbed to the sixth floor, her rang weighing a ton. When she came off the stairs, she froze. This floor was different. The lights in the ceiling shone brighter than anywhere else in the ganghouse. Most of the room stretched out like an alley and became much narrower the farther it went from the doorway. To the right, a glass division extended from the wall where Lena stood.

"Welcome to the target floor," she said.

"You guys built this?" Sarah asked.

"Yep. We needed somewhere we could practice, and it's something to do when you get bored."

"I should have brought a book instead of brass knuckles."

Lena snorted. "Don't tell me you've become a pacifist."

Sarah shrugged.

"OK," Lena said. "I'll explain it to you another way. We're here to practice shooting your rang gun so it only goes off when you want it to. Does that sound fair enough?"

It did. But it didn't help the feeling that Sarah wore a killing machine on her forearm. "I know how to follow orders," Sarah said. "I'll do whatever you want."

That only seemed to annoy Lena, but Sarah didn't care. Lena could make Sarah shoot her rang and ride into whatever hell hole this city had under the glass streets, but she couldn't make her like it.

"So this is how it's going to be from now on?" Lena asked. "You need to lighten up."

Lighten up. Seemed that was the one "up" Sarah would never be able to follow. She had enough trouble *shutting* up, because even though she'd wanted to bite her tongue, the next words flew from her mouth. "I can't."

"Can't what?"

It was out there now. Might as well say it. "I can't go crazy."

Lena smiled, even though it was a little sad. "Is that what you think happened to all of us? We all went nuts?"

"I don't know."

"Don't stop being honest now."

Sarah swallowed.

"Maybe you're right," Lena said. "Maybe Oubliette is more like an insane asylum than a prison. But it made us that way. And like it or not, Pao, you're here just like the rest of us. We briefed you on what's expected of you, how things work here. I want this to be the last time I have to talk to you about this. Do you want to live?"

"Yes." It came out more softly than Sarah had wanted, so she cleared her throat and said again, louder. "Yes."

"Then do what you have to so you stay that way. Whatever battle is going on underneath all that blue hair, get it taken care of and fill your role in this gang. Got me?"

"Loud and clear," Sarah said.

"Now let's move on to more fun stuff."

Sarah faked a smile. In time, the inability to hide her feelings would dissolve. Lena made it sound so simple. If you lost your mind, oh well. You still had your life, and wasn't that something? Sarah liked simple. But this was complicated.

"Step over there and face the targets," Lena said.

So that's what the two blotches on the far wall were. They looked like burned-in drawings in the shapes of women. Shadows.

"I guess you figured out how you shoot the rang."

"Not really," Sarah said. "It just… happened."

Lena raised her left arm and bent her wrist quickly as if she was knocking on a tabletop. "Quick. Intentional," she said. "There's a sensor right above your wrist. When you do that, it fires the rang. Go ahead and try."

"Now?"

"Sink or swim, Pao. Sink or swim." Lena backed away to stand behind the barrier.

Sarah breathed and raised her right arm at one of the targets. She ground her teeth and fought against the urge to squeeze her eyes closed when it happened. She flicked her wrist down like Lena had shown her. The blue ball fired from her arm and zipped down the long hallway. Damn, it was fast. It hit the wall just above the target's shoulder and flew back toward Sarah. She stepped away and flinched.

"Keep your arm up," Lena shouted.

Sarah cringed but did what Lena said. The ball of light returned into the rang and Sarah eased a bit, blowing out air she'd been holding.

"The only rang shot you don't need to avoid is your own," Lena said. "After you fire, it'll zip back into your gun after it contacts glass. And there's plenty of glass around."

"So it can't hurt me?"

"Oh, it can damn well hurt you. You'd just have to be reckless or suicidal." Lena looked away for a moment, like a ghost had walked in.

Sarah knew she probably should have kept it to herself, but something had been gnawing at the back of her mind, and she felt it was as good a time as any. "Is that what happened to Loveless?"

"Is that what they told you?"

"No one told me anything," Sarah said. "But I knew it had to be something that didn't mess up the truce."

Lena nodded and kicked at a nonexistent object on the floor. "She was spiraling into depression for a while. Nothing we did could cheer her up. It happens. One day some sheilas just wake up and don't feel like living anymore. So she did what she did. She always said she wanted to go out with a rang blast to the head. Always kept her word."

I'd rather be murderous than dead, Sarah thought, and hated herself for thinking it. "I'll shoot again," she said.

"OK. Remember, the shot will bounce around until it finds your rang. Always try to fire in a straight line." Lena backed behind the barrier.

Sarah flicked her wrist again, this time keeping her arm steady. The shot hit the middle of a target's chest and returned to Sarah's rang with a final, buzzing pop.

"Easy as that," Lena said. "You are the one in control. Remember that."

Lena was right. The power was Sarah's to wield. If she ever let it get away from her, that's when she would begin to crumble. Just like the rang shot, Sarah could release her rage when, and only when, she decided. Her grandmother used to talk about the yin and the yang. Pull too hard in one direction, you'll be snapped back far into the other. It's all about balance. If Sarah tried too hard to be sane, she would end up going crazy. But she always sucked at gymnastics, especially walking the balance beam.

Sarah chuckled.

"Well," Lena said, "I'm glad to see you're having fun now."

Sarah lost track of the time they spent there on the sixth floor shooting their rang guns. Lena showed her how to use the glass to her advantage and bounce shots off the wall to hit her target. She taught her to always be mindful of how her wrist rested against the gun, mainly while riding her cyclone. To set the safety when in doubt. After some discussion on how the Daughters avoided shooting each other and what their hand signals meant while riding through the streets, they took a break and ate some manna while sitting against the wall.

"So I heard you know some martial arts," Lena said.

Sarah nodded and chewed on her food.

"I can't tell if you're really humble, or like to keep secrets."

"You're the one with the big secret. I'm just trying to follow the ups."

Lena laughed. "You need to share all your hidden skills with the rest of us. Your parents taught you how to fight?"

"I went to Wing Chun class since I could walk. But my father used a more aggressive style. He took over my training when he knew I was coming to Oubliette."

"You mean when he had your mother send you here."

"I don't blame them," Sarah said. She didn't. It was the government that had forced them into near poverty. That's where she placed her hatred.

"You probably won't find anyone here as forgiving toward their mother."

"So what's with all the stuff you wanted the dwellers to bring back from Grindy's? Are we attempting an escape?"

Lena's face lit up at that, her lips curling into a mischievous smile. Sarah was just glad she could change the subject.

"Come on," Lena said. "I'll show you."

CHAPTER 23

Oubliette gave little, but what it did offer was plenty of spare parts and time to think of all the wondrous things you could build with them. Lena had been planning some nasty inventions for some time, and now with a dweller mob to help she could realize her visions. It was going to be a blast.

After watching the dwellers entertain themselves with old songs and dance battles, Hurley Girly and Dipity rode in, dragging two big boxes attached with wire cables. The cyclones lowered, and the accompanying dwellers got off and began handing out the assorted junk. A factory line of sorts formed from the first two dwellers, and soon a big pile of scrap gathered on the ganghouse floor.

"What's all this for?" one of the dwellers asked.

"We're making tampons," Hurley Girly said.

Dipity dragged a spare metal door from the pile. "I don't think this is big enough for you, Hurley."

Several dwellers muffled laughter and Hurley Girly extended both middle fingers.

"I do have plans for that door," Lena said. "Dipity, help me haul it up to the top elevator."

"Elevator?" Sarah asked. "Then why do we always take the stairs."

Lena considered nicknaming Sarah "Detective Pao".

"You grab hold of that door with Dipity and I'll show you." She led the way up the black stairs.

Sarah breathed hard carrying the lower end, but Dipity had no trouble with the door's weight.

"You want me to swap places with Pao?" Dipity asked.

"No," said Lena, "it's good exercise for her." Sarah would need all the help she could get before the shipment came.

At the final landing, Lena stepped over to a wall around the corner. The only difference between it and the flat plainness of the others was a thin line shaped into a square.

"Set the door down before Pao falls over and dies," Lena said.

They dropped it, Sarah crouching on the top step and wiping sweat from her eyes. Lena put her hand to the right of the wall square and the elevator door slid open. Air rushed up from the empty shaft, bringing with it metallic particulates that danced on the stale wafts escaping the darkness.

"Come here, Pao," Lena said. "Look at this."

Sarah crawled over and peered into the shaft. "Where's the lift?"

"They never put it in," Lena said.

"Oubliette never got finished when the UCNA took it," Dipity said. "There's lots of shit here that's incomplete."

"The worst being the Sludge River left uncovered." Lena crinkled her nose at the unsolicited memory of the river's smell.

"At least we have showers," Sarah offered.

"Yeah, and without toilet paper we have to take one after every shit." Dipity crossed her arms. "So why did you have us bring that heavy-ass door up here, Horror?"

"You'll see when I get some dwellers up here to install it," Lena said. "You guys are going to see all the surprises I've prepared for the ganghouse."

"Don't we need some of this stuff for when we take the baby?" Sarah asked. "Or are we not doing that anymore?"

Lena folded her arms. Detective Pao sounded like the perfect nickname.

"Shit," Dipity said. "You should know by now Lena doesn't change her mind."

Sarah wrinkled her face, looking even more confused.

"This *stuff*," Lena said, "is for when they come to steal her back."

CHAPTER 24

A knock rapped Dolfuse's back door. He was early.

"Senator Dolfuse," the man said in greeting when she let him inside. He wore glasses and a black leather hat to cover the stubble of a shaved head. A thick gray coat topped his short frame and he carried a large bag over his shoulder, the kind she would have expected Bobby to be lugging around somewhere in the east.

Martin, as to be expected, couldn't attend the viewing of the drone's flight through Oubliette. However, as promised, she'd sent Dolfuse's current visitor, Eric Lundgate, to make sure the drone worked properly. Spangler had sent a one-word text a few days before saying, "Done." Everything was set, and Dolfuse was pleased as punch. The vice president could stay away as long as she wanted.

"You can set up in the den," Dolfuse said. "It's just through there."

Lundgate tipped his hat and sauntered around the corner Dolfuse had directed. He had a wobble to him and Dolfuse hoped he was better at programming than getting around her house.

Who's to say we'll see anything? It's probably a wasteland.

"Want me to connect to the television?" Lundgate poked

his head from the den. He'd removed his jacket but left the hat. "It'd give us a bigger picture."

"You can do that?"

"Oh, sure. It's just plugging in a wire."

"OK, then."

Coffee. Coffee sounded good right then. It was nearing six o'clock at night, but she'd need something to hold in her hands and maybe even put to her mouth to keep her nerves in check.

"Would you like some coffee?" Dolfuse shouted from the kitchen.

Lundgate poked his head back out to say, "No, thanks," and promptly disappeared again.

The Oubliette file lay on the kitchen counter. Dolfuse quickly opened a drawer and dropped the envelope inside. She was tired of looking at the damned thing, and she had it all but memorized at that point.

At first, Oubliette became a penal city around the time Europe froze over and international trade shut down completely. Food was rationed and vouchers for future children had to be purchased at a hefty price. However, the government provided free sterilization for any who wanted it. Those the UCNA deemed spots on society got a one-way ticket to the darkness of space. Then the Supreme Court decision in the now infamous Dow vs. McCain case fit nicely with what finally became the rule of the land.

With all the criminals gone and the population still on the rise, Dow vs. McCain became a way to keep the population down for the foreseeable future. The resulting law gave mothers full ownership of their children until the age of eighteen, barring termination outside the womb.

When a child turned ten, the mother was given the option to transfer rights to the child to the government, by either selling those that met the criteria to the military, or sending the girls who didn't to Oubliette. The boys who didn't measure up still went to the military, they were just never seen again. Dolfuse had once caught Bobby joking about using these boys as "target practice". She didn't find that funny.

With her mug filled, Dolfuse took a breath and marched to the other room. The coffee table had become a small command center with a sleek laptop and a separate pad filled with buttons. Lundgate was at the back of the TV and with a small push of his arm the screen went from silent digital blue to a static-splashed image of starry space and the choppy roar of thrusters.

"The picture is terrible," Dolfuse said.

"It's better than nothing." Lundgate shrugged and trotted over to his bag on the couch behind the coffee table. "We're almost ready." The rustle of plastic met his hands as he dug into his pack. When he brought them back out they clutched an expensive-looking bag of melting jelly beans and an over-sized Scourge soda bottle. "There," he said. "Now we're ready."

CHAPTER 25

Sarah had grown more confident in riding her cyclone, but it didn't help too much as she rode at the end of the Daughters' "V" pattern. They were headed into dangerous territory and maybe a fight, a *real* fight. She hoped Lena knew what she was doing.

Sterling hadn't said much before they left. Every time Sarah had tried to catch Sterling's gaze, she'd walked away. It had to be that Sterling still disagreed with stealing the baby, but loyalty to the gang, and losing the fight with Lena, forced her into doing it. Sarah didn't want to think it was something she'd done.

All the Daughters remained quiet, even Hurley Girly. Sarah didn't know if they kept a ceremonial silence before the coming storm of rang shots, or if they all were as on edge as Sarah. Either way, she decided to conform to the stillness, and besides, she had nothing to say.

Eventually breaking the silence, Lena called from the front. "We're about to enter their turf. Keep your mouths closed and don't attract any attention."

The gang turned off a ramp and rode below a new set of buildings Sarah hadn't seen before, though they weren't any different. They had the same cookie-cutter glass as the other giants in the Daughters' neck of Hell. The feeling here, though, was definitely not the same. Sarah couldn't figure out if it was just nerves, or if the air really did taste a little sour and feel more humid. That didn't make sense, but the eerie vibe around this part of Oubliette stayed.

Lena signaled for them to follow her down an alley a block up. When they'd slowed to a halt in the shadow of the buildings, Lena sliced a hand in front of her throat, telling them to kill the cyclones.

"We walk from here," Lena whispered. "Keep your eyes peeled and your rangs ready."

They all hugged the wall and waited for Lena to crane her head around the corner. After a few seconds Lena nodded and they continued down the street. Sarah adopted the same crouching run as the other girls, excitement mixing with dread.

Lights distinguished a building at the end of the street. It had sharper angles than its surrounding counterparts, and red light shone from inside.

A large, garage-type door rose in the front of the building. The Amazons screamed in ghostly harmony as they hovered out of it on their cyclones.

Lena dropped to her stomach, prompting Sarah and the others to do the same. Farica led the parade, and the rest of the Amazons followed in single file. They turned to their left when they hit the street and picked up speed once all of them had made it outside.

Sarah made sure to look at each of the Amazons, but none of them carried baby Rory. A dweller peered out of the ganghouse and watched them leave before closing the door with the push of a button. The Amazon cyclone hums grew farther away. Their ganghouse returned to silence.

"Hell yeah!" Hurley Girly whisper-shouted. "Let's raid that place."

"Shut up," Lena said. "We'll give it a minute."

Sarah released a tense breath, thinking of the worst possible thing that could happen – the Amazons trapping them in the middle of the street. At any second, the Veil would ripple over Oubliette in welcome of the new shipment.

This had to be quick.

"Alright," Lena said after an eternity. "Sign language only until we're inside. Let's go."

Sarah pushed herself up and ran behind the others. The garage door had no windows for them to see into, and Lena was already heading for the side of the building.

"Dipity," Lena called as she ran, "stay here and keep watch."

Although she was visibly disappointed, Dipity nodded.

Hurley Girly had a tough time containing her bubbling giggles, so Ava punched her in the arm as she raced past her. Shaking her head, Sterling grabbed Sarah by the jacket and pulled her along.

This is a back way in, Lena signed.

Sarah looked around but could only see impenetrable glass and the Veil flickering above. The shipment must have just broken through.

You first. Lena pointed to Sarah.

Where?

Something like a manhole cover lay under her feet, but it was shaped like the top of a screw. Hurley Girly walked up, rubbing her punched arm.

Help me with it, Lena signed to Ava. *We have to twist it open.*

The two of them grabbed small handles in the screw's top and began to walk it counterclockwise multiple times. The manhole cover extended deep.

Sarah signed to Sterling, *Have you seen any of these screw things before?*

Sterling nodded her head.

The screw danced loosely in Lena and Ava's hands when they took it out. They breathed heavily as they set it against the wall. Sarah braved a look into the dark pit below.

Give me your hands, Lena signed and held her own out.

Her hands were the same size as Sarah's but rougher. Making sure to keep her head away from Sarah's rang gun, Lena lowered Sarah into the hole.

"I'm touching the floor," Sarah whispered when she felt her feet against a hard surface. Her amplified voice and foggy breath bounced off the darkness, and the small bit of light from the hole above. She quickly covered her mouth.

"Guess sign language is out." Lena's voice bit, even as a whisper.

"Is now a good time to tell her about the alien rats that live below the city?" Hurley Girly said.

Sarah trembled and raised her rang, aiming it to and fro. The rang's glow helped her see a little better. Piping and wires surrounded her. It was less like a sewer and more like what she imagined the guts of a spaceship would look like. She searched every dark cranny for movement or fur... or scales. The Daughters above snickered with hands over their mouths, and Sarah knew there were no monsters down there.

"Keep moving, Pao," Ava said. "The only intelligent life

out here is everybody but Hurley Girly."

They laughed more and Sarah found herself smiling a little as she crawled through the tunnel. Thumps sounded behind and the other Daughters followed by the light of their rangs.

"Shit," Hurley Girly said. "It smells like something died down here."

"It'd be a fitting place to put what the Amazons don't finish eating," Lena said, and it didn't have the same humor the conversation had been flavored with.

Sarah smelled it, too. And it reminded her that they were infiltrating the lair of a gang of cannibals. Alien rats would be a better alternative.

"Since we all might die," Hurley Girly said, "can you tell us why you got shipped, Lena?"

"No, goddamn it."

They all had to squat to avoid bumping their heads. After several feet into the growing sticky musk of rotten things, they came to a dead end. Sarah looked left, then right, but they had no other way to go.

"What now?" she asked when the Daughters stopped behind her.

"It's above us," Lena said.

Sarah lifted her rang and saw the bottom of another of those screw-like manholes. Lena got on the other side of it and Sarah helped walk it around, unscrewing it. The bottom had no benefit of handles, so they had to place their hands flat on the cool of the metal. Two and a quarter turns in, Sarah had to stop and catch her breath.

"Hurley Girly," Lena said. "Help me finish."

The smell became unbearably worse. If she hadn't been

worrying more about covering her nose, Sarah would have kicked herself for having to let Hurley Girly finish what she couldn't. But her arms and thighs were still burning from the little she did. The two women finished with the screw quickly, judging by the red light pouring in from a newly made crack around the cover.

"It's not budging any more," Hurley Girly said through grunts.

Lena pushed at it as well with no change. Both of them released their holds and the screw spun back down. They were back in darkness, and both Lena and Hurley Girly huffed from their effort.

"There's something on top," Lena said.

All of them got under it then, Sarah squished between Sterling and Ava. Whatever was above them, preventing them from getting into the ganghouse, it would only budge an inch or so and no more.

How many Daughters of Forgotten Light does it take to open a manhole? Sarah thought.

"Alright," Lena said. "Fuck this. All of you, back up. I'm going to blast this sucker open."

"So much for stealth," Ava said.

"Wouldn't it just bounce right back?" Sarah asked.

"It's metal, not glass," Lena said. "And we'll just have to see."

Sarah stumbled backwards. The other Daughters huddled around her as Lena took a crouching position and steadied where she would place her shot. There was a good chance the ball would bounce back into Lena's face. In the gathered blue glow of rang guns, Sterling's face held what could have been interpreted as worry. It said something to be concerned for the safety of someone who had, not long ago, beaten you to a pulp.

A flick of the wrist and Lena's rang fired. It was too quick and too short a distance to see the blue ball. Instead, an explosive *thoom* rocked the tunnel, and the screw blew upwards in a shower of sparks. In the wake of the shot, red light and a huge pile of debris fell into the hole, covering Lena in gunk and dust. Sarah crawled closer to Lena. The resulting rubble showed shattered bones, some still covered in skin and hair. The screw had been covered with discarded body parts.

"So that's what that smell was," Ava said.

"Let's get the hell out of this hole." Lena hacked and spit. "Pao?" She waited until Sarah nodded. "There can't be any witnesses. Do you understand what I'm saying?"

Sarah flinched. A sick burning feeling had tried to froth up from somewhere deep. Objection? An instinctual guarding of her innocence? She didn't know what it was. She just wanted to crawl back to the Daughter ganghouse. But she remembered the yin and yang, its black and white blending in curves that made it circular and whole. She breathed and swallowed it down, whatever *it* was, and again nodded.

She helped pushed the others out of the hole with a shove to the rear end or by kneeling and letting Sterling use her thigh as a step stool. Hurley Girly and Ava each grabbed one of Sarah's arms and yanked her into the main room of the Amazon's ganghouse. With ringing ears, Sarah aimed her rang from one side of the room to the other, ready for an attack.

The body pile was mostly bones, but the Amazons had certain parts they apparently found no use for. Sarah wanted to puke.

"Well, that's just unsanitary," Hurley Girly said.

A door slid open with an electric hum. In the same second, a dweller howled bloody murder and ran at them with what looked like a laser cutting-torch.

"Holy shit!" Ava said.

Sarah raised her rang, shaking. But Hurley Girly was quicker and blasted a hole through the oncoming dweller's chest. The blue ball bounced on the wall behind and returned from where it had come.

"Circle up," Lena shouted, and the Daughters put their backs together in a reverse huddle.

Sarah kept her rang up, eyes darting around the ganghouse. The red light around them had no direct source; it bled from the walls with a rise and fall of hypnotic brightness. The ganghouse had become too quiet after Hurley Girly had put down the screaming dweller.

"Heh... heh... heh," came laughter from a greasy voice.

It was above them. The Daughters raised their heads. A cage hung from the ceiling, made from pieces of manna boxes and glass. A dweller sat inside, both hands around the bars as she pushed her face between a gap.

"I am the watcher," she said. "I see everything."

"What the hell is that?" Ava said.

"Strangers," the caged dweller said. "Strangers in our house. My ladies will know about this. I see all!"

"Pao," Lena said.

Sarah knew what Lena wanted. Why couldn't it have been someone else, a sheila trying to kill her? That would have been easier. No, it had to be a crazy, feces-covered wretch in a cage.

No witnesses.

Sarah raised her rang.

"I am the watcher. All I do is watch! Watchwatchwatch watchwatch–"

The blue rang ball flew and smacked against the glass of the cage. Coarse laughter filled the ganghouse like a siren as the cage spun round and round from the force of the shot. Sarah tried to aim for another hit, but couldn't see the dweller in the demented centrifuge.

"You missed me." The dweller laughed and pointed a crooked finger at Sarah.

Hurley Girly huffed. "Are we just going to stand here with our thumbs up our asses all night?"

Lena groaned. "We need to shut this bitch up before–"

A faint cry. And not that of some dweller driven psycho from living under the rule of the Amazons. It was Rory, somewhere down a long hall to Sarah's right. Then it faded as quickly as it had come, as if someone had run with the baby into another room.

"You girls ready to do what we came here for?" Lena asked.

"Yeah," said Ava. "And let's get out of this haunted house before any freakier shit happens."

"Come back and see me!" cried the caged dweller.

Lena took off down the hall and the Daughters followed. Plenty of doors lined the hallway, but Lena passed them all until she got to the last one.

"This is it," Lena said. She paused with a hand to the glass, probably waiting to hear another cry for confirmation. But none came. She pushed the button to open the door and the gang pushed into the room.

There had to be at least fifty dwellers in here. All of them held some kind of tool or blade and had been cutting meat from dead limbs or building a piece of furniture. They now stood, facing Sarah's gang, all eyes on the Daughters.

"Fuck," Sarah said.

Rory rested in the arms of a bald dweller on the other side of the room who screamed, "Protect the baby!"

The dwellers raised their makeshift weapons and roared. Sterling and Hurley Girly shot their rangs as the nearest lunged for them.

"Wait!" Lena shouted.

Twin balls of light ripped through two dwellers and Hurley Girly's shot found another in the throat before ricocheting back to her.

"We can't hit the baby," Lena said. "Back into the hallway."

Ava cursed and was the last to back out of the room as two dwellers took swings at her with their hammer and laser cutters. She hit the door to close, but even Sarah knew it would only slow the dwellers for a second.

"There's a shitload more than I thought," Ava said, breathing heavy.

"We need Dipity," said Hurley Girly.

"No time," Lena shouted. "V pattern. Now. High in back."

Sarah knew her place in the "V" but didn't understand the rest of it. The dwellers poured from the room and stuffed the hallway like a mad river. Lena got on her stomach and the other three crouched at either side or behind. Sarah remained standing and kept her rang away from the other Daughters.

"Light these bitches up," Lena said.

Their rangs fired like muffled cannons. Sarah flicked her wrist and watched the cluster of blue balls zip into the oncoming dwellers. When hers returned, she kept firing. The hall became a symphony of bright chaos and blood, bodies flopping to the floor to add wet percussion. The dwellers showed no fear, no chance of being scared off. Whatever the Amazons had done to them, a rang blast to the face was a welcome thing.

The last dweller stood alone, looking down at her dead sisters. She kept her head down as she padded through the blood in a *splat, splat* of each step.

Run, Sarah thought. *Please, don't make me do this.*

The dweller charged.

CHAPTER 26

Lena got up from the floor as the blood trickled toward her. Pao's rang had blown off the final Amazon dweller's head, and Lena was glad she'd gotten to teach their ass a thing or two.

Staying in their formation, the Daughters stepped over the mounds of bodies and peeked into the room the horde had come from.

The bald dweller stood by the closest wall, still holding the baby, but she also held one of the laser cutters near the child's face. "This baby is an Amazon," she whispered.

"Don't do anything stupid," Lena waved a hand behind her to tell Sarah and the rest to stay back. "Your gang will be pissed if anything happens to Rory."

"And to die an Amazon," the dweller continued like she hadn't heard a word Lena had said, "is better than to live as anything else."

Lena held her hands out, palms up. "Give her to me."

The dweller laughed, deep, right from the gut. The laser cutter buzzed and Rory cried. With a shaky arm, the dweller sent sparks over the soft, black tufts of the baby's hair.

"It doesn't have to be this way," Lena said.

The dweller stopped laughing, her expression losing any

emotion. "Yes, it does." Her arm moved toward Rory's face.

Lena yelped. Blue light sprang from her rang gun and hit the wall behind the dweller, bouncing off the glass and ripping through the dweller's head. Lena dove. Rory fell into her arms, screaming even louder from the sudden drop. The dweller's body landed beside Lena, who curled herself around Rory and began heaving in choking sobs. The laser cutter, still engaged, burned into Lena's jacketed shoulder. Ava kicked it away before it could cut through the fabric.

Sarah and the others gathered around Lena. The baby quit crying, too interested now in the woman wailing and petting her tiny head. After a minute, Sterling put a hand to Lena's shoulder.

Sitting up, Lena wiped her wet eyes with the back of her jacket sleeve. "Let's see if we can find some of that manna juice," Lena said. "Then we really need to go."

They did a quick search of the room, but spare parts of glass and metal proved the only things to find. Without Lena having to say, they avoided any areas where the dwellers had been cutting meat. No juice or even any manna could be found and Lena had the sickening feeling they wouldn't find any. It wasn't long before they gave up and hurried back to the main room.

The caged dweller was screaming gibberish as a laser cutter was finishing a dome-shaped cut on the other side of the front door.

CHAPTER 27

"Wow," Lundgate said again. He'd been saying it for the last half hour.

His repetition didn't even annoy Dolfuse. She was thinking the same thing. It was phenomenal, despite the static and occasional skipping of the video feed. Only, Dolfuse's mouth had stayed wide open in awe, and she couldn't find the nerve to say anything. Oubliette was a marvel, a city made of ethereal glass that glowed dimly in the dark, matching, if not exceeding, the size of Manhattan.

Martin's files had painted a different picture in Dolfuse's mind, with no help from the nearly-propaganda posters from Oubliette's early days, decreeing it to be a hell for criminals.

"My nephew," Lundgate said. "He's been playing this game with his friends at school. They pretend to be on Oubliette, formed a little utopian society, farming imaginary vegetables in the sandbox. I thought it was going to be bad enough explaining that nothing grows out there. But this... If this wasn't classified, I wouldn't know what to say to him."

Dolfuse had no advice, so she kept silent.

Following its programming, the sperm-like drone detached from the shipping box and focused on a crowd that had developed around the shipment, hundreds of girls and women. And some had even come on motorcycles, strange machines on orange wheels of light.

A single woman stood before the crowd, older than the typical shippee. They hadn't opened the shipment yet, but they were arguing about something.

"Why can't we hear what they're saying?" Dolfuse shifted in her seat. The blipping audio was beyond annoying.

Lundgate shrugged. "Honestly, I'm amazed we have video."

Dolfuse could have popped him in the head.

One of the women got off her motorcycle and pointed angrily at the one in front of the shipping box.

The older woman raised her hand, seeming to try easing the heated situation.

"What's going on?" Dolfuse whispered.

"I haven't seen this show either," Lundgate snorted. "How should I know?"

The biker looked to the ground as if stuck in deep contemplation. The video skipped and she was pacing in front of the other bikers, flailing her arms violently.

"They're peeved about something," Lundgate said.

The video skipped again and all of the bikers stood in front of the box, right arms raised toward the older woman.

"Is that some kind of threat?" Lundgate chewed on a Twizzler.

The angry group descended on the woman, punching first, until she fell to the ground. Then they began kicking and stomping. A ripple swelled in the crowd behind them and the onlookers scattered, scrambling over each other to get away.

"Oh, my God," said Dolfuse.

The drone began to fly away.

"Where's it going?" Dolfuse asked.

Lundgate sighed, like he was bored. "The crowd is scattering. It's following the most concentrated group."

The last choppy images Dolfuse saw of the shipping box were the door lowering, the shippees walking out, and orange balls of light flying from the angry women's fists, tearing into them. The girls dropped in an instant, and then the murderous orbs returned to the bikers.

Dolfuse leapt to her feet, covering her mouth to muffle a scream.

"Oh, hell," Lundgate said. "You don't see that every day."

CHAPTER 28

Lena handed Rory to Sterling. It hurt to hand her off after all it took to get her. "Go back through the hole," she said.

Hurley Girly wasted no time and jumped into the pit. Ava went next and took the baby from Sterling. On the other side of the Amazon's garage door, one of the OC kicked out the piece they'd cut. It fell to the ground with a heavy *thwam*.

"You next, Pao," Lena whispered. *This is what a leader does*, she thought. *It was my fucking plan anyway.*

"No," Sarah said.

Shamika stepped through the opening. "Fancy meeting you here."

Sarah didn't move. Goddamn it, she was going to make this a shitload worse.

"We were just leaving," Lena said.

"Without one of your girls?" Shamika waved her hand and the rest of the OC entered, holding Dipity at rang point.

Sweat dripped from Dipity's dark hair, down her face.

"You alright, Dipity?" Lena asked.

Dipity nodded.

"She's fine," Shamika said. "I don't want trouble, Horror. In fact, I'm willing to let all of you leave here like you came. You saved us a lot of wet work."

"Really?" Lena knew there was a catch. *Just keep her talking.*

"For sure." Shamika smiled, flicking a curl of hair from her eye. "I'll trade you what I took, for what you took."

"Oh, ho, ho!" the dweller in the cage said. "This is too good. Lots to tell my ladies. Loads and loads. I'm watching all of you."

Shamika lifted her head. "What the fuck is that?"

"Whatever do you mean?" Lena said, returning the grin.

"Don't play that shit with me. We ain't got much time before the cannibals get back, and you're going to need us to back you up when they see what you did." Shamika looked around toward the hallway and the pile of dead dwellers. "Give me the baby, and we'll give you back your girl."

Sarah breathed loudly, moving from one foot to the other.

Shamika noticed, too. She laughed and smacked one of her gang against the arm. "Relax, kung fu. We don't want you passing out. Horror might end up leaving you on the floor for the Amazons to snack on."

"We don't leave our girls behind." Lena looked at Dipity, staring her square in the eyes.

They stayed still, not a quiver. She barely even blinked. Lena couldn't sacrifice her thirdincommand. No way in fuck. The baby would be well cared for with Shamika. But how could she abandon the child, after everything she'd done to bring her gang to this point. After she was so close to having what she never thought she could have again.

You going to bend over and take this, Horror?

She had only one choice.

But Sarah made the decision before Lena could say or do anything. She shot her rang at the wire holding the cage above, and insane laughter came down as the dweller plummeted atop the OC. Lena grabbed Dipity as the others dodged the shattering glass.

"Go!" Lena yelled.

They jumped into the manhole. Lena had never moved that fast in such a small space, and Dipity stayed close on her heels. Out on the street, they ran for the alley where their cyclones waited. The others had gotten there quickly, every girl having to fend for herself at that point. They all knew where to meet up.

Lena rounded the corner to see Ava and Hurley sat on their bikes while Sterling bounced the baby in her arms to soothe her whines.

Huffing, Dipity bent over the front of her cyclone.

Damn it, Pao! Lena turned around to smack Sarah in the head for royally fucking them over, but she was met with nothing but empty street.

"Where's Pao?" Ava asked.

Lena could have ripped her hair out. "Ah, shit."

CHAPTER 29

Sarah had fallen. When she lifted her head, the world was spinning and the leader of the all-black gang blasted a rang shot through the dweller inside the dropped cage. Before Sarah could get to her feet, hands grabbed and did it for her.

Even dizzy, Sarah slipped from their grasp and kicked one in the gut. The other got the side of Sarah's palm to the throat.

Shamika – *right, that was the head's name* – rushed over and grabbed Sarah by the hair. Sarah braced herself for a light ball to the face. It would have been fitting – karma. But the back of Shamika's hand was what hit her, smacking her even dizzier, straining her neck when her head whipped back.

"You got guts, sheila," Shamika said. "I'll give you that. But you just ruined any chance at peace between our gangs. What the fuck were you thinking?"

Blood beaded at the corner of Sarah's mouth. Fighting the urge to tongue the injury, she glared at Shamika. "I made Lena a promise."

Shamika snorted. "Well, I'll make *you* a promise. If we don't get that baby returned to us, where she belongs, then I'm going to put your head under my cyclone wheel until we can't tell who you are anymore. Fair?"

"Not really."

"Get this bitch out of here." Shamika waved her hand.

The two holding Sarah walked her out the door and down the street. She didn't understand their motive. If they wanted to kill her, they could have just done it right there in the Amazons' ganghouse. It would have been quick, and may have even laid all the blame at the Daughters' doorstep. Sarah's throat tightened. Why the hell was she thinking of good ideas for the OC? She really wished her mind would shut off sometimes.

"Where's your cyclone?" one of the OC girls asked.

"What?" The lump in Sarah's throat wouldn't go away no matter how many times she swallowed. "Why?"

"You don't think we're stupid enough to have you ride with one of us, do you?" the other one said. She shook as if she'd overdosed on coffee.

"You're... not killing me?" The thought relieved Sarah, but at the same time a new terror tickled at the back of her mind.

"Not yet," the jittery one said.

Lena and the rest had taken off, leaving Sarah's cyclone by itself in the alley. The Daughters would come for her. Do whatever it took. Wouldn't they?

The OC girls walked behind her as she rode her cyclone slowly to where Shamika and the others waited. They'd told her that if she even thought about trying to escape, they'd have rang shots in her so quick she'd look like a smoking piece of Swiss cheese. When all of them had gotten on their bikes, they surrounded Sarah and sped from the Amazon ganghouse. Sarah had no chance of getting away.

The OC wheels glowed black and purple, and were bigger than the other gangs'. Every so often the girl riding behind her would nudge the back of Sarah's cyclone. She didn't know if it was a warning to speed up or just because she didn't like her.

The gang crossed the Sludge River, and climbed a steep rise where there were fewer dweller buildings. Soon they came to the top of a glass mountain overlooking the Sludge. At the edge stood the Onyx Coalition ganghouse.

It was modest in comparison to the Amazons' head-quarters, and more refined than Sarah's own ganghouse. It could have been a doctor's home nestled in the Californian hills – at least from what she'd seen on TV.

They weaved through big glass barriers that made the front of the ganghouse look like a battlefield. The OC expected trouble. Lights flashed on from under the house's eaves when the group rode a hundred or so feet from the front door. The house had no windows, at least not anymore. Some kind of metal covered them.

Shamika got off her bike and knocked on a glass wall at the front. The wall split in the middle and a short black dweller nodded to the gang's head. They rode into the ganghouse, but this area didn't look like the main room, not like where the Daughters parked their cyclones. This was like a fancy hangar for a private jet. It was so clean it sparkled, and burn lines in the floor designated where each of them pulled in and shut down their bikes.

"You can put yours over there," Shamika said, pointing to the far wall.

Sarah parked her cyclone and waited until one of them grabbed her and pushed her forward. Two more got behind her as they all entered the house. Sarah hurried along before they could sneak in a few punches.

Inside the main room, a big window looked across the expanse of the city. Oubliette – it was truly stunning when you viewed it from a distance. Here sat the most exquisite furniture made from the city's glass – chairs, tables, even a few useless bowls and plates. Sarah couldn't keep her astounded sigh to herself.

"Beautiful, isn't it?" Shamika said, with no intent to hide her pride. "We have Oubliette's best glass cutters. Who do you think helped make your cyclone?"

"I thought Grindy built them."

"With our girls doing all the work!" Shamika looked at Sarah as if she was gum on her boot. "Grindy designed them, yeah. Got them working."

"Your ganghouse is very nice," Sarah said, trying to ease the mood, if only to save her hide for a moment more.

"Don't get too comfortable," Shamika said. She beckoned Sarah with a curled finger and led her down the hall to a white door. "Inside."

"What's in there?" Sarah asked.

Shamika rolled her eyes and opened the door. "Not a damn thing." She shoved Sarah inside and closed the door before Sarah could turn around.

A lock clicked as Sarah felt around in the dark. Shamika had been telling the truth. The closet-sized room was empty, especially of light. Nothing but slick glass walls surrounded her, and all she could do was listen to the sound of her breath, and hope her gang hadn't forgotten her.

CHAPTER 30

Dolfuse's drone flew over the city. The women who'd fled the center where the shipment had landed dispersed three different ways, hurrying as fast as they could without the benefit of motorcycles. Dolfuse watched silently, tense, as the television showed the drone soaring right above the surface of what could only be a river. The small amount of light coming from the buildings cast the occasional glimmer against the water, but other than that it was just a deeper, winding shadow amongst other darkness.

The drone detected more motorcycles with differently colored lights, and flew lower to follow.

Lundgate had abandoned his snacks. Who could eat after seeing what had happened to the shippees?

This other gang numbered only five, travelling like a flock of ducks. A twirl and a dive and the drone circled the motorcycles, keeping up with them along the street. The video jumped, putting the drone closer and showing something poking out of the top of the lead biker's jacket. Dolfuse rose from her couch and squinted at the television. *Was it…?*

"Is that a baby?" Lundgate said.

Dolfuse's gut twisted. It felt like the hairs on the back of her neck had ripped themselves free. "That can't be. Who would do such a thing?"

"This is going to send a wrench so far up that shipper warden's ass she'll be shitting iron for months."

Dolfuse turned back to him with scrunched brows.

"Oh." Lundgate's eyes widened. "Uh, pardon the French, senator."

"What did you mean about the warden?"

His eyes focused on the screen, Lundgate said, "Well, I mean, there's a baby on Oubliette. That's a huge deal. Illegal as hell. It's definitely going to ruin the warden's credibility, yeah?"

"I suppose it would."

They'd throw Beckles from her ivory tower the instant they discovered she hadn't noticed a smuggled child, or if she'd been behind it. But Dolfuse didn't see the warden making it easy on anyone who would try. And she had all those guards religiously loyal to her. Then there were all those shippees who'd yet to be sent to Oubliette.

Dolfuse had to warn Spangler. To hell with Beckles. She couldn't let her friend go down with the warden. Spangler could quit and they could formulate a plan, a defense when it came to the authorities interrogating him. And the questioning would come.

"The motorcycles are stopping," Lundgate said.

Dolfuse turned back to the TV. The gang stopped in front of a wide, one-story building. When their wheels disappeared, they leapt off their bikes and ran to the front door.

CHAPTER 31

"Fucking shit!" Ava said.

"How could we have lost Pao?" Dipity asked. "She was right behind us."

Sterling, the last inside, closed the door.

A hot geyser of hate filled Lena's gut. She flexed her hands into fists, pacing the darkened front of Grindy's shop. She wanted to hit something, but Rory gurgling from under her chin kept her from blowing her top.

Such a beautiful girl.

At least the night hadn't been a complete fuckup. She smiled and bounced the baby against her chest.

"So how are we going to get her back?" Hurley Girly asked.

Rory had to be the most precious thing Lena had ever seen. Even though they looked nothing alike, Lena knew she'd been destined to be her mother. Circumstances, fate, whatever they called it, had brought them together. Maybe there was a God out there, and he paid back his debts even if it was a little late.

"Hey, Horror!" Ava shouted.

Lena jolted, scaring Rory into a whine.

"What are we going to do about Pao?"

"Or was all that talk back there about never leaving our girls behind a bunch of bullshit?" Dipity raised an eyebrow.

"That's why we're here," Lena said. "We need Grindy's help." She turned and rocked Rory as she walked away.

"You think she will?" asked Ava. "We've pissed on everything she's tried to hold together."

"She's a Daughter," said Lena. "Always has been. And there's no more truce for her to defend."

"Where the hell is everyone?" Hurley Girly asked. "They should have been back by now."

"Someone get the lights," Lena said.

Sterling walked over and tried a switch. The dark remained as the light switch sounded an empty *click, click*. Something was definitely wrong. As they eased through the rows of shelves filled with spare parts and unfinished inventions, shadows played tricks on Lena, flickering at the periphery and making her dart her eyes from one junk-ridden cabinet to another.

A *clang* to their right. Hurley Girly crouched into shooting position. Her ball shot out and the hairs on the back of Lena's neck rose. Hurley Girly had successfully murdered a metal cylinder that had rolled off one of the shelves.

They continued on to Grindy's office. It had been left cracked open, and Lena pointed a finger at Dipity and Sterling to get on either side of the door, while Ava and Hurley Girly squatted further back, facing it.

With a nod from Lena, Dipity pushed the door the rest of the way open. Hurley Girly screamed and Sterling bent over, away from the door, dry heaving. The other two did much the same.

Their reactions told Lena everything, but she wasn't

ready for what she found. She let Rory wrap a tiny hand around her finger and stepped to the open door.

They'd cut Grindy to pieces. Her arms, legs, and head had been nailed to the wall, her face contorted in an inhuman grimace. Where her torso should have been, were the words, *No Mo Truce*. Blood covered the floor. They must have done it here. Who? The Amazons, who the fuck else?

Lena nestled Rory deeper into the jacket and covered the baby's nose as she moved in closer. She found the torso. It lay on top of Grindy's desk, stripped of clothing and most of the flesh.

"These fuckers," Lena whispered, "are going to wish they never messed with us."

An ear-splitting scratch came from outside, along with equally detestable laughter. The Daughters sprang to life, casting down their misery, and huddling against the shop's front door with their backs. Shit was about to get real, but if the Amazons wanted in, they'd have to be stronger than Lena and her gang.

"Daughters," said a high, singsong voice that could only belong to Farica. "Come out and play!"

The other Amazons whooped and copied Farica's taunt.

"I'm going to kill them." Ava rose, and Dipity had to pull her away from the door before she could open it.

"Wait," Lena said.

Hurley Girly pointed. "We can go out the back. If we leave now, they might not see us."

"On foot?" Dipity asked.

"There's no way we'd make it," Lena said. "But you're right about the back. They're going to wise up and come at us from both sides eventually."

Farica shouted through the door, "We found some gnarly weapons in there that Grindy's been making. I think she was planning on arming the dwellers with these fucking things." Something tapped against the street. "Can you believe that? Looks like that blade thing the grim reaper is always carrying around. Sharp glass, too. We gave a bunch of them to our dwellers. I tell you, those crazy sheilas were almost surgical when they cut into Grindy."

Ava scrambled to get out there. It took nearly all of them to hold her back.

"And now we're going to use them to fuck up your cyclones."

That was the last straw as far as Ava was concerned. Lena didn't know if Ava found some jolt of adrenaline to give her ultra strength or if the other Daughters had loosened their grip on her, but Ava opened the door and got off a shot before Dipity could close it back, just in time, as rang shots hit the glass door in a buzzing *thump, thump, thump*.

"My foot!" one of them screamed. "Ow, ow, ow, ow, ow, fuckity fuck!"

More laughter came, but it was from Ava, maniacal cackling. "My rang ball is still out there."

The Amazons were cursing, screaming, and yelling things like, "Duck!" and "The damn thing's over there!"

The back door crashed through. Lena and the others raised their rangs, ready to shoot the incoming Amazon, but it was Ava's ball of light come back home. When it returned, Lena yanked Hurley Girly to her feet and they all ran for the back door. Lena followed at the rear.

Loud humming filled the room from behind. Bursting through the door, one of the Daughters' cyclones hurtled in without a rider. Instinctively, Lena held Rory tighter, as if she could have prevented the oncoming wheels from crushing and burning both her and the child.

Sterling shoved Lena out of the way. When Lena fell onto her back, head smacking the side of a shelf, Rory cried so hard she gagged tiny baby coughs. The cyclone kept coming, throwing Sterling to the ground and rolling over her legs. Unable to scream properly, Sterling moaned like a drowning lawn mower. Tears streamed from her eyes and into her gaping mouth.

The cyclone slammed into a wall. It stayed in place there, buzzing and moving only slightly to one side.

"Get Sterling on that bike," Lena yelled at Hurley Girly. "Go to the ganghouse. Get ready for an attack."

They hurried to put Sterling behind Hurley Girly, and the two of them were out the back door in seconds. The other Daughters followed on foot, not bothering to wait around for the Amazons who'd surely be coming through the huge hole in the front of the shop. Lena tried to comfort Rory, who steadily whined as the Daughters crouched along the side of the building. Hurley Girly's cyclone wheels glowed in the distance before disappearing around a curve.

What the fuck had Sterling been thinking? Sure, Lena was glad to still be alive, for Rory to be OK. But now it was Sterling whose life was on the chopping block. How could she be so stupid? After all the hell Lena had put Sterling through, why did she sacrifice herself? If Sterling lived, she could never walk again, probably couldn't ride either. It was something they'd take care of later, if they were lucky enough to talk to her again.

"Run for the cyclones," Lena whispered. "They're

probably coming through the front now. If you see any of them, shoot until they're on the ground."

They ran, and Rory's cries bucked with the movement. When they got to the front, one Amazon waited on her bike, raised her rang. Lena fired; all of the able Daughters did. The Amazon was too slow, and the shots ripped into her, sending the cannibal flat onto the street.

Lena jumped on her cyclone and held up her rang to catch the returning ball. "Grab her rang."

By the time Hurley Girly nabbed the weapon, Amazons were rushing from the front of Grindy's. The Daughters rode away as orange rang shots flew past overhead. Lena had to swerve to deflect one with the back of her cyclone. Farica and her girls had wasted time shooting when they could have been on their cyclones and catching up. But there was only one way back to the Daughters' ganghouse, and the Amazons always had more than one card up their sleeves.

CHAPTER 32

"How can we get info on these women?" Dolfuse asked. Lundgate probably had no clue, but she had said it more to herself than him.

"I guess they would have that info at the shipping port," Lundgate said. "I don't know, though. It's just a guess."

Of course, fate would have her go back to that snake pit and run the risk of having to see Warden Beckles again. Spangler would be pissed as well. She'd already squeezed him dry for favors. But she had to know. Who was the biker woman? Who was the baby? How could she possibly be sent to Oubliette?

"Man," Lundgate said. "This is better than a movie – static aside. Martin is going to love it."

Dolfuse looked at him from the corner of her eye. "How well do you know the vice president?"

Lundgate stared at the ceiling, tilting his head from side to side. "Just a little. She's had me do different things for her. But I wouldn't say we're best friends or anything."

"Do you know why she's so interested in Oubliette?"

"I could guess." He wrinkled his brow, throwing her the occasional curious glance as the drone flew behind the warring gangs.

"Just for my own curiosity."

Lundgate nodded. "Yeah, she's like a human math problem. I've been trying to figure her out for a while. But I have a theory."

"I'm listening."

"Well, if the enviroshields break down, or the EA come a-calling, we're pretty much screwed. And based on how big I'm guessing this city is from what the drone's been showing us, there could easily be enough room for a few hundred thousand."

"So why not pack up and move everyone to Oubliette?" Dolfuse said, nodding. It would make sense.

"Not everybody."

There's the catch. "And I wonder how the lucky few would be selected."

Lundgate shrugged. "I don't know. I haven't thought that far. Anyway it's just a theory. I couldn't see us leaving all these people to die in the cold."

"We send children to die on Oubliette and in the army," Dolfuse said, softly.

That got Lundgate uncomfortable. He sighed, hunching his shoulders, and tried to focus on the television.

"And what about the women on Oubliette now?" Dolfuse asked.

"I guess they'd have to be removed."

CHAPTER 33

Lena, Dipity, and Ava flew through their front door, and Hurley Girly locked it behind them. Sterling lay on a manna box couch, shaking and gasping. The burnt mess of her legs shimmered wet under the lights, red skin showing through the holes in her pants.

Something slammed against the front door.

"I want my baby!" Farica shouted from the other side. "You all brought this on yourselves. I was being good! I followed the truce. You're the bad guys here. Not us!"

Lena spit. "We need to get Sterling upstairs."

No, Sterling signed. The effort seemed to give her more pain. *I'll hold them off.*

"Are you fucking nuts?" Lena leaned over her. "You've already done enough."

I'm dead anyway.

"The hell you are!" The last word came out wobbly, as Lena fought the tears bubbling up.

Sterling smiled. *Let me.*

Lena stormed away, determined to keep her mind from spiraling into the other side of insanity. But maybe it wouldn't be such a bad thing to let the monster out. But not now, not with Rory around.

"Ava," Lena said, "you're with me. Hurley and Dipity, get the turrets ready."

"But we never got any extra rangs," Hurley Girly said.

"Use the one you took off the Amazon."

"But–"

"Just fucking do it!"

Rory began crying again. Guilt immediately gripped Lena, right in the gut. It wasn't just the baby. It was the landslide of everything she'd done to call down the shitty predicament they were in.

Lasers sawed through their door.

Lena popped her neck and sighed. "Does everyone have a fucking laser cutter but us?"

CHAPTER 34

Farica rolled the scythe in her hand as she waited for her sheilas to finish cutting into the door. She'd cut Lena's throat first. Yeah, she bet Horowitz tasted sweeter than all the rest. She'd been marinating in crazy more than the others.

This was justice, the Daughters brought this on themselves. Nobody liked the fucking truce, but Farica and her Amazons would have upheld it. With the steady supply of meat coming in every quarter, why the hell would they disrupt that?

Because the meat would still come, even if we were the only gang left. Farica grinned, watching light glint off the scythe's blade.

A common misconception was that the cannibalism had started on Oubliette. Twenty years before, though, a story had ripped through the headlines about a family living off the grid in the wilds of Montana. It had been during the worst years of the famine. Nothing was growing, and most rural communities didn't have access to government-issued foodstuffs. Not that it could really be called "food."

The Altstadt family had been raided by UCNA special forces after several travelers in the area had gone missing. What they'd found was worse than any horror movie:

filleted cadavers piled up in a barn, booby traps for anyone dumb enough to come snooping around the property. Several agents had been killed without a shot fired.

In the end, though, most of the Altstadt family was put in the dirt, except for a girl named Farica and her younger siblings who'd hidden in a cellar. The one boy was handed over to the military while the girls were immediately processed and shipped to Oubliette.

Hands washed clean, as far as the government was concerned.

And once she got to Oubliette, Farica gathered her sisters and formed their own gang, named after the game they used to play in the woods, imagining themselves as warrior women who ate their enemies. Time and violence had made her the last original Amazon.

Daughters of Forgotten Light, Farica thought, *what a fucking mouthful*. And what did it even mean? Well, Farica would make sure they were forgotten soon enough.

"It's done," her right arm said.

"Ladies," Farica said, smiling at each of her gang, "try not to kill Rory when you're blowing holes through these bitches. Yeah?"

They nodded in unison, building up a momentous energy Farica could almost feel in the air. She kicked at the triangle shape that had been cut in the door. When it fell, the Amazons raised their rangs and entered two at a time. Shit, she was so amped about killing the Daughters, she'd almost forgotten that one of her gang still lay dead in front of Grindy's. Just another thing for the Daughters to pay for.

The main room was empty.

"Where are they at?" her left leg whispered.

"They want to play hide and seek," Farica said.

The Daughters' cyclones sat over by the wall, abandoned quickly and without an effort to line them up all neat. Farica had them running scared. So what do you do with prey that's running? You keep up the chase until they drop from exhaustion.

"But we're the best at this game aren't we, ladies?"

The Amazons grunted agreement. Their right leg and left arm rushed to the stairwell. Farica and her second-in-command followed. The two in front opened the door and hadn't even touched the first step when a cable tightened and pulled at something at the top of the stairs. Rang shots blasted toward them, tearing one Amazon's arm off and hitting the other right in the gut.

Blood splattered Farica's face as she and her second split from the doorway before the balls could hit them. The armless Amazon's screaming filled the stairwell. The one who'd gotten hit in the stomach mouthed silent words as blood pooled over her lips.

The Amazons' second-in-command ripped the cable from the door with a curse. The blood had gotten in her mohawk, polka-dotting the purple. Farica bent over the sheila who'd taken the hit to the arm.

"God, it hurts!" she screamed.

"Shit, I'm sorry," Farica said. She raised her rang to the woman's head. "I'll do you a solid. No one should suffer like this."

"No, Farica! Please–"

Pzzzt.

And that was that.

The sheila with the gut shot no longer mouthed anything,

or breathed. Farica's last Amazon stared at her.

"You still want to see this through," Farica asked.

"Fuck yes," she said.

"Alright, then. Let's take our time. The Daughters have been busy. And I don't want any more surprises."

When they got to the second floor, Farica poked out her scythe to attract any rang shots. But after a few minutes of waiting, and then searching the second floor, they found it empty. And each floor after that was the same.

"This is starting to piss me off," Farica said, waiting outside the entrance to the last floor.

"Maybe they left," her second said.

"No. Their cyclones are all here and there's no other way in or out."

"How do you know?"

Farica squinted at her. "I have my dweller spies, just like everyone else."

"They didn't seem to do us much good with that rang trap."

What a cheeky brat. But she was right. When Farica got out of here, she'd be cleaving flesh to teach her dwellers how to be loyal.

"OK," Farica said. "If they aren't on this floor, I'm going to hope they jumped. Be careful to–"

There it was. Rory's cry. Coming from the other side of the door.

"You hear that too?" Farica asked.

Her second nodded.

"Go."

They crouched onto the top floor, lined with bare walls and jagged corners. Another cry shot through the quiet hall, and Farica flicked two fingers toward the sound. Her sheila took the lead, both Amazons keeping their rangs aimed for any of the thieving bitches to pop out.

When another cry came, Farica's sheila got excited. She leapt from her crouch and ran for the door from where the crying had come.

"Wait, stupid!" Farica whispered.

The door opened, sensing the Amazon's running approach, and she went through with ease. Her screams only started halfway down the empty elevator shaft, probably when she realized she'd fucked up. And then they vanished from hearing, replaced with a low *thud*.

"Damn it!" Farica crawled to the open elevator door. She peered over the edge, holding on to the stability of the outer wall. It was a long, dark way down. She sniffed the air, listening. How had they made it seem like Rory was crying from the elevator shaft?

CHAPTER 35

Lena held two fingers over Rory's lips. She had no way to rock the baby to keep her quiet, not when she clung to the inside of the elevator shaft with her other hand. What a dumb, stupid fucking thing she'd done. But it had worked, hadn't it? One less Amazon to deal with.

Farica stood at the door, sniffing at the air like some feral animal. Lena wanted to bring up her rang and shoot the bitch in the chest, but she could see only the tip of Farica's nose from where she hung, and even if she could somehow manage a shot, she'd run the risk of falling nine stories with Rory at her chest.

Just stay quiet, pretty girl.

Farica started making clicking noises as if she was calling a kitten for supper. Rory closed her eyes. Something wet and warm spread across Lena's chest, the tangy smell of piss with it.

Ah, fuck!

The scythe blade swung into the shaft, striking just inches from Lena's face. Farica pulled it back, scratching glass with the sharp point. It sent a screeching into Lena's ears, a spasm down her back. Where were Hurley Girly and Dipity? They could just run out and push this shitbag into the shaft and end this godforsaken noise!

Rory scrunched her face, stuck out her bottom lip, looking ready to cry.

The scythe blade flipped and swung to the other side of the elevator shaft. Farica did the same thing – striking as far as she could reach and then pulling the blade along the metal in a torturously long scratch.

Then there was silence and Rory calmed down, relaxing her face back into infant slumber. Lena kept her breathing tight, quiet. If she knew Farica as well as she thought, the bitch would be waiting there, listening and smelling for them.

The elevator door closed, and Lena loosed a breath. It had to have been only a few minutes, but it felt like forever before Hurley Girly and Dipity opened the door.

"Take Rory," Lena told Dipity. The baby looked so tiny in Dipity's monstrous arms.

"I guess you're keeping that name for the baby then?" Hurley Girly asked, offering Lena a hand.

"It's a good name." Lena shuffled out of the shaft and got far from the open door. "She pissed all over me, though. I'm going to need a shower. But first – where the hell were you two?"

"Hiding in the next room," Dipity said. "We figured we could wrestle her down if she tried to come in. But there was no way in hell we were going to come at her with only one rang."

Cowards. "What about Ava?" Lena asked.

The Daughters' right arm herself ran around the corner, shaking her head. "These Amazons are dumber than hell. I waited forever in that room. They never checked it."

"Guess Farica figured she should hit the road while she still could," Hurley Girly said.

"She's not out of here yet." Lena placed Rory back into her jacket. "Let's hurry downstairs and grab your rangs."

"Don't you think one of us should stay back and hold the baby?" Ava asked.

"No," Lena said.

CHAPTER 36

After taking their rangs, Farica stepped over the two dead Amazons at the bottom of the stairs, and wished them a whispered goodbye. She hurried for the front door, now with a rang on each arm, striking the floor with the bottom of her scythe with every other step. She might have been outnumbered for now, but she'd be back to finish the Daughters, with more dwellers than they could count. Hell, fuck a gang, she'd be leading an army. And then Oubliette would be hers, and she could do what she wanted, kill who she wanted, fuck who she wanted, all without the weight of a goddamn truce.

Beside her, a Daughter popped out of a manna box couch, roaring a gurgling cry and aiming her rang gun at Farica. The ball fired from her arm before Farica could react. But it was a poor shot and went low, grazing Farica on the side of her knee.

"Shit!" Farica screamed, firing her own rang with even less success.

She limped and jumped for the bitch, making it to her just as the woman's ball of light returned to her rang. Farica swung her scythe down, cutting through the air with a low whistle that ended in a pleasing *thunk*. The blade had gone through the Daughter's head, down into her throat. The sharp glass was visible through her open mouth. The dead woman's eyes rolled back, leaving only the whites.

How the fuck could they have missed her when they first came in? Farica saw she had made herself a hole under the couch seat. Her legs were a mess, a puddle of blood under her knees, but not from what Farica had done to her. It looked like the Daughter wouldn't have made it much longer anyway.

"You're welcome," Farica said.

She pulled at her scythe, but the damn thing was stuck. She yanked and yanked. Nothing. She was going to have to put her boots on the dead Daughter's chest for leverage. As if she couldn't have gotten dirtier.

CHAPTER 37

Lena waited with Ava as Hurley Girly and Dipity grabbed their rang guns from the turrets at the top of the first flight of stairs. The two dead Amazons the guns had taken out still lay at the bottom. Seeing them filled Lena with a sudden fear, and she thought of Sterling. Lena shouldn't have listened to Sterling and her stupid death wish. They could have found a way to save her.

She ran to the main room.

Farica had a foot on Sterling's chest, pulling her scythe from the Daughter's head. It was an understandable time to scream, to cry, to show any form of emotion, but Lena emptied out and all that remained was Horror.

The others were still in the stairway when Lena shot. The Amazon raised her scythe and deflected the ball back to her. Using her left arm, Farica fired, sending Lena rolling on the floor to avoid it. She normally wouldn't have been so slow on the return. But she was holding Rory.

Stupid!

"You're dead," Farica shouted. "All of you. And you know it." She stood at the hole in the front door and dropped something.

It wasn't until it hit the floor that Lena recognized it as

a rang gun. She rolled behind a manna box as Farica fired from outside, the light ball striking the discarded rang. The explosion blew everything at the front of their ganghouse to high hell.

Lena cradled Rory like a cocoon just before the manna box slammed into her back. Glass pelted her head as dust filled her nose and mouth. She coughed for several minutes, spitting out the burnt grit on her tongue. When she stood, Rory made a terrified face, but she couldn't hear the baby's cries. Muffled voices came from behind. Ahead, huge chunks of debris blocked the exit. It would take a while, but they could clear it away. Farica, however, would be long gone.

She set Rory down on an opposite couch and cradled Sterling, lowering the dead Daughter onto her back. Lena didn't mind the blood. She already needed a shower.

Lena closed Sterling's eyes and mouth before the body would become too stiff to do so. They'd have to bury her. And Grindy. That was the second thing they had to do. The gang couldn't do anything else until properly mourning those they'd lost and they couldn't properly mourn until they'd hunted Farica and removed her from existence.

But what about Sarah Pao?

The other Daughters came back and circled the couch. Gasps and breathy curses all around her, but Lena had nothing more to give. What Farica did to Sterling had hollowed the head Daughter. Lena knew what she wanted to do, what she *had* to do, but there was no rage or misery to go along with it. It was just an urgent item on her to-do list. Maybe after everything was checked off she could allow herself to cry.

"Hurley Girly," Lena said. "Go squeeze some juice out of a manna loaf for Rory. She needs to eat. Ava, you, me, and Dipity are going to kill that redheaded rectal itch for good."

Dipity cleared her throat. "We have to get Pao back."

"I know," Lena said.

"We'll have to give Shamika the baby," Ava said.

"No." The harshness in Lena's voice was a surprise, even to her.

Ava threw her hands into the air. "Why is it so fucking important to you, Lena?"

"She has a name." Lena stared into Ava's eyes. "She's not an it, she's a person." She groaned and rubbed her face, trying to scrub away some of her exhaustion. Logic pushed away emotion. "But I know you're right. We're going to need to be on their good side. And we need Pao back. I'm not going to stand for one more Daughter dying."

"So we go to the top of the hill, then?" Dipity asked.

"Not yet. We have to clear this shit away so we can get outside. Farica couldn't have gotten far. Revenge first. Then we bury our own. Then we retrieve our own. I need a minute with Rory. By myself."

Ava and Dipity nodded as Hurley Girly came back with a cylinder full of milky liquid. When they'd cleared enough of a hole to fit through, Lena took Rory outside. On Earth she would have said she was getting some fresh air, but there was none of that here, just the same recycled staleness.

Rory opened her mouth when Lena put the cup to it, hungrily sucking up the juice. Lena thought she could almost see a smile. The baby's happy wriggling in her arms brought a grin to Lena's face and, God, did it hurt. She didn't want to let Rory go, no matter the benefits of letting the OC get their way.

"It looks like God's an asshole," she whispered to Rory. "He couldn't let me keep my first, and he won't let me keep you."

A sound buzzed from above. It wasn't like a cyclone, or a rang shot. It was something she'd never heard before – soft, but definitely out of place. She stayed still, keeping her head down, eyes on the baby. But at the corner of her sight, just above the short building across the street, something was hovering.

CHAPTER 38

"This picture sucks!" Dolfuse said. "Can you get a better look at her face?"

"Only if she raises her head or if I do some quick programming for it to get closer, if it doesn't fly off first. You wanted to stay covert, didn't you?"

Dolfuse had to know who this woman was. She had dark brown hair, pale skin, a slim build, but from what Dolfuse had seen the woman was stronger than her appearance let on.

The baby drank something from a cup. An ache swelled in Dolfuse's stomach, and it was stupid, she knew, but in that moment she wanted to be the one holding her, not some murderous biker a million miles away. Who was this woman?

"Program it to get closer," Dolfuse said. "I doubt any of them have the slightest clue we're watching them."

Lundgate shrugged and had the drone move in closer. It didn't advance for almost a minute, then the picture jumped and the woman raised her head, shooting her right arm forward. A brilliant blue light filled the screen and then there was only static.

"What the hell just happened?" Dolfuse yelled.

Lundgate pushed at buttons randomly as the static flickered on the television. "I think she just blew the drone to hell," he said. "Pardon the swear."

"Can you back up the recording?"

"Sure." He rewound the video to just before the ball of light left the woman's arm.

"Pause it," Dolfuse said. "Right there!"

The image froze on the woman's sneering face. All the evil in the world and beyond the stars was contained in that one look.

"I guess they found out we were watching," Lundgate said.

"I'd like a copy of this."

"Sure thing," he said. "And I'm just joshing you about the covert thing. I mean, so what if they know we sent a drone. It's not like they can do anything about it."

Lundgate laughed, but his words stuck with Dolfuse, like taffy between the teeth. These women were capable of building machines and weapons out of the leftovers Oubliette's founders had never gotten to use. They'd formed a ruthless society and had years of stewing in their hatred of Earth folk. If Martin planned on leading an expedition to Oubliette, she was in for a very rude welcome.

CHAPTER 39

"Motherfuckers are spying on us," Lena said, storming back in to the ganghouse.

The Daughters jumped to attention.

"Who?" Ava said. "The OC?"

Lena put Rory on a couch to sleep. "Come with me and I'll show you."

Outside, Hurley Girly kicked her boot against a big chunk of the machine. It was still smoking and had more jagged edges than Farica's teeth.

"I'm pretty damn sure it's not the OC's," Lena said. "This had to be from Earth. Doesn't look like anything Grindy's dwellers would build."

"Might have come in with tonight's shipment," Dipity said.

"That's what I'm assuming." Lena nodded. "And I sure as hell don't like it."

"Why the fuck would they care about what we're doing out here? Why now?" Hurley Girly asked.

"Cause something's changed," Ava said. She looked at Lena and, almost like telepathy, her stare told Lena everything she needed to know. They knew about the baby.

While her knowledge of military strategy was lacking, in every war movie she'd seen, they always sent recon before attacking. If they could send one flying machine, who was to say they wouldn't send more, with guns. Shooting the damned thing down probably didn't help matters either. If the UCNA didn't attack Oubliette, they sure as shit could let them all starve to death.

Lena sighed. "We're going to have to ration manna even more than we already have been."

"Ah, shit," Dipity muttered.

"This is too much to deal with," Hurley Girly said. There was a moan in her voice that sounded like a blizzard of crying would erupt, the kind that hit you so hard, you lost all your breath with each sob, and tensed into a silent, open-mouthed mess.

"What we don't have time for is pissing and moaning. Sterling wouldn't want that. We've got to be proactive. Otherwise we'll all be gone and forgotten. And no one is going to cry for us."

"There more than likely won't be a shipment coming," Ava said. "Not anymore."

"So we're going to have to find a way out of Oubliette," Lena said.

"I'm with you there," Dipity said. "But that's something we should've already figured out by now. And with Grindy gone..." She looked away.

For fuck's sake. Was everybody going to choke up today?

"We can worry about the details later. We need to find Farica. Let's get everyone loaded up." Lena rubbed her tired eyes. "And we need to go get Grindy's body."

• • •

They looked for Farica, in all of the typical areas and then the not-so-obvious. The Amazons' dwellers were gone, too, so there was no one to coerce into giving up the last of their leadership. No one hid in the Core, or in the sewers under the Amazon ganghouse. It was as if Farica and her minions had found a way off Oubliette, just when the Daughters were in desperate need of the same. It took a lot for Lena Horror to call it quits on the search. Time was a'wasting, for Sarah, for them all.

They dragged the dead Amazons from the stairwell and fished the other out of the bottom of the elevator shaft. The last one had made a bigger mess than they'd bargained for, and it was going to take a lot longer to clean up – yet another reason to get Pao back. But Lena figured if they were leaving Oubliette anyway, what was the point? Unless it began to smell.

Ava and Hurley Girly put the dead Amazons on the back of their cyclones while Dipity gave Sterling much more care and laid her on the back of her seat. The Daughters of Forgotten Light took the ride slow and steady, both to keep an eye out for the OC and Farica, and so the bodies wouldn't fall into the street.

When they got to Grindy's, Lena waited in front of the door with Rory asleep in her jacket. "I need at least one of you to help me. But if the rest of you want to stay behind, I'd understand."

Lena's sheilas looked at each other.

Ava spoke for them. "No. We're all coming in."

The front door was still a wreck from when the runaway cyclone burst through, and the already dark shop seemed even dimmer than before, probably because they knew what they would find. But something was different.

Carrying a light, a woman in a white shirt and jeans roamed the shelves like a ghost. Lena had to rub the fog from her eyes and remember there was no such thing as ghosts. It was Taylor. She was humming, but it wasn't a song.

"Taylor," Lena called, low enough not to startle the dweller.

"Huh?" Taylor said, moving closer. "Who's that?"

"Lena Horowitz."

"Oh. Hi, Horror." Her eyes were red, cheeks wet. But her face was blank.

"We've come to take Grindy," Lena said.

"She's not here."

"What? Who took her body?"

Taylor laughed and shook her head. "She's at the shipment. She'll be back in a little while. Why aren't you sheilas there?"

The sight of Grindy nailed to the wall must have snapped Taylor's crackers. This was no time for the dweller to go loopy. She was probably the best chance they had to get off the city.

"Come with me," Lena said, moving toward Grindy's office.

"What are you..." When Taylor saw where Lena was headed her face widened, like she'd suddenly become aware. She snarled. "No!"

Lena grabbed Taylor in a headlock.

"Oh, shit," Ava said. The Daughters got out of Lena's way.

"No!" Taylor screamed again, swatting her arms and

stumbling on her feet as Lena dragged her to the office.

This whole city brims with brats like this, Lena thought. Someone had to do some fucking growing up around here and face the hell in front of them.

She kicked the door open and shoved Taylor inside, onto her knees.

"Look!" Lena said, pointing at the body parts stuck to the wall.

Taylor cried, the way Lena thought Hurley Girly was going to earlier, reaching her hands out to Grindy's remains. She bent down to her knees and sobbed, the sound muffled by her folded body.

"Grindy is dead," Lena said. "We can't change that."

"I loved her!" Taylor wept into her knees.

"I know you did. And I swear to Christ we're going to make sure Farica gets what's coming to her. But we're going to need your help. And we're going to need you focused."

Taylor lifted her head, casting glimmering eyes at Lena. "What could I do? Grindy–"

"Put a lot of faith in you. Hell, you practically run this shop."

"Used to."

"No," Lena said. "I think you have one more big job in you. And this one's going to be a doozy."

"Like what?"

"We'll talk about it later," Lena said. "Let's give Grindy the sendoff she deserves."

The Sludge River was not just the waste collected from every unfortunate resident of Oubliette. It wasn't just the means by which every woman's waste got recycled underneath the streets by the same energy that lit the city's dwellings and gave gangs the means to blast each other to oblivion. It was also where the dead were put to rest.

The Daughters rode to the river bank opposite the OC's glass hill. They'd brought Taylor along on Lena's cyclone. It was only right for her to be there. If anyone could find a shred of happiness on Oubliette, it had to be cherished. And if lost, it had to be honored, remembered. Whatever hatred Lena thought she had for Taylor, it was gone with the truce. And Lena needed her.

Ava and Hurley Girly unceremoniously chucked the Amazons into the dirty water. Lena would have spit after them, but she didn't want to ruin the farewell to the dead she actually gave a shit about. She grabbed Sterling while Taylor and the others each took a piece of Grindy. They stopped at the Sludge's edge and put the dead Daughters into the river.

"Even though she'd left the gang a long time ago," Lena said, "Grindy was a Daughter. And once a Daughter..."

"Always a Daughter," the others said.

"She was our greatest friend," Lena said as the current picked up the bodies. "The Earth forgot her, but her sisters will always keep her here." Lena put a fist over her heart. "Her light will go on forever."

How many times had she said this same thing for all the others? It was second nature now. Like waking up and eating. She wondered if it would be the last time she had to do it. She'd do her damnedest to make it so.

"Grindy was the most important person in my life," Taylor said. "A genius engineer, a visionary, and a tornado in the sack."

That put a smile on Lena's face, on the rest of the Daughters'.

"I'm going to try and make her proud," Taylor said.

"Sterling," Lena said. "She was the most level-headed of all of us. I never thought I'd see her…" Lena took a slow breath and started again. "I always thought she'd be the one saying something about me as I drifted away. She couldn't talk, but she had more to say than any sheila on this dump. I don't know much about Islam, or what she believed. But she was the heart and soul of this gang, and she will never be forgotten."

They all pounded fists against their chests.

Lena squeezed her fist as tight as she could, feeling the pain, committing it to memory and seeing Farica's ugly face in her mind. "Her light will go on forever."

CHAPTER 40

Sarah found it funny how time could be lost when you were in a dark place and had nothing to orient yourself to besides muffled voices and drowned-out laughter. If the OC gang member who had opened the door told Sarah she'd been in there for a thousand years, she would have believed her.

Instead, the short, black woman grabbed her by the arm and led her to the main room. The overhead lights stung her eyes, and she had to squint until they adjusted. Others in the OC surrounded Shamika, who had her foot propped on the arm of a chair like some general at the front of a boat.

She turned her head to Sarah when she entered and tossed over a manna loaf. "Here you go."

Sarah dug into it. She never thought she would have been glad to see the tasteless muck, but she chewed on it like it was steak. The OC watched her eat, faces slack with indignation. One sucked on her teeth. Another's right eye twitched. Five of them, including the one who'd brought her out of the dark room.

"Thank you," Sarah said. Someone had to change the mood, and being rude would get her nowhere. Not yet.

Shamika laughed. "Damn, I can still smell the new on you."

The others laughed, too, their faces softening, if only a little.

"What do you mean?" Sarah asked.

"This city hasn't changed you, not completely. Your eyes are still wide with wonder. Your face hasn't aged with the stress of day-in-and-day-out fighting and struggling."

"I guess I got here at the right time." Sarah relaxed a little. It was good to hear from someone else that she hadn't yet dropped into the deep end of whack-job-itude. She was still the same person, no matter the things she'd had to do. *Balance*, she thought.

"Yeah, well if you hadn't noticed, the truce is fucking gone. Done. You'll get plenty of opportunities to lose your head, little girl."

"I'm seventeen," Sarah said.

"Oh," Shamika raised her hands in mock apology, "my bad. You're grown. And we're just a bunch of crazy bitches floating out here in space." She dropped her arms. "You don't know shit."

"That's not what I meant," Sarah said.

The gang resurrected their hateful faces, and Sarah had the sinking feeling that no matter what she said, they already had their minds made up about her, what she thought, and who she was. They'd probably dare her to say they were wrong.

Sarah put down the manna loaf. "What are you going to do with me? Am I in your gang now?"

The way Shamika reacted, Sarah thought she should have become a comedian. Her head snapped back and she cackled like it was the funniest thing ever said. "If your gang doesn't show anytime soon to trade you for the baby,

I'm afraid we won't have a use for you."

Sarah swallowed. She knew they didn't mean she could walk out the front door. One of the OC stroked their rang, making Sarah's skin crawl. She wanted to throw up.

The sixth OC member came through the front door. "We've got visitors," she said.

Shamika turned. "The Daughters?"

"Yep. And they've got the baby."

Shamika was in Sarah's face in two steps. "Come with me, little girl."

The OC sure liked to grab arms. Shamika squeezed at the spot the other OC had left sore, and forced Sarah out under the stars. They hustled behind one of the barriers soldered to the glass ground, and Shamika held Sarah out to the side, poking out her head for a quick second.

Lena stood there, where the path up the glass mountain curved around to the OC ganghouse. She held Rory cradled in her arms, easing her way toward them on foot. The other Daughters waited farther away, sitting on their cyclones.

"Stop right there, Horror," Shamika yelled.

"I've come to make a deal," Lena shouted back.

"We won't shoot unless you say something stupid," Shamika said.

"We'll trade you for Pao."

"Who?"

Me, Sarah thought. Shamika had never cared to ask her name.

"Sarah," Lena said. "The only one over there not hiding behind glass like a bitch."

"Easy there, Horror." Shamika put the end of her rang gun at Sarah's head.

A flash of what had happened to Dandelion crossed Sarah's mind and she tried to keep absolutely still.

Lena raised her left palm and nodded once. "My mistake. I've just had a long night."

"So we get the baby?" Shamika asked.

"I've got something a lot better."

Ava got off her bike and hustled toward Lena.

"I only want the kid," Shamika said. "But what would be better?"

Lena laughed through a sigh, shaking her head. "I've got some information. Something big. We'll let you in on it if you give us our Daughter back."

"Motherfuckers," Shamika said under her breath. Then, loudly, "The baby for your sheila. That or nothing."

Ava grabbed Lena's shoulder and the two bickered silently until Lena decided to stop talking. Ava finished whatever she was saying with hard eyes that seemed to say, "Don't screw this up."

Lena groaned and turned as Ava walked back to her cyclone. "We'll give you the baby for Pao, and your help."

"Help with what?" Shamika asked.

"We can talk about it after we've made sure no one is going to get shot."

"OK," Shamika said. "But we talk about it here, in our ganghouse."

"Shall we trade, then?" Lena said.

Shamika came out from behind the barrier, still holding onto Sarah's jacket, but dropping her rang. Lena walked to meet them, and when they were feet away from each other all three women stopped. Lena stared at them, not moving. When Shamika cleared her throat, it brought Lena back into motion. She kissed the baby and held her out. Rory croaked gentle whines.

"Now let Pao go," Lena said.

Shamika huffed and released her hold. Sarah stood there in a haze. It was too easy – all of this. Lena was giving up the baby, something she would never have done, even if it meant her and all the Daughters would die. Something must have been going on, something worth Lena using a little sanity for a change.

Sarah trembled, despite her whispered chides for her body to cooperate. She was walking like a shit-faced snail.

Lena had to pull Sarah the rest of the way over. "Alright, then," she said. "Are we all happy?"

Shamika cooed and nuzzled Rory. "She's where she belongs. All's right on Oubliette once again."

"Well, that's where you're wrong," Lena said.

Icy tension gripped Sarah right in the gut. Oh, God, please don't let her do something stupid. Sarah held her breath, waiting for Lena to draw her rang and bring down every OC ball of death on them. Shamika looked up, glaring at Lena. She must have thought the same thing. Her right arm twitched.

But Lena remained calm and kept her arms where they were. "Let's talk about it inside. OK?"

Shamika nodded and entered the ganghouse with Rory. Lena waved for the other Daughters to come up.

"Thank you," Sarah said. She sincerely thought she'd be dead by now.

"Don't mention it," Lena said, keeping her eyes on the approaching Daughters. "You're our sheila. And that shit you pulled with the dweller in that cage was legendary."

Sarah smiled. It lasted about as long as it took to see there was someone missing amongst the Daughters.

"Where's Sterling?" Sarah asked.

No one said anything. If they weren't coward enough to look at the ground, they just stared at her with blank faces. All Lena could do was shake her head.

Sarah thought she was going to cry. She felt the surge come up, but what left her mouth was a roaring scream toward the green Veil, one that made her throat sore and dropped her to her knees. The tears did come then. But she felt more like beating someone to death than wallowing in despair. Shamika had been wrong. Oubliette *had* changed her. It had only taken until that moment for it to show.

Sterling. Why Sterling? Sarah couldn't even bring herself to ask what happened. She didn't want to know. It would be worse to know. Maybe later... maybe later. No, now!

Ava patted Sarah on the shoulder. With a spin, Sarah clutched Ava's arm and flipped the woman onto her back. She bent over to start pummeling her face, but Dipity moved in, and Sarah had to take her down with a sweep of her leg. A reared-back fist sent Hurley Girly stumbling backwards with her hands up in supplication.

Lena. Where the fuck was Horror? Sarah would show her what terror really felt like. Turning, Sarah spotted Lena standing in the same place. Sarah was going to tear her smug-ass face off!

Huge arms wrapped around her before she could get close to Lena, and her gang's head stared at her sadly, as if she pitied her. Goddamn it, she didn't want pity, she wanted Sterling back. Sarah lost any will to fight as Dipity's arms tightened a little more to hold her still. She hadn't noticed it until then, but a ringing filled her ears, and as it faded she heard Dipity repeatedly tell her it was OK. But it wasn't.

When Sarah's eyes had dried up and she promised the Daughters three times she wouldn't attack them, they walked – some limped – into the ganghouse. Shamika twirled Rory around the main room, holding the baby under the arms. Lena stopped short and glared at Shamika. Maybe Sarah wore a similar disposition. But fuck Lena. The baby was alive. Sarah had truly lost someone she cared about. Lena had no right to feel anything. She hadn't cared about Sterling at all. Not like Sarah had.

Every so often, over the next half hour, Sarah felt bad about how she was thinking, that it wasn't Lena's fault. But she quickly argued it away. Sarah had the right to be angry, and Lena should have protected Sterling. The way Horror had beaten Sterling the other day, it would make sense Lena had let her die.

Shamika handed the baby to an OC and took a seat. "So what's this shit about?"

The other Daughters sat too as Lena spoke, but Sarah remained standing. This wasn't the time to relax. She didn't even catch most of what Lena said. Something about a flying drone. All of them needing to get off Oubliette.

Good fucking luck, she thought. She stared at a piece of glass wall, feeling hollow and too warm inside.

Lena said something about Farica being the only Amazon left. Well, that was a comfort at least.

Sarah really needed to hit something.

"How do I know you're not full of shit?" Shamika asked after Lena finished. "I mean, I feel awful about what happened to Grindy. And that fucks it up for everybody.

But this thing about a drone spying on us, it's way too crazy. Even for you."

Hurley Girly came forward with something in her arms. Sarah hadn't noticed it until then. She hadn't even caught what Lena had said about Grindy. What had happened to Grindy? Her anger was steadily subsiding. She couldn't afford to drift off and miss anything else.

The hunk of metal Hurley Girly dropped on the floor was charred around the edges and had a big eye with a cracked lens.

"Looks like a robot sperm," one of the OC said.

Shamika toed it with her boot. When she lifted her eyes to Lena they became softer, more accepting. "What are we going to do?"

"We need to fix or at least make one of those sensors the shipments have on them," Lena said. "This last shipment should have a fresh one. It's the only way we can get through the Veil."

"Those things get fried as soon as they come through," said Shamika. "There ain't much left to work with."

"I'm pretty good with that kind of shit," Ava said.

"OK." Shamika pulled her curls back. "Even if we busted our asses and somehow lucked out and fixed the sensor, what are we going back in? Those shipment boxes don't have controls, and I don't see a ship lying around."

"We'll have to build one," Lena said.

The entire OC laughed. Most shook their heads. One murmured, "Bitch, please."

"It'll be hard," Lena continued, undeterred. "But if we all come together on this, all of the dwellers under us, we can do it. There was a time we didn't have cyclones racing down these streets, you know."

"And how big is this ship going to be?" Shamika asked. "There's no way it'll be able to fit every sheila on Oubliette."

"No," Lena said. "It won't be big enough for everybody."

The anger Sarah had put on hold was making a comeback. How was Lena any better than the dickheads on Earth who thought they could decide who was worth saving and who was only fit for the shipping box?

"The dwellers will have to draw for a spot," Lena said.

Shamika rubbed the bridge of her nose. At least someone shared Sarah's feelings on the subject. "Why in the hell," Shamika said, "would the dwellers help build this ship if there's a chance they won't be able to leave on it."

"Well," Lena said, "they won't know until after it's built."

"Oh, Lena," Shamika said. "You're one cold, heartless bitch."

"The alternative is all of us starving to death out here as we sing 'Holding Hands to Hold Back the Cold.' And damn, ain't it great that we all decided to stay together instead of getting off our asses and having a few strong sheilas get off this shithole city?"

Shamika grinned. "OK, Horror. I get your point."

"And I don't plan on letting the ones who stay here die. First thing we'll do is send a shipment with manna. Then we'll work on getting them back to Earth."

That's better, Sarah thought.

"Cause the shippers are just going to bow at our return and let us do whatever the fuck we want."

"They won't be breathing by then."

"Ooh!" Shamika rubbed her hands. "This is getting better. I like a little revenge with my hostile takeover. So we send manna, and then bring back everybody we left behind. Then what?"

"Not everybody," Lena said. "We have to get rid of Farica and her dwellers."

Sarah wanted that same thing. At least, it's what she thought she wanted. The excitement she'd expected in avenging Sterling wasn't there. Instead she felt exhausted, and so damn overloaded with warring thoughts. How could you have balance when the light and darkness inside you kept fighting for dominion? When you couldn't tell them apart?

"One Amazon and her loony followers?" Shamika said. "No. I'm not worried about them."

"They could be a problem," Lena said. "The quicker we–"

"The quicker we build the ship, the quicker we can get off this city," Shamika said. "You want my help, my gang's and my dwellers', for this psycho mission? Fine. I'm down with that. I see the purpose. There's no love lost between the Amazons and my gang, but I'm not wasting time hunting down cannibals. Not when we need to use every bit of our time in getting through the Veil. Got me?"

Lena's eyes moved from Shamika down to Rory. Her stare on the baby remained as she said, "Fine."

It was unclear if any of this was going to work, in Sarah's mind, and she didn't have much to be sure of any more. It sounded like a fool's errand. But the pieces she'd been able to grasp from what Lena had told Shamika painted a horrifying picture. If the UCNA was sending drones to capture video, video showing what was happening on Oubliette, especially in the last few hours, they would have seen a bunch of psychotics running the asylum. And they would do something about it.

At least now the gangs had something to work toward together instead of fighting. But that was the tricky thing about Oubliette, Sarah had learned. There was always a fight around the corner, and someone always ended up dying.

CHAPTER 41

The shipper port was the last place Dolfuse ever wanted to return. Besides the joy of seeing Spangler, the whole place gave her a headache. Warden Beckles' threat didn't make things too welcoming either. But this time, Dolfuse walked through the doors with a strange confidence. She wasn't entirely sure where it had come from. Maybe accomplishing her task had unearthed something inside her. She liked it. She felt unstoppable.

"Hello," Dolfuse said to the red-cheeked guard, with a burst of enthusiasm.

She'd taken the guard by surprise. The woman got to her feet, mouth agape.

Dolfuse laughed to herself and spoke before the guard could get her mind right. "I wanted to come by and tell you I'll be pushing for a vote on that matter we discussed the last time I was here. I have to say, you inspired me so much I couldn't wait to bring it to the floor."

The guard smiled. "You mean–"

"If the bill passes, which I'm sure it will, anyone sixty-five or older will have their rights given to their first-born child."

The guard frowned. "I'm the middle kid."

Hell's bells.

Think fast, think fast. Dolfuse's pathetic lie was crumbling at the foundation and her confidence with it.

"Not to worry," Dolfuse said. "How many siblings are older than you?"

"Just one. My brother."

"Aha!" Dolfuse raised a finger, pretending some lightning strike of an idea. "I can change the language of the bill to allow only first-born daughters to receive the rights. How does that sound?"

The guard's smile returned. "Yeah, that would work!"

"Glad to hear it." Dolfuse smiled at her, cheeks hurting. "Say, since I'm here, would it be alright to go say hi to my old friend upstairs?"

The guard nodded. "Sure. Thanks for coming to tell me about the vote."

"No problem," Dolfuse said as she slipped through the scanner. "My pleasure and duty as an elected official."

Dolfuse would have discarded her false smile as she left the guard to celebrate, but it became a genuine grin at having weaseled her way into the shipper port. Was this how she used to be when she first came to Washington? Full of poise and bullshit? She'd been burned out for a long time, she'd known that for a while. But this personal mission – not the task Martin had given her, but Dolfuse's own agenda – had sparked her back into life. She wasn't going to waste it.

She continued smiling as she neared the control room, thinking about the absurd lie she told the front guard. Most of the Senate and Congress were composed of people over sixty-five. There was no chance in hell a bill like that would pass. There was no bill. Not any more. It had been shot down the minute a young senator from Quebec had mentioned it, simultaneously killing his career.

Spangler sat at the main controls, like he always did when Dolfuse came to visit. She adored his predictability, but this time he didn't get up when she entered, didn't say anything.

"I tried calling you," Dolfuse said.

"I've been busy."

"You've never ignored me before. What did I do?"

"Didn't the warden tell you never to come back here? What are you trying to do to me?"

Dolfuse sputtered her lips. "I'm not afraid of that sasquatch. What's she going to do to me? I'm a senator of the United Continent. She likes to swing her member around like she's more important than she is, but I'm good at dodging cocks."

Spangler snorted and covered his mouth. "Stop it." He giggled. "I'm trying to be serious. What's gotten into you?"

"Do you think you can do me another favor?"

Spangler's face sank. He sighed.

"Not sneaking anything off like before," Dolfuse said. "I just wanted you to look someone up. I would've had you do it at my place if you'd ever picked up your phone."

"I'm trying to stay out of any trouble."

"You have access to records of all the shippees who've left this port. I just need you to find one woman. Who she is and why she was sent up."

Shaking his head, Spangler said, "We can't ask their mothers why. It's just their choice. The rest is confidential, Linda. There are privacy laws."

"For shippees who've already been sent up and forgotten? Give me a break. Besides, this is a matter of continental security."

Her lies were multiplying, crossing lines she never thought she'd compromise. She'd never lied to Spangler before. Not once. But this time, she had to play a little dirty.

Spangler whispered a prayer. It was that surrendering sound that meant he'd given in to her pressuring. "Who is she?" he asked.

"I don't have a name. Only this."

From her bag, Dolfuse gave Spangler a printout of the last image the drone had captured, the woman who'd shot light from her arm.

"She doesn't look familiar," Spangler said. "Not that I can remember the thousands of faces who come in here."

Thousands. Oh, yes. Something she'd forgotten to ask him. About all those shippees being kept underground like a human stockpile. Did he even know? Later, she decided.

"Judging by how old she looks, I'd guess she was shipped before my time."

"So you're going to run a facial recognition program?"

He pushed himself away from the control panel, riding the wheeled seat to a computer in the corner. Dolfuse went to lean over his shoulder.

"Yep. And to save time I'll run it within certain parameters. Caucasian girls who've been shipped from before five years ago."

Dolfuse cleared her throat. "By the way, would it be possible for someone to ship a baby?"

"What?" Spangler said.

"If someone wanted to smuggle an infant in one of your

shipments, could they get away with it?"

"You mean like a drone?" Spangler asked, focused on scrolling through the hundreds of pictures. "Why would anyone do that?"

"Ten year-olds get shipped."

Spangler shrugged. "Hypothetically, someone could bribe the guards. They'd ship their own mothers for the right price. But I wouldn't let that happen. No way in hell."

After a few minutes of watching the computer wade through endless pictures, Dolfuse said, "I got an email from Bobby."

That got his attention. He turned around and had to push up his neon orange glasses to keep them from falling off his nose. "Crazy. So, he's coming home?"

Dolfuse nodded. "He wants to start a family."

"That's great."

"No. I screwed up big time. I gave my baby up when I didn't have to. He'll find out. He'll–"

"Never have to know," Spangler said. "You can start over. With another baby."

She felt a headache coming on. She hadn't even meant to come to Spangler to spill her emotions like some seppuku samurai. But it always seemed to happen anyway. He was trying to help, but he was saying the wrong things. Dolfuse wanted him to tell her she was a horrible person and she deserved to feel as bad as she did. People telling her that she was brave or that they understood what she must be going through, even if they didn't know the complete truth, *that* made it all stale and plastic and wrong.

That old question popped again in her head: how could anyone just forget someone? Especially someone that had grown inside them.

"This sounds terrible to say it out loud," Dolfuse said, "but there was big part of me that just knew Bobby wasn't ever coming home. And I couldn't raise a baby without him. I didn't want to do it without him." The computer scrolled on, until a familiar face flashed onto the screen. "That's her!"

"What?" Spangler spun back to the computer and the picture of a soft-skinned girl with big brown eyes and thin lips. "Are you sure?"

"Compare it to the picture I gave you."

Spangler held up the more recent photo. He hummed agreeably. "You're right. She's gotten a lot rougher around the edges but... Lena Horowitz. She was shipped about ten years ago."

"Is her mother's name listed?"

"Renee Horowitz," Spangler said. "45 Blinkley Circle, Mechanicsville, Maryland, is the address."

"That's only about an hour and a half away," Dolfuse said, after searching it on her phone.

"You going to go talk to mama and find out what I can't tell you?"

"Pretty much."

Spangler wrinkled his brow. "This has something to do with your baby, doesn't it?"

Dolfuse smiled. *Dodge and divert.* "Let me ask *you* something. Why is Beckles holding back girls from every shipment?"

He leaned back as if he'd been snake bit. "What are you talking about?"

"The good warden is keeping shippees for herself. Could

be a thousand. I saw where they keep them below ground, but I just don't understand why she's doing it. Don't tell me you don't know."

He was going to lie to her. She saw it in the way the wrinkles at the corners of his eyes twitched. He even opened his mouth, like he would, but then his face relaxed. He couldn't lie to her.

"Why don't you ask me yourself?" came the warden's voice from the ceiling.

Dolfuse jumped and turned to Spangler, who backed up and looked above. At the door, a group of guards charged in.

"Wait!" Dolfuse shouted, not knowing what else to say.

"You can see firsthand how wide I can swing my member," Beckles said through the unseen speaker. It was the last thing Dolfuse heard before the guards dragged her and Spangler from the room.

CHAPTER 42

"What are your bets up to now?" Lena asked in the dark.

They'd gathered in the ganghouse's main room, bringing down their manna box beds or claiming one of the couches. It reminded Sarah of slumber parties she'd seen in movies, never having been lucky enough to go to one herself. She'd had to travel a million miles for this moment – cracking jokes in the dark with other girls. She just wished the food was better.

Pizza. God, what she wouldn't do for a pizza, the deep dish kind where they put the inorganic tomato sauce on top. She'd only had it once, on her twelfth birthday in lieu of a present, but the memory of it stuck with her even now. But the manna was at least filling.

The Daughters agreed it would be best from then on to sleep together in the main room. Hurley Girly had gotten too excited when Lena first suggested it, and Lena had to explain it was to be close to the cyclones if the need arose for them to make a quick exit. Sterling's cyclone sat in the corner, cold and neglected. Sarah avoided looking at it.

The new sleeping arrangements worked just fine for Sarah. She hadn't told any of them, but she slept like crap and would almost scream when she woke up alone in the dark, forgetting where she was for a few seconds.

None of them had forgotten what they'd seen in the Amazon ganghouse – the religiouslike devotion of the dwellers. Farica had enough followers to retaliate, it was just a question of when. Tomorrow, the Daughters and the OC would start building a ship and find a way to get through the Veil.

Sarah's skill set didn't fall among mechanical things, and she wasn't sure how much good she'd be. Fighting and sign language were her strengths, but she'd lost a reason to do either.

Don't think, she told herself. Instead, she focused on what Lena had asked about their bets. "Our bets?" she asked.

"About why Lena was sent to Oubliette," Ava said. "I'm up to five manna loaves."

"Parts off my cyclone and two loaves," Dipity said.

"I keep putting up a good pussy-licking," Hurley Girly said, "but these bitches keep turning me down."

"Ain't none of us want that shit," Dipity sputtered her lips.

"I was hoping one of you would match my bet and reseperate," said Hurley Girly.

Ava said, "It's 'reciprocate,' you dumb fuck."

Sarah laughed, and damn, it felt good. They all laughed.

"I think Lena was deep into drugs," Hurley Girly said. "Her mom tried to get her clean, but when she wouldn't..." she clapped her hands "...off to Oubliette."

Lena remained quiet, not giving a hint to whether or not Hurley Girly was right.

"Poverty shipping," Dipity said. "Gotta be."

"None of you are thinking about it," Ava said. "You're just throwing out the laziest story that pops in your head.

And none of them have been right."

"What do you think, Ava?" Sarah asked.

"Her mom sold her to the military, but she got kicked out for some reason," Ava said. "That's the best I can assume."

"What about you, Pao?" Lena asked in a sleepy voice. She moved on her bed, creaking the box.

"I don't know," Sarah said.

"Guess."

Sarah thought over everything she knew about Lena, what she'd seen and heard. Her gang's leader was crazy for sure, but also calculating and patient. Lena didn't have a lust for the more base desires like Hurley Girly or some of the dwellers. But she'd been obsessed with stealing Rory. The baby meant more to her than to the other gang leaders. Shamika wanted the baby because of race. Farica out of spite. But why was Lena so adamant about it?

"A boy," Sarah said.

The other Daughters laughed.

"It's a good guess," Lena says.

"I'm not done," Sarah said.

They got quiet.

"A boy," Sarah said again, "and the baby he gave you."

Silence. For a minute, Sarah thought she'd pissed Lena off or they'd all gone to sleep without listening to her. But then there was the sound of lone, slow applause.

"Wait," Hurley said. "She's right?"

"She's not getting my shit if she *is* right," Ava said. "She didn't bet."

"Lena?" Dipity asked.

"A rough guess," Lena said. "But she's gotten closer than any of you."

"Oh, I've got to hear about this," Dipity said.

Hurley Girly gasped. "You had a kid?"

Lena sighed. "I guess I might as well tell you, since there's a chance we'll all be dead soon." She'd spoken softly, but the next thing she said rose in volume and anger. "But I don't want to hear shit while I'm speaking. I hate talking about it, and I'd rather just get it out and be done with it!"

"OK, Horror," Ava said. It was the kindest Sarah had ever heard her speak. "We're listening."

"I grew up with a boy named Jeff," Lena began. "My mom didn't like me hanging out with him at first. He was black, and his family were devout Catholics, and she would have rather gutted me for a sacrifice than see me date some 'negro gentile.' But since we were just friends and his parents were the only company she'd had since my dad died, she got over it pretty quickly.

"Me and Jeff spent all our time together. He was taller than a lot of the other boys and had gray-blue eyes, like the Atlantic Ocean on a rainy day. That's the picture I always saw when I looked into them. We were never official as far as boyfriend and girlfriend, but we never dated anyone else, even when we got to senior year."

Sarah figured they all knew she meant high school. It sucked that none of them knew what Earth was like as a legal adult. No cigarettes or alcohol. No voting. No choice. They were never given a chance to grow up. Just get older.

"We were satisfied in our relationship," Lena said. "It was perfect how it was, whatever it was. Then came that night in the back of his pickup.

"We were out in some field in the boonies. He told me his parents were selling him to the military. I thought he was joking at first. He liked to pull that kind of shit with me just to see how I'd react. But then he started crying, and I knew he was for real. He never cried. I couldn't believe it. His mom was so nice, I never would have thought she would do something like that.

"I hugged him for a long time. When he finally quit sobbing into my shoulder, he lifted his head and kissed me. One thing led to another. Don't even ask me for the details. I can barely remember, it just happened. I didn't have any hesitation, either. It was like he was always destined to be my first – and I guess my last.

"I found out I was pregnant a month later. We told his parents first. They decided against sending him off to war, told him we had to get married and they would handle the paperwork for getting a child allowance. I was ecstatic. We both were. We'd accidentally found a loophole that would keep him at home, and we could start a life together after we got my mom to sign off on it.

"But she wasn't so keen on the idea. Didn't speak to me for a week after I told her. I swear she didn't even let me finish. Just got up in the middle of our conversation and locked herself in her bedroom.

"Then one day she comes to me smiling, saying she's excited to be a grandmother and she wants to take me shopping for a wedding dress. I was so surprised and happy I jumped in the car without a second thought. I asked her when we could have the wedding, something small and quiet. She said we would take care of it right away."

Lena made a sound like she was going to vomit.

"You OK?" Ava asked.

"Shut up and listen," said Lena. "When we pulled in to

this blank, gray building, I thought we'd arrived at some swank dress shop that didn't even need a sign on the door. I strolled ahead of my mom, but knew I'd walked into a clinic as soon as I saw the ugly nurse behind the window.

"My mom blocked the door and screamed for help to restrain me. I slapped her across the face, but two big guys in scrubs pulled me to the back before I could run."

Sarah stifled a gasp. She knew what was coming because all stories were like that. The ending came inevitably, like a train chugging toward a cliff, no matter how much you hoped for a happy conclusion. Lena hadn't always been crazy. She'd just been through hell even before coming to Oubliette.

Lena must not have heard Sarah's gasp because she kept talking. "I was stripped and strapped to a table, my feet in stirrups. It was obvious what they were going to do, and it was legal since I was still seventeen, and that gave my mom right over me and my baby.

"I fought as hard as I could against those men, against the restraints. I lost my voice from all my screaming. But they were able to get a needle in me. When I came to I was still tied down but in another room. My mom was nowhere around. Sometime later, after I'd cried for the hundredth time and screamed for my baby and for someone to get me the hell out of there, a doctor came in and told me the fetus – that's the word he used – had been burned out, and that the shippers were on their way to take me into custody.

"My bitch of a mother had signed the papers while I was unconscious. See, she knew. She knew she had to send me to Oubliette, because I would have hunted her down and killed her the first chance I got. I'd burn her out the way she'd had them do to my baby. But I was robbed of that, too.

"And that's why I'm here on this hell hole with you fine ladies."

No one said anything. It was a long time silent in the dark, and Sarah fell asleep before anyone spoke again.

CHAPTER 43

"I'm having the worst case of déjà vu." Beckles tapped her fingers against the top of the desk, her knuckles dry and red.

Dolfuse could understand what Beckles meant. Beckles wore the same outfit from their last rendezvous, and Dolfuse could have sworn the same cold, neglected steak sat on the warden's desk.

"I don't know what this is all about," Dolfuse said, "but I am a senator of the United Continent, and I have seen enough evidence to make your life a living hell."

"Shut your mouth, you uppity bitch."

Dolfuse's insides caught fire. She wanted to say a whole lot of things to this bear of a woman, this bully.

Beckles grinned, apparently aware she'd gotten a reaction from the senator. "I have even more evidence against you. And I'm the one who can make your life a lot more complicated, even without turning you in for smuggling an infant out on one of my shipments. But no matter. We both know we've reached a point way beyond looking the other way."

"The baby? I had nothing to do with tha –"

"Save it." Beckles raised her palm. "That poor child. If I'd been more vigilant, squeezed my fist tighter, it would have never happened. It's not right. But neither you or anyone in that cesspit of Washington have to worry. I've learned my lesson."

Dolfuse breathed so hard through her nose, it made a whistling sound. "Let's talk about something else, then," she said. "What are you doing with all the shippees who should have already been sent to Oubliette? And don't tell me there was no room or they weren't broken in yet. I can sling bullshit as deep as anyone else, you included."

"It's my business." Beckles patted the sides of her hair, turning to the enormous window behind her. "And none of yours. The only reason you're still here and breathing, my dear senator, is that I haven't quite decided what to do with you. I can't let you go. You'll run off to your superiors and that would speed things up. And I don't want to eliminate you, since you might be valuable… should something happen."

Who did this woman think she was? God. She'd said as much. At best, she had a messiah complex. There was no bargaining with her, then. Dolfuse's best option was to make nice and wait for the cavalry to show. She looked around the warden's office and wondered, not for the first time, why she'd been the only one the guards had brought in here.

"Where's Spangler?" Dolfuse asked.

She heard a scream, muffled by glass. Then Spangler's body fell past Beckles' window, arms and legs flailing on his way to the pavement five stories below.

"I'm afraid we had to let him go."

Dolfuse punched and kicked at the guards beside her,

yelling and clawing to get a hold of Beckles. She tried for the steak knife on the plate, but before she could grab it thousands of volts of electricity ran through her body, sending her to the ground in a convulsing mess. She felt saliva run from her mouth, her hands and feet clench, her teeth clamp down. She could do nothing about any of it.

All my fault. All of this. The words kept repeating in her mind.

When the guards quit prodding her with their stun sticks, she sat up slowly, waiting for her head to stop spinning. Her mouth had gone cottony.

A buzz came from Beckles' desk.

"Yes?" the warden said.

A woman's voice told her police had arrived out front. Dolfuse eased a bit.

Beckles glared at Dolfuse, as if it was her fault. The warden hit a button.

Push all the knobs and switches you want, Dolfuse thought. *You're finished.*

Outside the window, a large metal sheet lowered to block out the day, and an electric screen came to life where the window had been, showing hundreds of boxed images from the shipping port's cameras. One image showed police in SWAT gear running to the front door just before another metal piece slammed down to keep them out of the port. Elsewhere, the cameras showed every exterior window and door being sealed just the same. The port had been locked down. No one could get in.

No one can get out either, thought Dolfuse.

The police beat on the metal, searching for a way to breach. One of the policewomen in a bulky vest signaled part of the group to go around each side of the building. They scattered like ants.

How did they know to come? Dolfuse hadn't told Martin or anyone else where she'd be. She'd never told anyone about the army of stockpiled shippees.

Beckles picked up a microphone and sat on the top of her desk. "Broadcast me outside," she said into the microphone. There was a click and Beckles cleared her throat. "You are out of your jurisdiction. Leave now or we will resort to deadly force."

"We have a warrant," the lead policewoman shouted, though she looked all over as if she didn't know where to direct her cop-smug directives.

"I will give you thirty seconds, beginning now." Beckles began counting down from twenty-nine.

The policewoman backed up, raising her rifle. She spoke into the radio microphone at her shoulder, calling the other officers back to the front. Dolfuse wondered what Beckles planned to do if the police didn't leave. Keep the door sealed until they found a way in? And then what? Send guards against the police with nothing but stun sticks? This whole thing would have been amusing if Dolfuse hadn't been stuck in the middle of it. If her actions hadn't cost Spangler his life.

Guns drawn and heads bobbing in every direction, the police huddled at the front door in full force. Dolfuse considered grabbing the microphone from Beckles – she was only at eighteen... seventeen – and tell the police to come back with the army. But she was too weak, muscles still twitching from the stun sticks.

When Beckles reached the end of her countdown, she

pressed another button. Guns lowered from the front awning, aimed at the police. Laser cannons. It was so sudden, so unexpected, Dolfuse could only watch, not fully comprehending what was happening on the screen. The lasers bit into every police officer, cutting their armor and their flesh like tissue. Only one officer was able to get a shot off, straight into the air. Then she dropped like the rest.

Beckles pushed the button again, and the guns retracted.

Dolfuse stared at the pile of bodies outside the port. *This must be what Bobby sees every day.* How could you repeatedly see such terrible things and not go a little crazy. She even thought she might be losing her own head. But it couldn't be. This wasn't how things happened. The good guys were supposed to win.

"Follow me," Beckles said to the two guards holding Dolfuse by her arms. "And bring the senator. We're going to have more heat on us soon. We've run out of time."

They took her through countless plain white doors, down plain white halls, deep parts of the shipping port Dolfuse had never imagined. It went on forever, and she thought about going to sleep so later she could wake up from this nightmare. But one of the guards kicked Dolfuse in the back of the leg and told her to walk or leave the same way Spangler did.

She walked.

Motors hummed behind the last door they came to. Unlike the other doors, four guards stood in front of this one, carrying rifles.

"We're giving a tour," Beckles told them with a chuckle.

The guards saluted her and broke for Dolfuse and the others to pass. When the door slid open, the industrial churning escaped and filled Dolfuse's ears. The massive room reminded Dolfuse of a factory as they walked on a railing that crisscrossed from one end of the room to the other, all above rows upon rows of gigantic, open vats where metal blades mixed off-white muck.

"Welcome to manna production." Beckles had to yell. "We can survive inside this port for the next hundred years with what you see below you. Besides it tasting like cardboard, it'll never go bad."

Dolfuse stared at her, imagining if she could get a hold of one of the rifles and end this coup before it started.

"But that's not the best part," Beckles said.

Her oversized boots clanged as she moved to the middle of the manna room and turned right. The guards hurried Dolfuse along, and when they'd reached the wall, another door opened to a similar space, albeit much quieter. The guards held Dolfuse off to the side as Beckles walked on. Fifty feet below, gathered in square formations, stood hundreds of shippees.

A microphone attached to the railing shrieked feedback when Beckles stopped behind it, looking onto her horde of shippees. The warden raised her arms. "Do you want to go to Oubliette?"

The shippees stayed quiet. Not an army. Not some overwhelming force, but a bunch of girls who had no clue why they'd been kept behind. Some shook their heads, shifting nervously in their white uniforms.

"I asked you," Beckles said, louder, more angry, "if you want to be sent to Oubliette."

This time the shippees screamed in unison, "No!"

"For many months," Beckles said, "some of you over a

year, we've trained you, separated you from the chaff being shipped out. Held you from being forgotten. Why?"

She paused. None of the shippees tried an answer.

"Because I don't want to ship you away." She pounded a fist against her broad chest. "*I* want to give you a second life. Those sanctimonious bureaucrats out there couldn't give a damn if you were never heard from again. To them, you are nothing. Are they right?"

"No!" came the shippees' answer. Now they sounded more like an army. They even stood straighter.

Dolfuse's head swam.

"Then take up your weapons." Beckles spread her arms.

At each side of the room, guards poured in with carts stacked with guns – rifles. Dolfuse thought she even saw a cart of grenades. The guards handed a weapon to each shippee. Handling the weapons like professional soldiers, the shippees performed a quick, uniform check of the rifles and methodically placed them butt to ground, resting against their leg.

"You're going to have to fight to stay on Earth," Beckles said after the guards returned from where they'd entered. "Are you with me?"

The shippees cheered in the affirmative, raising their rifles to the air.

"Then so be it." Beckles beamed, proud of herself, proud of the twisted moral code she'd infected into these desperate women. "Get ready, ladies. This is where we make our stand." She raised fists above her head.

The shippees chanted a grunt.

Dolfuse shook her head. Even as deluded as Beckles was, the chances of the warden succeeding looked quite high. Most of the military fought overseas. At home, only a scattering of Continental Guard and a few police remained.

Dolfuse could have laughed herself to death.

Beckles had played the system against itself, masquerading as some modern Julius Caesar, savior of the continent. She wanted to burn society down and rebuild from the ashes, using the shippees to do her dirty work. It was all so clear now. Dolfuse just wished she had figured it out while she was a long way away from where the revolution would begin.

CHAPTER 44

"Fuck this fucking thing!" Ava slammed the drone sensor onto the glass table. Most of the green in its center had been charred black after passing through the Veil.

"You'll figure it out," Lena said, trying to restrain herself from slapping Ava for almost destroying the only hope they had.

Grindy's shop was alive again, bustling with dwellers and gang members from the OC and the Daughters. It was what Grindy always wanted – everyone working together. Who knew all it would take was killing off most of the Amazons and an impending threat of no more shipments?

"Just try to relax," Lena told Ava.

Look who's talking.

"It's stuck in there," Ava said. "The thing's been melted to the casing."

"Most shit just needs a little time and finesse."

"We have neither of those."

Lena zipped her jacket. "This is your priority. You're our sheila on this, so take Grindy's office if you need the quiet."

"It still smells like blood in there." Ava shuffled to the office, looking at the sensor like a frustrating puzzle.

Lena sighed as she watched her go. She hadn't been

blowing smoke up Ava's ass. Her second-in-command was the best around at that sort of thing. Whatever she needed to get the sensor fixed, Lena would see that she got it.

Taylor stood at the back door, guiding in dwellers and members of the OC who were carrying large pieces of glass and cyclone engines from the dead Amazons' discarded bikes. Two of them were stuck in the door and unable to follow directions, much to Taylor's annoyance. When she yelled for them to stop, the line bumped into each other and a dweller dropped a cyclone engine on an OC's foot. The black woman screamed curses and not-so-idle threats at the dweller, who was smart enough to back away into the crowd.

Taylor hollered as well, stomping and pacing and mumbling to herself. "Take her over there to rest," she told another two dwellers. They helped the injured OC limp to a chair.

Lena put a hand on Taylor's shoulder. "Like herding cats."

"I hate cats."

"How are your blueprints coming?"

"Grindy was the better designer," Taylor said. "All my sketches look like refrigerator art."

"It doesn't have to be perfect," Lena said. "Keep it up."

Lena walked away before she would say what she really thought. These bitches were moving too fucking slow. She knew it wasn't Taylor's fault, or Ava's. But she wanted to blame someone and she was honest enough to know she wouldn't point the finger in her own direction. Was all this just some pointless attempt to prolong their inevitable end?

Her beliefs had always been contradictions – she believed in destiny, but she also believed she could choke the fuck out of fate to make the bitch do what she wanted. Better keep her hands around that throat a little while longer.

Shamika sat on a manna box couch, lifting Rory above her and making stupid faces. The baby stared at her with the cutest what-the-fuck face. Lowering Rory, Shamika turned to Lena and raised an eyebrow.

Lena guessed she'd been gawking again, but hell, she couldn't help it.

"You got a problem?" Shamika asked.

Lena swallowed her pride. It tasted like weakness. "No," she said. "I was just going to ask if you could come help me gather laser cutters."

"I'm busy," Shamika said, and promptly returned to playing with Rory.

Oh! She was such a... Lena could kill her! If only she didn't need her help in getting off Oubliette, she'd skewer the pus-filled twat's eyeballs with her own fingers. Lena focused on breathing through her nose and stomped over to where Dipity was stacking glass.

"Something wrong?" Dipity asked.

"No."

"OK, then."

"I just want this to go smoothly."

"You have a Plan B?"

The question hit her like an unseen rock. "Like what?"

"Say we can't get through the Veil, even if we can get a ship built and flying."

"I try to stay positive, Dipity. There is no backup plan."

Dipity snorted. "So no going out the easy way?" She put a finger to her head and mockfired.

"Don't even play like that."

"I'm just saying. If the end looks definite..."

"I'll claw and scratch until I'm ripped from this life. You can bet your ass on that."

"Well, since we're still in this, me and Hurley Girly were talking about taking the Core. It would kill the Veil and be all the power we'd need to fly out of here. It's not like we'll need the Core much longer anyway."

Lena groaned and rubbed the spot between her eyes. "Don't you think it'll suck when all the air and gravity gets turned off and we all get sent flying into space?"

"Oh, yeah," Dipity said. "Sorry, Lena. I haven't gotten much sleep. But we can still drain the Core enough to where the Veil is still up."

"No. No point in killing the goose that's still shitting gold," Lena said. "We still need clean water, and light to see what we're building. And besides, I'm not going to leave the ones who stay behind without the Core."

"Oh, you were serious about that?"

"We're coming back to get them."

Dipity shrugged and walked away to retrieve more glass. She passed Sarah, who was pushing around a frizzy-haired dweller in a wheelchair. Sarah made whooshing sounds as the woman laughed and held on for the ride.

What the hell? This isn't the time to be giggling like a bunch of assholes.

"Pao," Lena snapped.

Her gang's ass halted, still smiling. "Selene wanted to pretend she was riding a cyclone."

"I couldn't give a fuck. There's work to do. Get over there and help with the laser cutters."

Tears filled the eyes of the dweller. A flash of anger crossed

Sarah's face, but then it dwindled into a sad hanging of her head, her blue hair dingy from the last few nights. Lena wasn't sure how much of it was from blood. After wheeling Selene over to a dweller, Sarah began sorting tools.

So this is what a piece of shit feels like, Lena thought.

What was wrong with her? These sheilas were trying to grasp the smallest amount of happiness in these last days, and she was destroying it.

But all of them had only this one shot. If she had to be the bad guy to save their asses, then so be it. They'd thank her later, and if they didn't, oh-fucking-well. She'd know she'd done the right thing, even if they hated her for doing it.

She spotted a cyclone engine and headed off to carry it. There was a lot more to be done in so little time. A lot more.

CHAPTER 45

Tanks arrived at the shipper port. Beckles laughed, nearly choking on the tiny pretzels she'd popped into her mouth. Dolfuse had been given a pinch off a manna loaf she'd steadily been squishing between her fingers. How could she eat when she'd been sated on thoughts of every wrong move she'd made?

Spangler, I'm so sorry.

The guards beside her ate nothing. They'd exchanged their stun sticks for rifles.

They all sat once more in the gloom of Beckles' office, watching a screen that showed several tanks approaching. One of the iron beasts even traveled on the railing usually reserved for the monorail. Then, they began firing.

Dolfuse flinched at every hit against the port. The shots sent heavy vibrations throughout the building, but after the smoke had cleared the entrances were still sealed and intact, and the port stood as erect as ever.

"You shits are going to have to do a lot better than that!" Beckles screamed at the screen, spitting pretzel crumbs onto her chest.

"They'll get in eventually." Dolfuse cleared her throat. "Don't you think?"

Beckles turned with an annoyed curl of her lips. "This port is made of Gareth fiber. Same material used–"

"Used in the enviroshields," Dolfuse snapped. "Yes, I know."

Beckles squinted an eye at her. "Are you not enjoying your stay with us?"

"I just want to know what the hell you plan on doing with me. The wait and anticipation are what's killing me. Whatever it is, just get on with it."

"Do you not see what I'm trying to do here?"

Dolfuse dropped her piece of manna to the floor. "The only things I can comment on are the facts. You killed my best friend and sealed us in with your own private army. Forgive me if I can't see any merit in any of that."

"Spangler was disloyal and dishonest," Beckles said. "I couldn't have any further dealings with someone like that. As for the shippees, I'm giving them something in return for their service."

"The benefit of staying a few minutes on Earth, just to be blown away by some tank shell?"

"We've already talked about this, senator." Beckles wagged a finger. "Those bastards won't be able to get in here."

Dolfuse wasn't so sure. And it scared her, seeing that they'd have to resort to destroying everyone inside the port. But maybe there was a way to get on Beckles' good side, find a weakness, exploit it.

"It's not that I don't appreciate what you're trying to do…" Dolfuse began.

Beckles raised her brow and put a finger to her lips.

"I don't believe in all this shipping either," said Dolfuse. "But there's a more diplomatic way of doing this."

"Don't try to pump me up with sentiments. If anyone could have helped end shipping, you were it."

There goes that plan, Dolfuse thought.

For some reason she could understand if Beckles was a psychotic, someone who just wanted to take over and be the one with all the power. It was more difficult wrapping her brain around someone who thought they were fighting a righteous crusade.

"But let me get this straight," Beckles said. "You say you're against shipping, but you sent your *infant* daughter to a place where you had no idea what went on, and knew you would never see her again. Senator, you may see me as crazy or reprehensible, but even I would never stoop to the levels you have."

"That's not my daughter. I had nothing to..." *Could it be?*

The guards beside Dolfuse chuckled under their breath. Dolfuse bit her lip and let the wave of revulsion pass over her.

"Hm." Beckles scratched her chin. "We'll see if that's true when this is all over. But you certainly are an anomaly."

"Choice," Dolfuse said harshly, like lightning striking the desert.

"What?"

"You're giving these women no choice. They're going to fight for you, because the alternative is too terrible. Their mothers were given all the power in deciding to send them away, but no one gave them a choice. No one cared to hear their voices, or cared whether they lived or died. So who gets the right to choose and who doesn't?"

"I'm the one who gets to choose from now on," Beckles said.

"I see now," Dolfuse said to herself.

"You *will* see," Beckles said. "I think I've decided what to do with you, senator. At least for now." Beckles pointed to the two guards. "Show her what shippees have to go through when they arrive at our door."

"The whole process?" one of the guards asked.

"Cell and all," Beckles said.

"You're not going to get away with this!" Dolfuse screamed as the guards dragged her from the office.

Beckles turned back to the screen and watched the tanks continue their pointless barrage.

The guards threw Dolfuse into a large shower room where a single large hose lay near a ruststained drain in the center. They stripped her. Of course, she fought them, but struggling just seemed to make it easier for them to get her clothes off. When she was naked and crouching in a corner, they threw bleach powder on her. That's when one of them grabbed the big hose and smiled wide.

The water stream was like a punch to the gut. The other guard grabbed a brush and began scrubbing at her with the rough strands at the end of the pole. Scratching, scratching, like she wouldn't have any skin left. She screamed and cried, even though she promised herself she wouldn't. Soon, the water and sandpaper scrubbing stopped.

They hauled her to an enclosed room with a single bench. A folded white uniform had been placed on top, along with shoes and a note attached to a necklace of ID tags.

I'll take these back when you're done, the note said.

Dolfuse would be glad to return them to Warden Beckles – down her throat.

"Put them on," one of the guards said. "Shoes, too."

Dolfuse trembled from the water cooling on her skin, and her still-slick body made clothing herself difficult. She felt like she'd be covered in mildew soon.

Through the white halls she went again, no longer fighting the guards' pull. They'd already done their worst. They led her to the main holding cells where shippee conversations buzzed loudly. A hive. That's what the shipper port was now – and Beckles their sadistic queen. Down metal stairs the guards pushed her, and the shippees dropped their talk as she passed, watching her.

"This is where you'll stay tonight," one of the guards said, extending an arm to an open cell.

Inside, a girl with a metal prosthetic arm cleaned her rifle. She looked up and the ponytail of her red hair fell from her shoulder. Dolfuse turned to see if the guards were going to force her to do anything else, but they'd left.

"I was wondering why they moved Clarissa out of here," the girl said. "It's not like they let us have a cell to ourselves. I haven't seen you before."

"No," Dolfuse said, looking around the room. A toilet stood against the back of the wall with a half-used roll of paper and a book sitting in a recessed shelf. "I'm new."

"I thought they locked the port down. No more shippees coming in."

"They did. I'm a special visitor. They're giving me the advanced tour."

"That makes sense," the girl said.

Dolfuse gave her a confused look.

"You know. Because you're old."

"Huh."

"Well, you're a lot older than the average shippee." The girl smiled, and Dolfuse couldn't help but return it. "I'm Rebecca." She put aside her rifle and extended her robotic arm. Dolfuse looked at it, noticing the twitching mechanical innards that made the fingers open and close.

Slowly, Dolfuse took Rebecca's hand. It was warm. She'd been expecting cold metal, but it was almost human – at least to the touch.

"I'm... Linda," Dolfuse said. No reason to go around telling bloodthirsty shippees, angry at the establishment, that a continental senator hid among them.

"You can have the top bunk."

"Are you sure?"

"Yeah." Rebecca returned to her seat on the bottom bed. "When the war starts I want to be the first one out the door."

A child eager to kill and die. Dolfuse thought it was the worst thing she'd seen all day. And there was a lot of competition for that spot.

"How old are you?" Dolfuse asked.

"I'll be eleven next month," she said, proudly. "What about you?"

"I just turned thirty-seven."

"Whoa!"

"You can count that high, right?" Dolfuse said with a weak smile.

Rebecca laughed. "Math was my best subject before I got sent away." Her happy attitude died with the last part. "My parents didn't wait a second into my tenth birthday before waking me up in the middle of the night and having these scary people in white uniforms put me in the back of a truck. Didn't like having a daughter born with one arm, I guess."

"But you have a prosthetic. That's the only reason they shipped you?"

"I got this new arm here at the port, so I could shoot a rifle. My parents never got me anything. They just thought everyone whispered about the family with the one-armed girl. Doctors didn't catch it while I was in my mom's belly, and then they were stuck with me. They told me so. Every few months they'd give me a countdown of how many more days they had to put up with me. 'Two years and three months more, Rebecca.' Thought they'd look good, for being so 'brave.' For making a tough decision. That's OK. I've made a decision, too. And after we take over, I'll pay Mom and Dad a visit." She clamped her robotic fingers into a fist that made a deadly *clink*.

Dolfuse shivered. "You know the warden doesn't really care about you, right?"

Rebecca flicked her green eyes to Dolfuse, still holding her metallic fist in front of her.

Dolfuse never thought she'd be afraid of an eleven year-old, but this girl had been fed pain on a daily basis and recently given the means to release it on others with the pull of a trigger. Still, Dolfuse dared to say, "She's just using all of you for her own reasons."

Rebecca shrugged. "If I fight, I get to stay. If I don't, I die or get shipped out eventually. That's what all of us decided."

"I can't argue with you there," Dolfuse said.

"I'm going to go play some cards, you want to come with me?" Rebecca walked to the cell's entrance and turned back to Dolfuse.

"No," Dolfuse said. "Thank you. I think I'm going to sleep for a few hours. But wake me if anything happens."

Rebecca nodded and waved goodbye with her robotic digits.

Dolfuse woke in darkness. The blast of a tank shell ripped her from a dreamless sleep, but the tanks continued their assault without a peep from the shippees scattered throughout the holding room. The shippees' silence was eerier than the tanks waiting just beyond the walls, especially compared to the bustle that had been outside her new cell just hours... well, she didn't know how long ago. A quick snore came from below her and Rebecca shifted in her sleep.

Dolfuse didn't blame the shippees for doing anything to avoid going to that hell in space. It was much worse than they knew. She wondered if Martin had seen the drone's video yet. Seen what Oubliette had become. Seen the baby. Maybe that's why the tanks had come. They were bringing that injustice to light.

Dolfuse tried to roll to her side and fall back asleep, but she couldn't. Thoughts of Bobby and Spangler flooded her mind and she breathed faster and shook with pent-up energy. She had to stretch her legs. Get her mind right. Find some way out of the predicament she'd put herself in.

She followed the few dim lights and walked the circle of cells on her level. She heard a rustling from within a cell and saw a large shape underneath a sheet – too large to be just one shippee tumbling around under there.

Farther down, she rested against the railing and looked to the bottom. It was a good twenty feet, enough to kill you if you landed properly. The rail cooled her palms at the touch and she found a little comfort in it. Her eyes began to adjust and she could see the bottom of the holding floor, like a faint moon. It looked welcoming. It wouldn't take but a quick shift in gravity.

No. Someone had to stop this madness. She was the only person in this nuthouse that could. She could grab Rebecca's rifle, shoot her way to Beckles' office and end this coup before it even got out of the port.

Her legs carried her as she rationalized it. Her father had taught her to shoot. It wasn't that long ago. And besides, what was the skill in it, you just pointed and squeezed. She could do this.

She stood feet from her and Rebecca's cell when the ceiling caved in. Fire and chunks of Gareth fiber exploded into the holding room, sending Dolfuse onto her stomach. The air filled with smoke. Dolfuse salivated uncontrollably and had to spit out the plastic taste that had latched to her tongue. Shippees flooded from their cells as an electric chirping, like a gigantic alien cricket, filled the room.

An attack ship, blacker than pitch and big as a whale, hovered through the newly made hole in the ceiling, casting bright green light onto the cells. Dolfuse had seen the aircraft before, seen the enormous cannons mounted on its sides. *Sweet Kiss*. The prototype Wickey had shown her the day she went to look at the drones. It was out for a trial run, and she and the shippees were its first test.

It fired, giving no warning. A few shippees were quick enough to shoot their laser rifles, but most caught a laser or were blown apart before they'd rubbed the sleep from their eyes.

Dolfuse crawled. It was all she could do as light and blood rained all around her. Screams and the *thwump, thwump, thwump* of each cannon or laser only spurned her to move faster before the entire floor crumbled below her.

She made it to her cell, staying on her stomach. Rebecca lay on the floor, pinning a pillow around the back of her head. A cannon flashed behind them, briefly revealing a tearsoaked face, a child's face, terrified beyond belief. Dolfuse knew just how she felt.

"Follow me," Dolfuse said.

Rebecca shook her head. "I don't wanna die!"

"You don't have to." Dolfuse grabbed her arm. "But we do have to get out of here."

Rebecca released the pillow and latched onto the back of Dolfuse's uniform. The senator grabbed the shippee's rifle and crawled from the cell. They'd stay low. Senator or not, she wore the same white as every other shippee, and *Sweet Kiss* wouldn't give her time to explain the situation.

The attack ship maneuvered in a circle, picking off assailing shippees with smaller guns, and decimating entire cells with its cannons. Dolfuse made it to the stairs and had to crawl over more than a few dead shippees before she and Rebecca reached the top. When Dolfuse looked back, *Sweet Kiss* fired a cannon and blew apart the stairs behind them. That's when Dolfuse and the shippee ran.

"Where are we going?" Rebecca asked.

"To end this."

CHAPTER 46

Sarah didn't know welding huge pieces of Oubliette glass and metal could be so fun. One of the OC women had offered to teach her how to do it if Sarah agreed to finish the job. Sarah didn't wield the laser perfectly, but she got used to the task easily enough.

"Am I doing this right?" she asked the OC member, who hadn't offered her name.

"Yep. Try to stay a little tighter, but that's it."

Sarah smiled behind the golden sparks issuing from her laser cutter. The other woman walked off and Sarah thanked her without looking up from her work. She really wanted to show Dipity and Hurley Girly what she'd learned, but Lena had sent them off to refill more canisters with energy from the Core. They'd been gone a while, and nobody said anything more about where Farica and her dwellers might be hiding.

Ava was too busy with the sensor to bother with anything else, and Lena seemed to have the weight of the city on her shoulders. Sarah guessed it made sense to feel that way. It was Lena's plan, and if something went wrong, everyone would blame her.

The lights went out.

Dwellers screamed and something clanged against the floor amidst shuffling boots. Sarah quit welding so she wouldn't mistakenly burn the wrong thing.

"Everyone calm down," Lena shouted. "We're still breathing, so that means we still have the Veil. Is everyone OK?"

Rory cried from where Sarah had last seen her, on a couch with Shamika, where they'd both fallen asleep.

"I'm just fine, Horror," Shamika said. "What the hell did you do?"

Lena didn't answer, and Sarah wondered how much restraint it took.

"Pao," Lena said, and lit a laser cutter to illuminate her face. "Come with me to the roof."

Sarah lit her own cutter and moved past crouching dwellers and overturned shelves until she reached Lena. They eased their way to the roof and came out to a blackened city. No lights whatsoever shone from any building, including Grindy's warehouse. Even the street looked darker, devoid of its glow.

"What happened?" Sarah looked all around.

"More than likely? Dipity and Hurley Girly took more power than they should have. But they've already been gone longer than I thought they'd be. So it was them, or…"

"Or what?"

Lena stopped talking. It gave Sarah the chance to hear the distant sound of a yelling crowd. It grew in volume by the second, but she could see nothing. Then, from a building a few blocks up, the unmistakable glow of orange cyclone wheels rounded the corner. A fathomless, dark mass followed behind it.

"Oh shit," Lena said.

"Is that what I think it is?" Sarah asked. Of course it was what she thought it was, it was plain as night. Sarah just wished she was dreaming and that Lena would slap her back into a safer reality. No such luck.

"I knew we should have found them sooner," Lena sighed.

"What are we going to do?"

"The only thing we can do. Fight blind."

CHAPTER 47

"Stop here," Rebecca said. She pushed Dolfuse behind a corner as shipper guards rushed by.

Dolfuse tried to steady her breath so the guards wouldn't hear, but it didn't matter. The sounds of death covered their steps, and the guards were too focused on finally getting to shoot something.

"How much farther?" Dolfuse asked after the guards had gone.

"We're almost to the manna room. Come on."

Since escaping the holding cells minutes before, they'd run until they heard someone coming, and hid until the danger passed. Once the young girl had calmed down, Dolfuse realized that Rebecca knew the ins and outs of the port, having marched down every corridor for the last year. And she knew where to hide if any guards – or invading soldiers – approached. She stopped again just beside a hallway when Dolfuse heard a familiar voice.

"Focus everyone on that attack ship," Beckles told a group of guards, who quickly hurried to join the battle.

Dolfuse dared a peek around the corner and spotted Beckles entering the manna room in a night robe.

How classy.

"Let's go." Dolfuse crept toward the manna room.

"No," Rebecca said. "If we go the other way, we can take the main stairs and get out of here."

"This is the best shot we have of not getting blown to hell – if we capture the warden," she held up the rifle, "then they'll be more apt to keep their fingers off the trigger. Now let's go get that bitch."

Beckles was standing halfway across the top railing when Dolfuse entered the manna room. The blades in the vats of goo spun like manic propellers below.

Whipping around, Beckles drew a handgun from her robe and fired. Rebecca pulled Dolfuse out of the way, but not before the shot ripped through the senator's hand, sending the rifle from Dolfuse's grip and into one of the giant manna vats. The shippee dragged Dolfuse across to the opposite railing, dodging another of the warden's shots, and coming to a rest at a large air conditioning unit.

"She shot me!" Dolfuse stared at the burned hole in her hand. No blood – the laser had seared the blood vessels. Pain, though, plenty of that radiated from the wound.

"Shippee!" Beckles yelled. Her steps clanged closer. "You should have stayed and fought like you promised me."

Rebecca tightened her lips and hung her head.

Beckles stepped closer. "This is all your fault, Senator Dolfuse."

"Senator?" Rebecca whispered.

Dolfuse would have retorted, but it was trouble enough gritting her teeth against the pain in her hand.

Leaning close to Dolfuse's ear, Rebecca whispered. "When I tell you, run and catch her from behind."

"What?"

"I'm going to distract her."

"No, wait." Dolfuse tried to grab her, but Rebecca bolted toward the other side.

"Now!" Rebecca yelled.

Dolfuse swallowed and clambered behind the air unit.

Keeping low, Rebecca zigzagged every few steps. Beckles took the bait and fired, but the shots whizzed over the shippee's head, or into the railing at her feet.

It was now or never. Dolfuse rounded the railing, keeping her injured hand tucked to her chest. The night robe flapped behind Beckles as she stomped after Rebecca with an itchy trigger finger.

Dolfuse charged when Beckles aimed another shot at the fleeing shippee. But the warden heard her coming and turned the gun around. Dolfuse had already leapt, knocking her head into Beckles' gun hand and wrapping her arms around her waist.

The two women landed on their backs and the gun slid across the railing. Dolfuse went for it, but Beckles pulled her back by the ankle. Pain ripped across Dolfuse's scalp when the warden took a tight grip on her hair, yanking back and slamming her head into the grated floor. Dolfuse squeezed her eyes shut, as if it would protect her. The metal greeted her nose and forehead with bludgeons and cuts – again and again and again.

When Beckles stopped to catch her breath, Dolfuse rolled over and kicked both feet into the warden's chest. The blow sent Beckles onto her back, but instead of pouncing on her, Dolfuse used the break to get to her feet. It gave Beckles enough time to do the same.

The warden swung a left hook, a surprise even in the

heat of the fight. Dolfuse cowered back, barely dodging the punch. Beckles grinned. Sweat covered her face, and one of her eyelids twitched. With her big arms, Beckles grabbed Dolfuse into a bear hug, and suddenly the senator could no longer breathe.

"I'm going to crush you till your eyes pop out." Beckles grit her teeth. Her arms tensed – as if they could have tightened any more. "And I'm going to watch it happen slowly."

Dolfuse's daddy always used to say she should never resort to using her fists when she could use her head instead. And so she did. A quick bend backward and Dolfuse used the momentum to slam her head into Beckles' nose, sending more pain through her own damaged face. The warden let go of her and staggered back, clutching the gushing wound. Beckles moved so fast, so preoccupied with her bleeding nose, she didn't see the railing behind her.

Hitting the metal, Beckles flipped over the side, screaming only once before sinking into a manna vat. When Dolfuse looked over the railing, the concoction had turned a bright shade of red. Dolfuse turned away, nearly vomiting.

"You OK, Linda?" Rebecca trotted over. "Did you let the warden escape?"

Dolfuse shook her head and thumbed behind her, toward the vats. "She thought she was God. I guess now she's the body and blood of Christ."

"Oh, gross." Rebecca stuck her tongue out, grimacing and showing her age. "What a way to go."

A hundred boots beat against the metal railing. Dolfuse didn't have to look up to know which side was coming toward them. Who else could it have been?

The senator got to her knees and raised both arms into the air, nodding for Rebecca to do the same. The UCNA soldiers met them with laser rifles aimed at their heads.

One with more bars on his shoulder than the others stepped forward. "Face down on the ground."

"Don't shoot." Dolfuse obeyed the soldier's command, placing her face against the railing, sucking in air from the stinging cuts across her skin. "I'm a continental senator."

They'd given Dolfuse a sandwich, just a slice of bologna between two pieces of bread, but it might as well have been a twelve course meal at a reservation-only establishment. She never again wanted to eat that terrible manna, let alone look at it. It all probably tasted like blood and guts now anyway.

She waited in Beckles' office alone, with soldiers guarding the door outside. They'd sworn she wasn't a prisoner, but she couldn't leave and they had to guard her. What else would they have called it, then?

The soldiers hadn't told her where they'd taken Rebecca. Although Dolfuse let them know repeatedly the girl had been the only reason she was still alive, and should be rewarded for it, the soldiers had simply nodded and carried the shippee off. Fear had coated Rebecca's face when they separated them, but Dolfuse assured her everything would be alright, and that she would keep her promise to protect her.

Finishing her sandwich and craving something to drink, Dolfuse leaned back in her chair and felt the dog tags around her neck shift. She lifted them out of her shirt and stared at her own name pressed into the metal.

Bobby would get a laugh out of this. The rest hadn't been so funny.

Dolfuse used to wonder how people who'd gone through something traumatic would be able to make it to another day without losing their minds. But she thought she might have figured it out, as she sat there, rubbing her dog tags between her fingers. It all felt like a dream, happening so fast, she couldn't replay it all through her head – the parts she didn't mind going over again, anyway. That's how victims moved on, they treated the experience as a dream. Dreams could be forgotten, for the most part, and the comfort came from knowing they weren't real.

She ripped the dog tags from her neck and looked at them one last time. A light shone on Beckles' magnetic frame that held so many of the same tiny dog tags, representing so many shippees who'd suffered more than she had. Those women couldn't wake up like she could. They were lost to the nightmare. And those left behind on Earth got to be the ones to forget.

Dolfuse cast the dog tags into the air. The magnet picked them up and sucked them into the countless horde. Just another addition.

The doors opened and Vice President Martin strolled in with a concerned face and open arms. "Linda, you poor dear!"

Dolfuse accepted her embrace, thankful to have any sort of contact besides a gun to the face.

"I rushed here as soon as they told me." Martin rubbed at tears that she obviously hadn't shed.

"They wouldn't let me leave."

"Yes. I'm sorry. With this whole mess, we couldn't let

anyone go until we knew who was who, and where to put them back."

Dolfuse returned to the chair. "There was a girl with me. She helped me escape."

"Oh?"

"I promised her that she wouldn't be shipped."

Martin puffed her cheeks. "Oh. Linda, I... You shouldn't go around making promises like that."

"I'm a politician. It's what we're best at. But I intend to honor it."

"That can't happen." Martin shook her head.

"Why in hell not?" Dolfuse sat up. "I'm a continental senator, you're the vice president. I'm not saying we can help all of these shippees, but this one, Rebecca's her name, she helped me when I was stuck in this torture chamber, and I demand that kindness be repaid."

"It's not like a crime that can be pardoned." Martin laughed a little under her breath. "Her mother made a choice to ship her. If we let this girl go, we'd be interfering with her mother's legal rights."

"What about the girl's rights?" A bad taste coated Dolfuse's tongue. She hated Martin with every molecule; she just didn't know it so completely until that moment.

Martin sat on the edge of Beckles' desk. "What rights? Goodness, Linda. What did they do to you in here? You sound like an anti-shipper."

"I'm seeing things for how they really are."

"Who would take care of her? You?"

"If there was no one else," Dolfuse nodded. "If it meant she wouldn't be forgotten."

Martin laughed again, harder this time. She flapped a

hand in the air as if dispelling a foul smell. "Anyway, she won't be getting shipped. None of them will."

Dolfuse wrinkled her brow. "What do you mean?"

"There will be no more shipments to Oubliette." Martin smiled proudly. "As of 0800 hours, Executive Order KMA-4 went into effect. You know, we initially thought of cutting off the manna supply and waiting for the inevitable. But the freeze and the EA weren't going to let up, so we had to take a more aggressive approach."

Dolfuse leapt to her feet. "What are you talking about? And there's a baby on Oubliette."

"Yes, I know."

"We have to bring her back."

"That video from the drone." Martin whistled. "I have to tell you, Linda, that's what did it for President Griffin. I was afraid she wasn't a hundred percent behind the plan, but when she saw all those ruffians killing each other, she couldn't sign the order quick enough."

"What did Griffin sign? What is KMA-4?" Dolfuse said through clenched teeth, trying to refrain from strangling the vice president.

Martin hopped off the desk. "Come with me, Linda, and I'll show you."

Trudging once again through the unbearably porcelain halls of the shipping port, Dolfuse wondered if she'd ever leave, or if she'd died and gone to White Hell. "What are you going to do with the shippees?"

"Military is going to pick and choose from them. Give some a second chance." Martin tucked her hands into her pants pockets.

"And the rest?"

Martin quickened her pace and Dolfuse saw that they neared the control room. She thought of Spangler. He wouldn't be in there like he'd always been before. Dolfuse tried to brace herself for the blow, remembering he was gone, but it still pierced her to see that her best friend's chair stood empty, that only soldiers stuffed the room.

It only got worse when she saw what waited on the other side of the glass in the launch room. Plumes of frozen air rolled off its sharp black wings, prepping it for space travel. Soldiers hustled at each side, ensuring the laser cannons' power cells were topped off. *Sweet Kiss*, the airship that had killed most of the shippees in the holding cells, was ready to wipe out Oubliette.

"You've got to be kidding." Dolfuse pressed her head against the glass, feeling the coolness against her flushed skin.

Martin stood beside her. "Oubliette will soon be free of heathens on motorcycles and anyone else that doesn't belong. We can escape war and the ice, and live there quite comfortably. Where's the joke in that?"

"The baby!" Squeezing her fists, ignoring the pain in her wrapped hand, Dolfuse fumed through her nose.

Martin put her mouth to Dolfuse's ear and whispered, "Your daughter."

Dolfuse's gut twisted, her breath staggered.

"I lost a lot of money on that Australian deal you screwed me out of. But I meant what I said about you getting things done. Killing you would have been a waste. And you played your part better than I'd hoped. I don't know who you thought you were kidding, wearing black all the time and trying to hide that swollen belly. When I got wind of you giving your child away, under the table... well, I have a way of getting others to do things for me. Did you see her on that drone video? Your baby?"

Dolfuse wanted to scream, to strangle the life from Martin. But her voice only croaked, her hands only squeezed themselves.

Martin took a step back and smiled. "You're going to go home, Senator Dolfuse. You've had a terrible time here, and I'm sure you're more than ready to get out of that awful uniform. Forget about the shippees and what's happening on Oubliette. After a day or two of rest, you can come back to work and stand with us, looking toward the future. Right?"

Nothing remained inside Dolfuse. Exhaustion clawed at her whole body and threatened to pull her under forever. What could she do? How could she fight? She wouldn't win. Even if she managed to kill Martin where she stood, the soldiers would rip her apart with a barrage of lasers. And they'd still send the airship to wipe out Oubliette. Her poor daughter. Poor Rebecca. Spangler. She'd let them all down. She had no choice.

Dolfuse turned to leave the control room. Her legs felt like concrete.

Eric Lundgate entered with a lollipop inside his cheek, tipping his hat to Dolfuse. "Where do I sit?" he asked Martin.

The vice president pointed to Spangler's chair.

Bastards, Dolfuse thought. *Every last one of you.*

"A shame you're going to miss it, though," Martin said as Dolfuse neared the door. "It's going to be a hell of a show."

CHAPTER 48

Lena should have known Ava was going to hate the plan.

"What do you mean 'no cyclones'?" Ava had been pissed since Lena dragged her from Grindy's office. "We'll ride out there, shoot Farica and the rest all to hell, and be back in time to finish this suicide mission we're on."

Lena stomped toward the back door, clicking off her rang's safety. "They might have Dipity and Hurley Girly. Those two should have already been back from the Core ten times by now. Besides, they won't see us if we're not riding the bikes."

"Horror's right." Shamika jogged to catch up, her gang following behind her. "With it dark like this, we can get the jump on them."

"Whatever," Ava said.

Lena opened the door to let Sarah and Ava through. When Shamika came up Lena said, "I told you we should have taken care of Farica sooner."

"Well, we will now, won't we?" Shamika smiled and patted Lena on the shoulder.

"Where's Rory?"

"I told Shakes to stay behind and watch her. It'll be fine, as long as she don't shake the baby." Clicking her tongue,

Shamika pushed through the door.

Lena sighed and followed. Was she the only one taking this seriously? Hopefully the dwellers holed up in Grindy's would help look after the baby.

Both the Daughters and the OC were waiting for Lena in the alley.

Shamika whistled. "OK, we need three of you on rooftops."

"I'll go," Sarah said.

"Good deal," Lena said.

Two of Shamika's gang agreed to go also.

"Three different buildings. One of you on top of Grindy's. Another on that one." Lena directed her rang light to a taller, darkened structure. "And that one over there. Don't shoot until we do. And for fuck's sake hurry. We don't have much time for you to vadge around."

Sarah and one of the OC ran toward the taller buildings while the last ran back inside.

"The rest of us should ambush them from the alley up the street," Shamika said.

The shouts of the approaching mob bounced across the glass city.

Lena didn't have time to give a shit about who led this circus or who thought up the best idea. "Works for me. Let's go."

She ran into the street.

Rolling closer, Farica's orange wheels glowed like Halloween, a thousand serial killers roaring for blood behind them.

Shit! Lena dove into the nearest alley and Ava scrambled right behind, landing on top of her. They got to their feet and looked behind them. Shamika stood in the middle of the street, hunched down, weaving from one side of the glass to the other until she dashed toward Lena and Ava, just before the glow of Farica's wheels could catch her.

"We got to hit 'em now!" Shamika whispered as she inched along the building, rang at the ready.

"Not yet," Lena said. "We have to make sure Dipity and Hurley Girly aren't with them."

Over the slow hum of Farica's cyclone and the vicious chants of her dwellers, a new, distant sound buzzed through the dark – other cyclones, maybe half a klick away.

Damn it to fuck!

"I'm shooting!" Shamika raised her rang, but stopped when she heard the unseen cyclones coming. "What is that?"

Lena sighed. "My best and brightest on their way back from the Core."

"We better shoot then," Shamika said, "before they get caught between the crossfire."

Lena reached out for Ava, touching her arm to make sure she was there.

"Let's do it," Ava said.

Lena nodded, even though Ava couldn't see. "Got to die sometime, right?"

"Right."

Lena tapped Shamika's shoulder. "On my count."

Farica's cyclone rolled into view.

"One." Lena raised her rang.

Shamika did the same.

"Two."

Ava stepped to her side.

"Thr–"

The Veil crackled, and for a second Lena held her breath, afraid the damn thing had finally given out and the last bit of air she'd ever breathe lay tucked inside her cheeks. But then she looked up. A flying craft broke through the Veil. Not a shipping box. Its massive size – like a jumbo jet – and jagged angles made that clear.

On the street, the ravenous dwellers stopped their rabble, and Lena didn't hear any more humming from distant cyclones, just Farica's around the corner. Blue-white light rained from the bottom of the craft as it descended, the light morphing into a dazzling wall. The radiance moved back and forth, over the buildings, almost like it was...

"... scanning," Lena whispered. She awoke from her awe and yelled, "Run!"

Ava and Shamika looked at her, the craft's beam illuminating their faces.

Lena staggered back, farther into the alley, keeping her eyes on the flying machine. When the light touched the top of a building – one of the buildings where either Sarah or the OC woman waited – the aircraft spun around with a high-pitched *whoom*. It opened fire immediately, blasting multiple laser shots into the structure. The top of the building crumbled in glass and fire, plummeting toward the mass of Amazon dwellers who screamed and ran back the way they came.

Farica's cyclone flew past the alley, dodging the falling debris as it crushed the dwellers around her. She pushed on, rolling over anyone in her way, screaming with more anger and fear than Lena had ever seen. Above, the craft shifted, nosing down toward the fleeing crowd. This time it shot a large ball of energy that exploded as soon as it hit the closest dweller. The blast sent a dozen of them into the air, limbs connected or not. Burning blood filled the street.

"We got to get to the cyclones." Lena ran the other way.

Ava chugged behind her. "We need to shoot that thing down."

"We can't draw attention to ourselves."

"My sheila was on that building." Shamika hollered at Lena's side.

"Could have been... mine. Ain't shit we can do now." God, she hoped it wasn't Sarah.

They stopped at the next street over. The aircraft busied itself with the Amazon dwellers – for the moment – so they backtracked to Grindy's, leaving the screams and explosions far behind, but not far enough.

Hurley Girly and Dipity held laser cutters for light when Lena entered the shop.

Dipity swallowed. "Lena, I don't know what happened–"

"Did Pao make it back yet?" Lena couldn't catch her breath, sweating. Fuck sweat, she'd nearly pissed herself.

"No," Dipity said. "Wasn't she with you?"

Hurley Girly thinned her eyes. "What's going on out there?"

"You dumbasses didn't see it?" Shamika marched straight for Rory. She took the baby in her arms and looked around for a cup of manna juice.

"We came back as soon as we could," Dipity said. "The Core messed up. We took too much power."

"No shit," Shamika said.

Hurley Girly huffed. "There was nothing wrong with the Core, Dipity. You just fucked up."

"I'll cut you, bitch!" Dipity lunged for Hurley Girly.

"Shut up!" Lena screamed. "Every last damn fucking one of you. None of this matters. There's some kind of aircraft flying around out there, blowing dwellers to hell. Didn't you hear it?"

Dipity lowered her laser cutter. "I thought I heard something."

"And Pao's out there." Lena wiped her eyes of stinging sweat. "We have to go get her if she's alive. But I'm not planning on getting my ass blown off just standing around here bitching about dumb shit. Let's ride."

"Where we going to go, Horror?" Shamika rubbed Rory's back.

Lena combed a tangle of hair over her ear. "I'm going to take down that ship."

"Have fun with that," Shamika said.

"I'm with you, Horror." Ava grabbed a laser cutter and popped her neck.

"You'd be the smartest person in this city," Lena said. "'Cause whether we like it or not, that fucking thing is here to kill every sheila on Oubliette. Shamika, you saw that scanning thing it can do. It'll hunt us down, level buildings to make sure there ain't one of us left."

Grindy's shop shook as something big flew over.

"You dwellers need to stay here until it's safe," Lena yelled for all of them to hear.

A few rebellious dwellers took the opportunity to run out of the front door. They were halfway across the street when a white light coated them like a UFO tractor beam from the movies. The aircraft turned them into jelly with a swift *ratta tat tat* of laser fire.

"Let's get the fuck out of here!" Hurley Girly bolted for

the back door.

Damn. Lena spit.

Every gang member rushed after Hurley Girly and jumped onto their cyclone. Lena sped down the street, away from where she guessed the aircraft flew. The others followed, probably thinking Lena had a plan. The truth was she didn't know what the hell she was doing, and all her instincts told her to race for the Core, stay underground, and die a slow death.

She looked back at Shamika following just behind. Rory lay tucked in her jacket, just like Lena had done. Was Shamika stupid? She'd get the baby killed.

Lena slowed, riding at Shamika's side. She couldn't believe she was going to say it. "Go to the Core."

"What? Why?" Shamika curled her lips as if she tasted something rotten.

"Rory will be safe down there till this is over. Take care of her."

"I don't need you–"

Electric sputtering, like a robot trying to speak, blurted behind them. The aircraft shone its light onto the cavalcade as it sped closer.

"Go!" Lena shouted.

Shamika broke off from the group as the street split into two ramps. Rory and her guardian went down to street level, the others went up.

Laser blasts flew down, biting into the glass street and barely missing the remaining cyclones. Several shots ripped into a slick black building to their right. The entire structure seemed to groan in pain as it fell, jagged shards raining down with it. The building collapsed onto the overpass and the glass beneath Lena shifted like an earthquake.

Lena tried not to look back, but she did anyway. The first thing she saw was Ava's face – pale and understandably scared shitless. Behind Ava and the others, the overpass crumbled under the weight of the fallen building.

The aircraft was on top of them.

"Someone try to shoot it!" one of the OC shouted.

Lena locked in her cyclone's speed and raised her rang, but Hurley Girly beat her to it. The aircraft dodged the ball of blue light, thrown off its chase for a few seconds.

A sheila screamed.

The glass street shattered under one of the OC. She fought to stabilize her bike, but the cracks slowed her down too much, preventing the wheels from grabbing any solid surface. She plummeted from the overpass as it fell to pieces below her.

"Speed up!" Lena yelled. She pushed her handles as far forward as they would go.

The end of the overpass lay feet away, but it might as well have been miles. Lena felt the glass under her cyclone crack and heave. She kept seeing herself and the others falling to their deaths, Sarah blown from the top of that building, falling just like them.

But with a few bumps, they made it to the end of the ramp and the crumbling glass didn't follow. When Lena returned her eyes to the street ahead, the aircraft banked in from around a building. Lena threw up the signal to split, and all of the Daughters jerked to opposite sides of the street. Some of the OC were smart enough to follow the pattern, but the one at the end hadn't caught on in time. The aircraft fired its cannon, scattering the OC woman and her cyclone all over the street.

The group took the next left.

Lena shouted, "This isn't working."

"What do we do?" Ava asked.

Lena shook her head. A shit idea came to her. Any other time, she would have tossed it away and gone back to the drawing board. But the terrible, awful idea was all she had. "I'll lead it away."

"Why would it follow?"

"They've seen my face before." Lena tensed her lips, a taste like battery acid covering her tongue. "Lead these sheilas to the Core. It won't be able to follow you down there. Do it. Next corner."

Ava raised her fist and yelled, "On me."

The acrid taste told Lena the aircraft had caught up to them. With a sweep of her arm, she shot her rang, clipping the airship's wing. Ava zoomed to the right as Lena continued down the street, alone. The aircraft wobbled in midair, but righted itself, only a smoky wing tip to show for Lena's effort. For a second, Lena thought it would follow the others – more targets equaling more fun – but it straightened and hurried after the lone leader of the Daughters of Forgotten Light. Lena's rang shot returned and she readied herself for what came next.

You can do it. Just like last time. It won't see it coming.

She steadied her breath, heard the energy building up somewhere inside the aircraft, felt the prickle of the hairs on the back of her neck.

Now!

She jerked back a handlebar and leaned forward with all her weight. She'd done it before, damned if she couldn't do it again. She flipped into the air, even higher than she had the night she crushed the Amazon. The aircraft fired continuously, following her with its shots, lasers punching into the building she sailed toward.

Reengaging all of her cyclone's wheels, Lena hit the side of the building, and if she'd closed her eyes she never would have believed it, but those bright blue, wonderful wheels were climbing the side of the building, straight up. The whole city seemed upside down, but she just kept riding. Hovering below, the airship rose to meet her, and she would have chanced a shot if she wasn't so scared of falling off the building.

Gravity shifted, and straight up suddenly turned into straight ahead as the damaged building plunged like a fainting giant. The aircraft flew at Lena's side, yawing to put her in its sights.

Gotta die sometime.

Lena turned, heading for the aircraft, locking her handles as far as they'd go. She put a foot onto her cyclone's seat, holding out her arms for balance, but also aiming her rang at one of the airship's engines. The cyclone soared off the building and she jumped, splayed out as if she could fly. Flicking her wrist, she fired. The shot hit the engine, spraying sparks and metal at Lena's face. She closed her eyes and opened her hands, hoping like hell they'd find what they were looking for.

The wing caught her. Her cyclone fell toward the street, but she held on. Spinning and shooting, the aircraft veered chaotically over the smaller dweller units, twisting Lena's insides and sending her cheeks flapping. She heard explosions and other sounds of destruction. Burning mechanical innards scattered with every spark from the gash she'd put into the aircraft's engine. Lena didn't want to look anywhere but at the piece of black metal in front of her, although she tried once.

The view was a whirling mess.

Slowing and rocking from side to side, the aircraft fought to escape the stall. A rooftop lay below, close enough she might not die from the fall, but far enough to scare Lena into holding on longer.

Fuck. She let go.

Lena landed on the balls of her feet and rolled as much as she could to absorb the fall. The airship nosed down and didn't stop until it flipped over, crashing somewhere below. Standing, she winced. Her left ankle ached from the fall, and it took more than a couple limping steps to peer over the roof's edge at the wrecked aircraft. A few pieces had been knocked off, but it remained in decent condition – better than she felt – but didn't move either.

The familiar hum of Lena's rang zipped toward her and she raised her arm for the blue ball to zip back into her gun. For a moment she stood there, hoping fruitlessly for a cool breeze to blow against her face. Some wishes just don't come true.

Soon, though. She stared down at the wrecked air machine. *Soon.*

Now for the hard part: climbing the stairs down to the street.

CHAPTER 49

When the spaceship broke through the Veil, Sarah didn't waste time deciding what it was or why it had come. Oubliette had taught her not to trust anyone or anything, so she ran from the roof and hid inside the stairwell. Later, when the screams and explosions and smell of powdered glass came, she knew her gut feeling had been right.

What the hell was going on out there? Sarah didn't believe in little green men, but she did subscribe to the unrepentant, destructive nature of the human race. Someone on Earth had sent that thing to kill them all. When the building shook around her, it became a choice between staying inside and letting the glass and metal crush her, or chancing an escape onto the street.

Her cyclone.

Lena had told them not to use the bikes, but circumstances had gone to shit, the board wiped clean. It was up to her to save her own ass, and Grindy's shop lay at least five blocks away. Before leaving the building, she waited with a hand against the cool glass of the front door. She listened – nothing. A quick breath did nothing for her nerves, but she poked her head out. The dwellers, Farica, and the spaceship, all were gone. At the end of the street, rubble cascaded in small rivulets of dust and glass – the building the OC woman had been on.

That could have been me.

Sarah crept onto the street, moving toward the ruined building, but stopped herself before taking another step. No one lay under all that broken glass and metal, no one alive anyway. No screams for help came, no hands clawing from under the debris. And having no time or reason to search for the dead, Sarah ran the other way.

Her footsteps echoed across the glass as if she was taking a hammer to it. If it had been an Earth street she snuck down, the noises of hovercars and newspapers blowing in the wind would have unsettled her. But on Oubliette it was the quiet. She'd have given her left hand for a noise, any noise, to help cover up her long trek. As if granting her wish, a low, sharp chirping echoed over the buildings. It was the spaceship.

Sarah hurried her steps.

Grindy's shop lay dark and desolate, just the way they'd left it. Her cyclone stood alone in the back lot. The others must have had the same idea and sped the hell away as fast as they could. She wondered how long they'd waited for her – probably not one millisecond. She couldn't blame them.

Inside Grindy's shop, something fell. Had the gangs even considered taking the dwellers with them? Those poor women probably still waited inside. Well, Sarah wasn't going to let them die like a bunch of useless animals.

When she entered, the door closed behind and sealed her in the sticky hot dark of the shop. She opened her mouth to call out, but thought better of it, having seen more than a few old horror movies, and Oubliette was just one giant haunted house.

Something solid and soft squished under her boot, burbling wet. Every muscle tensed. She refused to reach down and see what she'd stepped on. She stood still.

On second thought, to hell with the dwellers, she'd get on her cyclone and ride to the Core or back to the ganghouse.

A laser cutter sparked on in the middle of the shop, revealing a shadowy shape standing a few feet away. Sarah gasped, and the shadow turned toward her. It held the cutter against a dismembered head, burning the skin off the cheek and chin. Sarah staggered back as the laser cutter rose, illuminating a terrible face. Farica grinned with blood-smeared lips, before the laser light went out.

A pipe fell to Sarah's right. Something shattered to her left. Farica's demented laughter moved in behind her, and Sarah broke into a run. She'd only taken a few strides when her foot hit another of the solid squishy things on the ground. Before Sarah knew she'd fallen, her face hit the floor. She rolled away with her rang raised. Blood and burning flesh thickened the air, the smell of dwellers dead and left behind.

Something pinged on the floor to her right, so she swung her rang that way, giving Farica an opening from the left. The cannibal jumped on her, straddling Sarah's chest and wrestling against her arms. Sarah fought to get her rang close enough to blow away her attacker's head, but the Amazon was too strong.

Farica whipped her rang hard against Sarah's face before removing the Daughter's rang and tossing it across the shop floor. Head spinning, all Sarah's strength left her arms, and she was half-conscious enough to feel the Amazon throw her onto a table.

"You know," Farica said, "if I had my way, we'd all live happily ever after. You know what 'Farica' means? 'Tranquil leader.' Hey, that would have been nice, huh? Right?"

Sarah moved to roll off the table, but Farica slugged her in the stomach. Her breathy "Stop" became garbled with painful coughs.

"But it's all coming to an end. I see what my real meaning is now. You can't have tranquility when no one gets with the goddamn program. I'm going to help move this ending along. Like that old book, *Ten Little Indians*? Yeah," Farica nodded, as if her own words were revealing an epiphany. "I'm the final girl." Farica lowered the laser cutter.

The heat radiated against Sarah's legs, and her quickening pulse sharpened her senses. There was no fucking way she would lay down and die.

She wrapped her legs around Farica and took the cannibal with her off the table. The laser cutter bit at the sides of her legs, and Sarah screamed, but she refused to release her squeeze. Farica dropped the laser cutter in an effort to claw at Sarah's eyes. The cutter spun when it hit the floor, splashing light against the walls and shelves in a dizzying kaleidoscope.

With two fists, Farica hammered Sarah's privates. A rang to the face had been more welcome, and Sarah loosened her legs enough for Farica to crawl away. The Amazon stood and lifted her rang. Swiping a leg, Sarah tripped Farica, and as the Amazon fell, her rang fired. Orange light flew through Sarah's left hand, splattering her face with the flesh and blood that didn't get burned up in the ball of energy.

Only a charred stump remained.

Sarah screamed, scrambling to her feet. The rang shot returned to its owner and Sarah closed in behind it. Pain swelled throughout every muscle and tendon, but she distilled every bit of it into a rage that painted her vision red, even in the darkness.

Brass knuckles slipping onto her remaining hand, Sarah pounded into Farica's face, kicked her in the side. Farica pushed her away, fighting against Sarah's grappling, sending fresh jolts of pain through Sarah's tender stump, but also fueling her anger. Sarah grabbed hold of the Amazon's rang and ripped it from her forearm. By the time Sarah put it on and fired, Farica had thrown a shelf behind her and bolted through the back door.

Sarah chased the Amazon outside in time to see Farica's image dwindling in the distance, speeding away on Sarah's cyclone.

Another of Sarah's screams ripped across the darkened Oubliette streets, against what few buildings remained standing. Sarah didn't care if the spaceship heard her and hunted her down. What else did she have to lose?

Sarah guarded her injured arm as she limped down the street, one rang strapped on and the other hanging from her teeth. Even with no weather on Oubliette, she couldn't shake the chill that enveloped her, no matter how much she hugged herself, or moved her legs.

Black char coated the stump where her left hand used to be. At least she hadn't bled to death. And she didn't care if she had to stay behind to get it done when the others returned to Earth, but she was going to find that miserable shit, Farica, and rip her apart, one digit and limb at a time. Maybe Sarah would make Farica eat her own flesh, since she was so keen on devouring other people.

Sarah lowered her eyes to the street and kept walking – she didn't know where. Maybe, if she was honest with herself, she hoped that spaceship would find her and put her out of her misery. And if she was lucky, she would find Farica right before that.

Instead, she found Lena.

The glass street had started glowing again, fading in from nothing, and then glimmering brighter than it had before. It startled Sarah so much, she jumped and looked all around. The buildings lit up and just around the corner, Lena stood beside the wreck of the spaceship.

"Lena!" The extra rang dropped from Sarah's mouth as she yelled. She ran, tears streaming from her eyes.

Lena aimed her rang, but dropped it when she saw Sarah. The younger Daughter wrapped her arms around her gang's head and cried into her jacket; every hurt she thought she could swallow and forget flooded out of her eyes and mouth.

"Glad you're OK." Lena patted her back.

Sarah broke from the embrace. "I'm far from OK. I've been through hell!"

"I thought you were on that building this fucking thing blew up." She nodded toward the spaceship. "What happened?"

"Farica." Sarah shook her head, choking back tears so she could tell Lena. "She tried to kill me, she did this!" She held up her burned stump.

"Oh shit," Lena whispered, frowning at the missing hand.

"And she rode off with my cyclone."

Lena crossed her arms and spit. "Would you like some good news?"

"What could possibly be good about any of this?" Sarah could have hit her.

"This airship had a sensor to get through the Veil. And guess what?" She held up a thin green card, black electronic veins coursing through it. "It's still intact."

A humming buzz zoomed from around the corner. Sarah turned and raised her rang in unison with Lena.

Taylor pulled up to the curb. "Hot damn, Horror! You killed it!"

"I thought you'd be dead." Sarah lowered her rang, steadying her breath.

"I'm not that stupid," Taylor said. "I got the hell out of there as soon as all of you went after Farica. This is Grindy's old bike."

Lena pocketed the Veil sensor and stepped forward. "Got room on there for three?"

CHAPTER 50

"That's one gnarly wound." Hurley Girly inspected Sarah's nub with the curiosity of a sideshow patron.

Sarah pulled her arm away, tucking it behind the other. "Yeah, well, the bitch who did it is going to get ten times worse."

"You've gotten to be one cold mother." Hurley Girly whistled and jogged around to the other side of the airship.

Only six dwellers had survived the night, most of them under the Daughters' protection, and rather than wasting time and energy hauling the airship back to Grindy's, Taylor suggested they work on it where it lay.

"We've already built some good replacement parts," Taylor had said, "and the thing is in damn fine condition considering Lena dropped it off a rooftop."

Taylor asked Sarah if she'd like to go back with her to Grindy's and grab some extra tools.

"I don't know what good I'd be," Sarah said.

"I think I might have something to make you damn useful. Just be sure to grab that extra rang you took off Farica."

The rules said no dwellers got to use rangs, but if Taylor wanted some protection from here on out, Sarah wasn't

304

going to deny her. Everything had changed. But Taylor didn't ask for the rang until they'd gone inside Grindy's.

Rot and blood suffocated Sarah when they entered. The return of the lights revealed several dismembered and torn bodies strewn across the shop floor, one even hanging from a shelf.

"Don't pay any attention to that," Taylor said. "Unless it's going to help you focus on our goal."

"Why'd you bring me back here?" Sarah covered her mouth with the collar of her jacket. "I've only got one hand."

Taylor held out her palm. "Give me your other rang."

Like hell. "Why? I already gave you the other one." Sarah had been taken advantage of before, and while she didn't think Taylor was her enemy, trust had become scarcer than the dwindling manna supply.

"I'd been working on a prototype. Damned thing wouldn't fit over anyone's hand. But, I think it'd fit you just fine."

"What's wrong with the rang I've got?" Pain in the stump throbbed to the beat of Sarah's pulse.

Taylor smiled. "This is much different. Trust and follow, little bird."

Behind Grindy's shop, Taylor had built herself what amounted to a small shed where she'd tinker in her spare time. All kinds of weird, oblong "tools" covered its inner walls. Sarah couldn't tell what any of them did. Here something that resembled a laser cutter with two orifices pointed opposite directions, there something that looked like a nail gun.

"Let me see that other rang," Taylor said.

Sarah handed it over, after a moment of hesitation.

Taylor went to a manna box desk and bent over to dig through a pile of junk that clinked and shuffled against her searching hands. "Here it is." She turned back with a smooth, coneshaped piece of metal with straps dangling from the back end.

"What the hell is that?"

"Your new rang." Taylor set the conical piece on the desk and slammed one of the old rangs against the edge.

"Hey!" Sarah stepped forward, ready to strangle the dweller.

"This won't take but a minute." Taylor pulled away cracked pieces of the rang and removed a small cylinder that glowed blue. With the same amount of indifference, she broke open the other rang and took out its luminous orange core.

"Is that what powers the rangs?"

"You betcha. And I need both to supply your new gun."

Sarah bit her lip as she watched Taylor open one side of the new rang and slide in the orange cylinder, sealing it back with a *pop* of the metal. On the other side, she placed the blue core.

"And that's that." Taylor handed over the conical rang.

"How do I wear it?"

"Well," Taylor straightened out the straps. "You'll have to wear it on your left arm. Seeing how the truce is over, it shouldn't mean a damn if you're a southpaw or not, yeah?"

Sarah nodded.

"Anyway, I'll slip it over your... nub and secure it with the straps. Oh, one more thing. Keep your arm bent. You shoot it by straightening out your arm, pressing your..."

"Just call it a fucking stump or nub."

"OK," Taylor cleared her throat. "Your stump presses the inner sensor and fires."

A terrible thought sprang to Sarah's mind. "Wait. How am I going to be able to ride a cyclone?"

"You won't." Taylor looked away. "But to be honest, you wouldn't have been able to anyway. Not without a hand."

Tears burned in Sarah's eyes, at the back of her throat. Farica had robbed her of more than she'd previously thought.

But she fought back the weakness, and focused on her hate. "So what's so special about this rang?"

"In theory," Taylor grinned wide, showing grimy teeth, "multiple shots at once."

"Like a machine gun?"

Taylor shrugged. "Don't know. Like I said, it's a prototype and never got tested or used. Now's as good a time as any to try it out. Shoot out that way and give it a go."

"Maybe later." Sarah shook her head. "Besides, there's only one person I want to use it on. This thing better not blow up in my face."

Taylor made a *pfft* with her lips. "I'm confident in my design. It's not like you have a hand to lose now anyway."

Sarah punched her in the arm.

"Gah! Sorry. Come on, we've got a ship to fly off this shithole."

CHAPTER 51

Dolfuse turned to the other side of her bed and grabbed her phone, smearing her face against the drool-soaked pillow. Without even bothering to see who'd messaged her, she threw the phone across the room, where it smashed against the wall into a few dozen oblong pieces. She did manage to take another swig of bourbon before rolling over and closing her eyes.

If she could stay in bed for the next month or so, letting the memory of her daughter and Spangler and Oubliette disappear from her memory, she might be fine. It was what she used to do as a little girl when she was upset. All you had to do was close your eyes and wait for sleep as the tears dripped down your cheek, and when you woke up everything changed back to normal.

Back then she didn't have the assistance of Maker's Mark.

The phone *ding* had jarred her from an otherwise peaceful depression and she couldn't close her eyes again. The sun had shifted and the light straining through the blinds was now more orange than yellow, and at a sharper angle. She couldn't tell if it was morning or evening. Not that it mattered. She'd either shuffle to the kitchen to have bourbon and egg substitute or bourbon and bagged chowder. Her legs had gotten more stubbly than ever from lack of shaving. At least a week's worth. Damn, had she been cooped up that long?

She sat up, swinging her legs over the edge of the bed. No matter how much she drank, the pain in her injured hand wouldn't numb, and she'd been too lazy to change the bandage.

By now, the flying monster machine was blowing all of Oubliette to smithereens, her daughter included. At least the baby wasn't alone. She had a new mother before the end – Lorna was it? No, Lena. Horowitz. Someone else who knew what it meant to be discarded and forgotten.

It would be very enlightening to speak to someone who'd shipped their daughter. Someone who knew what it was like. Of course, Dolfuse had an acquaintance or two who'd shipped, one of her staff had even done it. But she couldn't let them see her so disheveled, what her mother would have called a "hot mess". No, she needed to see someone right then who didn't know her. Even better if that somebody could give insight into who Lena Horowitz was.

This new development gave her enough of a spark to hobble over to her computer, feeling her drunk even heavier on two feet. She searched for "Horowitz" and "Mechanicsville" – the town Spangler said Lena was from.

As Spangler had told her, Renee Horowitz, according to her search engine, lived at 45 Blinkley Circle, just under two hours away.

I can drive that.

But she was drunk! Not just a little buzzed.

The world is ending and I'm worried about a DUI?

To hell with the police. If they tried to pull her over, she'd just hit the gas pedal to the floor. And for God's sake, she was still a UCNA senator! She'd have their badges if they gave her any grief.

Anyway, she'd take the back roads as best she could.

Having made up her mind, she slid on a pair of tennis shoes, pulled a jacket over her rumpled, sad kitten shirt, and scooped up her keys as she strode out the door.

A horn blared behind Dolfuse as she swerved back into her own lane. "Damn old biddy!" she yelled to no one but the dash. It had been the third time she'd nearly wrecked, but for a drunken two and a half hour drive, that could be considered admirable.

Her car's navigation system, in a husky masculine voice, told her to take her next right. The destination would be at the end of the drive. When she turned, the road became gravel, her hover engines sending dust all around her car. An abundance of dark trees lined the path, and the moon was the only other illumination besides her headlights. Dolfuse considered that it might have been a terrible idea to come out here.

But since I'm nearly there…

Maybe Renee Horowitz would have a couple aspirin for her throbbing head.

"You have arrived." The navigation voice smoldered through her speakers. It reminded her of Bobby's voice.

The two-story house had that old-time country feel, one she recognized from growing up in the boonies of Arkansas. A large porch extended from the front where a swing hung from two chains. Darkness stared from the windows and a smoothed-out square of dirt by the eastern corner sat empty.

It was just as well no one was home. The time it had taken Dolfuse to drive from outside Washington had been used to ensure she stayed between the mayo and the mustard. She hadn't thought of what she'd say to Renee Horowitz.

Dolfuse ran her hand along the porch railing as she stepped onto the old gray wood. The cushioned porch swing felt cool against her back when she sat. With her heels, she rocked back and forth, looking at the peeling paint above her, at the black trees surrounding the Horowitz estate like an army of titans.

She imagined Lena sitting there on summer nights, reading or just listening to the crickets chirp. Then one day it had all been taken away. Why?

A pair of headlights cut around the bend, the car rolling on rubber wheels. Dolfuse forgot some people preferred the antique look. The vehicle cruised down the gravel like a golden whale, crunching the rocks in that wonderful sound Dolfuse hadn't heard since her daddy's farm. The shadowy figure in the driver's seat had short, frizzy hair, but that was all she could see.

The driver parked behind Dolfuse's hover car, but left the engine running. After opening the door, she stood, keeping one foot inside the car. "Can I help you?"

"You can if you're Renee Horowitz." Dolfuse got off the porch swing.

"Who are you?"

"I'm Senator Linda Dolfuse."

"OK?" The older woman shrugged.

"I'm here on matters of continental security."

"That makes no sense. I work at a small-town bank, and you're slurring your words. Let's cut the bullshit."

Dolfuse leaned against a porch post. "I would have used a lie if it would have worked. But I'm telling you the truth."

"You drunk?"

"I've had a rough couple of days."

Renee stepped out of the car and crossed her arms. Her ash gray hair had been cut close to the scalp and the wrinkles at the corners of her eyes looked more like the effects of stress than age. "What's this really about?"

"Your daughter, Lena."

With a swallow and stretch of her neck, Renee leaned in through her car's window and shut the engine off. She kept her head down as she passed Dolfuse, heading for the front door. "I don't have a daughter."

She disappeared inside the house, leaving the door wide open for Dolfuse. The senator's head spun, like she'd just gotten off a Tilt-a-Whirl, but she staggered in, one foot at a time.

"You look like you could use some coffee," Renee said in the dark. A light clicked on to Dolfuse's left, revealing a kitchen with yellow cabinets.

"And some aspirin if you have it."

"Ibuprofen, but it works the same damn way." Renee pointed to a chair at a small dining table. "Go ahead and have a seat. You can take a rest before you head back to... Washington?"

Dolfuse nodded.

"Yeah, well, I'm sorry you came all the way out here for nothing."

Dolfuse began to think Renee Horowitz was right. But nothing ever got done if you gave up. Drunk or not. Depressed or not. Dolfuse would get... something out of this.

"All I've got is an ancient can of Folgers." Renee clanged from cupboard to cabinet. Soon she sat down and stared at Dolfuse as the coffee maker burbled its brew.

"I know you have a daughter," Dolfuse said. "I've seen her."

Renee looked away, tensed her jaw. "Does the government make a habit of coming out at all hours of the night to rub people's faces in their own mistakes?"

"You regret shipping her?"

The hollow kitchen light glistened against fresh tears in the corners of Renee Horowitz's eyes. Her lip trembled. "Every day of my life."

"Why did you do it?"

Renee rubbed away the tears and cleared her throat. "What does this have to do with continental security? What do you mean you've seen my daughter?"

"We sent a drone to see what goes on," Dolfuse pointed to the sky, "up there. It's... not what we expected."

"Is she OK?"

"This is why I needed to talk to someone, someone I didn't know." Dolfuse couldn't help smile a little, anticipation with sadness weighing it down. "I wanted to see if I was the only one."

"The only what?"

"The only one who couldn't forget their daughter. They may have been sent away, but something else filled the void they left. The most unbearable agony I've ever felt. And the problem is that feeling comes and goes, always there, always ready to drag you under."

Renee stared at Dolfuse for a moment, then stood. "Come with me. I want to show you something."

Dolfuse followed her upstairs, Renee turning on the lights as they went. At the end of the hall they stopped at a room.

Renee nodded to the door. "In there."

Dolfuse opened it, feeling for a light switch along the wall. With a flick, the ceiling light, along with a dazzling string of pink Christmas bulbs curled into spirals on the wall, illuminated a pink canopy bed and purple rugs. Posters of bands and pop singers popular a decade before hung in random, nonsymmetrical spots. It was a girl's room, a teenage girl. One who was deeply loved, by the look of the décor.

So curious, Dolfuse thought. *Why do we discard what we love?*

Renee stood in the doorway, almost as if she was afraid to enter. "She was always such a good girl. Never stayed out too late. Did her homework. Went to temple every week. When she told me she was pregnant…"

Dolfuse moved to sit on the bed.

"Don't!"

The senator stopped and turned back to Renee. "Pregnant? What happened to her baby?"

"I had it taken care of."

"Did she want to keep it?"

Renee couldn't hold back the tears any longer. "Of course she did. She wanted to marry that boy. I couldn't allow it. I was so blinded by my rage and disappointment; I filed the shipping papers in a blur. It felt like someone else was controlling my feet to walk into that clinic, someone else moving my hand to sign my daughter away."

"But it wasn't."

Renee shook her head. "No. It was me. It was my choice. And I forgot the rule about choices."

"What's that?"

"They have consequences."

Oh, hell, did Dolfuse ever know that. She thought she'd come for answers, but being honest with herself she really came for something to make her feel better about everything that had happened. She only felt worse.

"Is Lena–" A sound from outside cut Renee off, something distant but speeding closer. A robotic chirping. "What is that?"

An icy chill ran down Dolfuse's spine. That sound. She knew what it was. She'd heard it before.

CHAPTER 52

"Alright, ladies." Lena wiped sweat from her face after they'd loaded the last cyclone into the airship. "Clean your gash and get ready to dash. We're flying the fuck out of here."

The OC, the Daughters of Forgotten Light, Taylor, and the few remaining dwellers all crammed into the cabin, leaving no room for comfort or discretion, all keeping quiet and staring anywhere but at each other as they shifted elbows and knees.

This is going to be a long trip, Lena thought.

Ava had volunteered to fly and shuffled her way to the cockpit.

"You sure she won't wreck this thing?" Shamika zipped Rory into her jacket and gave the baby a finger to suckle. It didn't ease the baby's crying.

Lena returned Shamika's smug face. "Ava can drive anything that moves. Isn't that right, Ava?"

"I'm also good at shooting mouthy bitches, too." Ava shouted over the warming engines.

They all laughed, even the OC sheilas, although not as loudly. The airship jerked off the ground, and Lena grabbed the side of the cabin to keep from falling out.

Damn it, Ava!

"Just working the kinks out," Ava said.

Lena looked at her fellow travelers before shutting the door. "I hope everybody has what they need."

"Oh shit. Hold up." Shamika hopped from the airship and stomped off toward a pile of manna boxes.

If it had just been Shamika, Lena would have told Ava to fly off. But the OC leader had Rory with her, and that gave the others no choice but to wait.

"Where the hell are you going?" Lena shouted.

Shamika searched the manna boxes with one hand, while keeping Rory close with the other. "Manna juice for the trip." She retrieved a small glass bottle and held it up as she ran back. "Got it."

The airship was three or four feet off the ground, Ava trying to keep it low enough for Shamika and the baby. Lena grasped Shamika's hands and pulled, but before Shamika could get a foothold into the cabin, a humming filled the air over the airship engines, and Ava cursed from the cockpit.

A blue-wheeled cyclone, unwomanned, zoomed toward the airship at a hundred miles an hour.

Ava lifted the craft, veering hard to the right, now twenty feet off the ground. The women behind Lena slammed into her and each other, but Lena kept hold of Shamika as she dangled from the airship door. Rory cried from Shamika's jacket, somehow knowing, like the rest of them, something had gone terribly wrong.

Shamika shrieked and a crop of red, spiky hair appeared at her feet. Farica, face caked in dried blood, gripped Shamika's legs with both hands. The Amazon screamed laughter as they soared farther up, up over Grindy's, up over the streets and the dweller buildings, picking up speed. They were nearing the Sludge River.

The OC women shouted for Lena to do something as Shamika kicked at Farica's head. Shamika's kicking yanked Lena forward onto her stomach. It took half of Horror's strength just to stay inside the cabin.

"Rory!" Lena yelled, her hair flapping into her mouth.

Tears spattered off Shamika's cheeks, and Lena couldn't tell if it was from fear or pain, or the false Oubliette air rushing over her eyes.

"She's going to fall." Lena reached for the screaming baby girl.

Don't you dare take her from me again.

Rory lifted a single, peachy palm from the jacket. Below, Farica grabbed higher onto Shamika's backside. The head OC stared at Lena, a million thoughts in that look. There was no way she could be that selfish, no way she would hold onto her pride with the same stubbornness she held the child.

"Take her," Shamika said.

Quickly, Lena released one of Shamika's hands and grabbed Rory, tucking the baby into the crook of her free arm. The kid didn't stop crying, but she felt so soft in Lena's arm, safe, where she belonged.

They flew at least a hundred feet over the dark, winding curves of the Sludge. Farica pulled at Shamika's shoulder. From behind, Sarah Pao pushed her way through and stretched an arm over Lena's head.

Before Lena could tell her to get back, she said, "Eat this," and fired.

It would have been bad enough if only one rang shot had

flown from the gun, but what blasted into Farica's head, torso, and across the Oubliette skyline, was a spectacular assortment of lights Lena hadn't witnessed since her last Fourth of July on Earth. Energy balls of blue and orange scattered like shooting stars, and Farica fell in a heaping mess of spraying blood and splintered bone.

The airship shifted violently, causing Lena and Rory to slip farther out of the open door. Shamika raised her arm and extended the middle finger, grinning like crazy. Only then did Lena see the sharp piece of glass protruding from Shamika's back, blood dripping down her jacket and flicking into the air. Before Lena could reach out for Shamika's other hand, the head OC let go. Falling through the sky, Shamika never wavered from her smile until she sank into the Sludge far below.

The airship sped on and up, gaining altitude by the second. Neither Farica nor Shamika rose to the Sludge's surface.

"You killed her," one of the OC screamed, grabbing Sarah by the hair.

Sarah twisted and snapped her attacker's arm in two moves, then kicked her square in the ass to send her out of the airship.

Lena shifted Rory to her other arm and raised her rang at the last two OC members. "I hope you sheilas aren't going to start shit."

They shook their heads and backed up as best they could.

"Good." Lena lowered her rang. "Shamika let go of my hand to save Rory. I never thought she was like that, but you knew her better than I did. In any case, welcome to the Daughters of Forgotten Light."

Lena shut the door. It became instantly stuffy inside the cabin, and too damn quiet.

"How do I get one of those badass rangs?" Hurley Girly pointed to Sarah.

Taylor harrumphed. "If you'd lost a hand first, you might have gotten that one."

Sarah eyed Lena from her periphery. Something passed between them, not altogether unpleasant, but not the fuzzy warmth of best friends. An understanding.

Remember your promise, Pao, Lena thought.

"The Veil is right ahead of us," Ava called from the cockpit.

"What'll happen if the sensor doesn't work?" Sarah asked.

"Don't jinx this." Dipity beat fingers against her lips.

Lena kissed Rory and patted her backside. *Fuck. Shamika had the last of the manna juice.* "We're about to find out one way or the other."

Pushing her way to the front, Lena looked through the cockpit's glass. She didn't see it at first, but slowly the green of the Veil grew brighter.

"Would you look at that," Hurley Girly whispered.

No one moved. Lena didn't think anyone even breathed. Ava pulled at the throttle and the force pushed every sheila a little farther back. Static erupted across the airship, then stars, billions of them. Ahead waited the Hole.

We're doing it. We did it!

The others hooted and clapped, but Lena knew there was still a long way to go.

"Um." Hurley Girly cleared her throat. "I was just wondering. What are we going to do when we get there. Back to Earth I mean."

"I tell you what we need to do," Dipity said. "We need to take out anyone who would try to send us back, or worse."

They all nodded their heads.

Sarah reached over and tickled Rory's chin. "We're going to need an overwhelming force to do that."

"Hey," Hurley Girly said, "We've got cyclones and rangs, plus your machine gun blaster."

"We'll need more than that," Lena said.

"Where are we going to get more than this?" Hurley Girly waved a hand at the women and machines around them.

"The shipper port," said Sarah.

The others groaned.

One of the dwellers said, "Fuck that" under her breath.

"The warden was keeping a lot of shippees behind," Sarah said. "There were tons before I got shipped. If they haven't killed them all, that's who we need on our side."

"Right into the lion's den," Ava said, pointing at buttons and controls for her own benefit. "I like it."

Lena nodded. "I'm with Sarah on this." She looked at the Hole, its gigantic white curves becoming larger the closer they flew. Lights and circuits lined the inside of the circle, something she never saw from Oubliette's surface. "But I hope you ladies don't mind if we make a quick stop before visiting our old friends at the shipping port. There's someone else I need to see."

CHAPTER 53

Dolfuse stumbled backwards. That sound. *Sweet Kiss*. Martin and the others were done wiping out Oubliette and they'd tracked her down somehow – taking care of any loose ends. Dolfuse would be damned if she'd let them get her.

She grabbed Renee Horowitz by the shoulders. "You have somewhere we can hide?"

"I... um..." She looked around her daughter's room. "The shed."

"You mean outside?"

"What the hell is going on?"

Dolfuse headed for the stairs. She could answer questions later, when she was certain a laser cannon wasn't going to blow her apart. "We need to go. Now!"

The shed outside couldn't keep out a draft much less the peering light of the attack ship, but approaching death didn't give them anywhere else. By the time Renee shut them into the musty, cramped space of the Horowitz shed, dazzling white light stabbed through the multiple holes and cracks in the walls and roof.

"What kind of trouble did you bring here?" Renee crouched, leaning against the wall.

Dolfuse put a finger to the older woman's lips.

Dust and pieces of gravel racked the shed. Dolfuse had to squeeze her eyes to shut out more of the stinging dirt. When *Sweet Kiss's* engines faded and the wind died down, a voice shouted as a thudding of footsteps ran across the yard, into the house. Glass shattered and objects fell to the ground. Dolfuse saw only shadows.

"They're destroying my house!" Renee whispered.

Dolfuse put her hand over Renee's mouth, staring right into the woman's eyes, hoping she got the damn message – that if she didn't keep her mouth shut, they'd find them and kill them as sure as Europe was a popsicle.

The soldiers rushed out of the house.

One of them shouted, "Check over there."

They were coming toward the shed. Dolfuse's stomach twisted into frozen knots as she clawed at the door, searching for a way to lock it.

"It only locks from the outside." Renee slumped to the ground, making no attempt to keep her voice down.

The door swung open, allowing blinding light into the shed. Dolfuse held up a hand to keep it off her face.

"Get them out of there," one of them said.

This is it, Dolfuse thought. *This is my punishment for everything I've done.*

They put her on her knees, outside on the gravel.

Renee grunted as she fell beside the senator. "Lena?"

Dolfuse squinted against the light. A group of women and girls stood in front of them, some wearing strange leather jackets and aiming hunks of metal from their forearms.

Oh, shit.

"My Lena!" Renee rose to her feet. "You're back."

One with blue hair shoved Renee to the ground.

"I've got this." Lena, Dolfuse recognized, stepped to the front, bending over her mother. "Don't talk to me like I've been on vacation."

The others stood silent.

Renee cried, lifting her hands toward Lena. "I'm so sorry for what I did."

"Where's my daughter?" Dolfuse searched their arms for her baby, but none of them held her. "My baby?"

"I don't know who you are," a big woman said, "but I'd shut the hell up."

"You can come live with me again." Renee wasn't going to let up. She seriously thought Lena would forgive her.

Lena crossed her arms. "What did you always say about how Adam had to toil in the fields? That it was his labor, his duty. And Eve suffered in childbirth? How that was her field?"

Renee had nothing to say to that. The tears came steadily and her hands shook as she cupped them and brought them to her mouth, as if praying.

Say one for me too, Dolfuse thought.

"Well, Mom," Lena raised her fist in line with her mother, "you planted me in Oubliette, and I've returned to give you the fruits of your labor."

Dolfuse flinched. She'd seen what came from the guns strapped to these women's arms. But Lena hesitated, her arm shaking as she bit her lip, wrenched her face. She screamed and stomped before firing her weapon toward the Horowitz house. The blazing ball of blue light flew through the second story window, through the roof, and then continued on toward the stars until it vanished from sight. Dropping her right arm, Lena used the other to punch

Renee square in her temple. The older woman flopped to the ground and didn't move.

"Where the fuck did your rang go?" a pigtailed blonde asked.

Lena spit. "Give me one of the extras. Taylor, why didn't my rang bounce back?"

"Oubliette glass," an older woman said. "It's a hell of a thing. Here on Earth, consider yourselves armed with only one shot. Well, except for Pao."

"Please don't kill me." Dolfuse covered her head, looking away from the psychotic women, but her sight found the unconscious but breathing lump of Renee Horowitz. Dolfuse looked back to her captors, determining she couldn't stop whatever they were about to do.

An Asian woman with blue hair pushed from behind the group. She held a baby girl in her arms.

Dolfuse pointed. "That's my baby."

Lena turned to look at Dolfuse's daughter, and then back to her. "Who are you?"

"I'm Senator Linda Dolfuse. I can help you. I saw you, on a drone feed. You're Lena Horowitz."

Lena immediately aimed her newly strapped gun at Dolfuse. The others raised their arms in sync.

"Please." Dolfuse fought to keep her voice from shaking, but it was beyond her control.

Lena stepped closer, sneering. "You sent that airship to wipe us out."

"No." Dolfuse shook her head. "I didn't know anything about that until they were already launching the thing. I tried to stop them. The vice president was behind every step of it. She used me like a pawn."

"She's full of shit, Lena," said another woman with Down syndrome and peanut-colored hair.

"That's my daughter she's holding over there." Dolfuse nodded toward the blonde. "Why would I want her to die? I didn't send the attack ship."

Lena scrunched her brow. "How can I trust anyone who'd ship their daughter? A baby, especially. Someone like that must be one cold bitch."

"I didn't." Dolfuse snapped. "It was the vice president. I thought the baby was being adopted. Martin had her shipped to punish me."

Lena scoffed. Squatting down, she signaled for Dolfuse to come closer.

Dolfuse hesitated, thoughts of getting pummeled in the face flashing across her mind. But after a moment, she leaned in.

"I'm going to let you in on a little secret." Lena put her mouth to Dolfuse's ear. "You have to own your mistakes. See, on Oubliette we get that. We make a bad call, we have to claim it." She turned to the others with spread arms. "Ain't that right, ladies?"

They nodded and hooted agreement.

"I can help you," Dolfuse said.

Lena smiled. "You will. But you won't get your baby back, if that's what you're thinking. Just be glad I don't feel like killing you."

Dolfuse nodded, her headache returning with a vengeance.

"For now," Lena added.

Dolfuse swallowed and looked around at the others, who laughed like it was a party.

Lena pointed to the house. "Let's grab some food from inside. See if there's any milk for Rory, too."

Rory, Dolfuse thought. *My baby's name is Rory.*

"Grab and go," Lena shouted to the women as they ran for the house. "We need to get to the shipper port before they figure out we brought back their airship." She turned to Dolfuse. "And you're going to help us."

CHAPTER 54

As they flew toward Washington Sarah kept her eyes on the senator, or the black woman who claimed to be a senator. Lena had been too quick to believe the woman, but at least they had their rangs trained on her and that was a tough thing to do in the cramped space of the airship.

Dolfuse stared at Rory as the baby drank some of the powdered milk they'd found in the cupboard. "They were controlling this ship with an ansible program," the senator said. "They might be able to take over again, see what you're doing."

"Not without this they won't." Ava threw back a chunk of wires and circuits that rolled to the tip of Dolfuse's shoe.

The senator shrugged, satisfied.

"What's the best way in?" Lena continued feeding Rory, eyeing Dolfuse like a murder suspect. "The most covert."

"Honestly?" Dolfuse said. "Probably returning to the launch room. I reason, if you go in that way, they'll think the airship returned back to where they launched it, autonomously."

"What's with you and your big words?" Hurley Girly asked.

Sarah laughed. "She means, if we don't go blowing shit

up on our way in they'll think it flew back by itself."

"Could work," Dipity said.

Lena shook her head. "I don't know."

"It's the best shot you have." Dolfuse rubbed her face like she was trying to wake herself from a bad dream. "Land anywhere else, or, as the blue-haired one said–"

"My name is Sarah."

Dolfuse smiled curtly. "If you go in guns blazing, they'll blow us from the sky before you can do... whatever it is you're planning on doing."

"That settles that, then." Lena leaned toward Ava in the cockpit. "You remember where the launch room is?"

"Unfortunately," Ava said.

A few minutes farther and the shipper port gleamed like a fallen star on the horizon. Spotlights surrounded it, the beams weaving throughout the sky.

"What's with all the lights?" Ava said. "I never remember it looking like a Hollywood premiere."

Lena kissed Rory's head as the baby blinked sleepily. "They have their guard up. Get us some altitude and come in from above. We don't want anyone with an itchy trigger finger to get spooked."

Ava took them higher, but stayed under cloud cover.

The sudden shift sent Sarah's stomach into a whirl, so she focused on the spotlights outside to settle her stomach. Blocky shapes sat in front of the shipper port, but it wasn't until they'd flown another few miles that Sarah realized what they were. "Tanks."

Hurley Girly clicked her tongue. "This just keeps getting better and better."

"Care to shed any light on this?" Lena asked Dolfuse.

The senator shook her head. "They probably kept the tanks and soldiers here after they stormed the place."

"So you were here for that?" Lena raised an eyebrow.

Dolfuse swallowed. "Yes. But I left as soon as I was able."

"What happened?" Dipity glared at Dolfuse. "Couldn't stomach a mass genocide?"

"Warden Beckles had me thrown into the shippee population. Just like you."

Everyone stared at the senator.

Dolfuse sniffed and looked away. "I don't care if you hate me. I deserve it. But I've been paying for my sins since they scrubbed me down and shoved me into a white uniform last week. And I made a promise to a girl inside that port. If you can help me keep that promise, then we'll get along just fine. I'll do whatever I have to." She stole a glance at Rory before dropping her eyes to the floor.

Sarah still didn't trust her, but she could tell the senator wasn't lying.

"And before you say it," Dolfuse added, "I know I still haven't been through the same things you have. I couldn't stand a couple days eating that terrible manna gunk. I'd kill myself if I had to eat it for years on end."

"You can get used to just about anything," Taylor said. She'd been silent until then, looking around, studying everything as if she were seeing it for the first time.

As they approached the shipping port, steadily coasting lower toward the hole leading to the launch room, the black tanks followed the airship with their long barrels while the spotlights continued their pacing. It reminded Sarah of an old movie about air raids in a war a long time ago.

"I can't believe they're not firing." Sarah stared down the

dark hole of a tank gun.

"They underestimate you," Dolfuse said. "Arrogance. They couldn't imagine any of you could fly this ship back here. To them, you're just shippees, and dead on Oubliette."

Lena passed Rory to one of the dwellers. "You keep saying 'them' like you had nothing to do with it. Even after spending a little time in the shipping port, you said it yourself. You're *Senator* Dolfuse."

"I'm not a part of anything." Dolfuse swallowed. "Not anymore. And you can call me Linda if it makes things kosher."

Lena laughed, obviously relishing the senator's pain. "Well, I sure as shit hope you can go along with us. At least enough not to fuck things up."

Dolfuse nodded.

Ava lowered the airship into the launch hole and everything went dark. Not even a fragment of the spotlights followed them. The ship's engine hum intensified as the sound bounced off the long cylinder. Sarah tried to look out and catch any light, but only darkness looked back, and the glow of the airship controls remained the only comfort. She should have been used to it by then – the dark. But old fears died hard.

"I don't know where the hell I'm going," Ava whispered. "I'm just going straight down until I hit bottom."

"Well go slow, then," Dipity snapped.

"You're doing fine," Lena said.

They descended into a large, bright room with a glass pane set in the wall straight ahead where people in two-piece suits and street clothes stared at them. Below, soldiers rushed in from a large doorway, gawking with their heads tilted back, rifles at the ready.

It had only been a few months since Sarah had been in this place, but at the same time it could have been a million years that she'd been on Oubliette. All the better, because this was not a homecoming. This was an invasion. And damn it felt good.

"They can't see us in here, can they?" Lena cradled her rang arm.

"No," Ava said. "This windshield is tinted."

The airship touched the floor and settled. The people on the other side of the glass stared from the control room just a few feet above.

"Who are those people?" Lena slapped Dolfuse with the back of her fingers to get the senator's attention.

Dolfuse pointed. "I don't know about the others, but that man there, Eric Lundgate, he programmed this attack ship when they sent it to Oubliette."

The man wore an ugly hat and a look of concerned confusion. This was going to be fun.

"Groovy," Lena said.

"What are we going to do about the soldiers?" Hurley Girly played with one of her pigtails.

Lena smiled. "Ava, when I tell you, blast every last one of these motherfuckers with everything we have. Don't forget those idiots in the control room."

Dolfuse cowered into a heap, hands over her face, mumbling to herself. Sarah shook her head. Some people couldn't take the heat.

"On my count," Lena said. "Three…"

Sarah leaned in behind Lena to get a good view of the show.

"...Two..."

Ava caressed the controls.

"...One. Shoot!"

The entire airship vibrated from the concussive force of the lasers and cannons. Ava fired everything at the soldiers directly in front of them before shifting to fire into the control room window. Everything outside the airship turned into a blinding expanse of multicolored light. The only gap in the inferno came when Ava turned the ship in order to aim at the soldiers behind and below, who'd begun to fire in return. Their shots hit, but did nothing to the airship's exterior.

"OK, ease up." Lena gripped Ava's shoulder.

The airship lowered and cooled, the declining whine of the guns giving way to the release of held breaths within the cabin.

"Sheilas," Lena said, "our lives depend on what we do here in a few minutes. We need these shippees, and we need the manna equipment. Don't let me down."

They all nodded.

"Open the hatch," Lena said.

Ava hit a button and nodded to Sarah. "Watch yourselves out there. I don't know if I got them all."

"I need you to stay here." Lena put a hand to Ava's shoulder.

"Like hell. I'm not going to miss out on any of the fun."

"Relax. You just killed more of them alone than we might see altogether. Besides, you're the only one who can fly this thing. If shit goes down, I want to know we have a chance to get out of here."

Ava turned around in her seat, keeping her eyes forward.

She clearly wasn't happy about staying, but she wouldn't go against Lena.

The rear hatch finished lowering with a metallic *wham* against the floor.

"Senator Dolfuse," Lena said. "Stay here with the others."

"Gladly." Dolfuse folded her arms.

Lena grinned. "Don't get too comfortable. I still have use for you."

Sarah followed Lena to the edge of the ramp, scanning the immediate area with her eyes and the end of her new rang. The heat inside the gun burned a little each time she waved it one way or the other in search of soldiers, but she could tolerate it.

With a hand signal, Lena told them the area was clear. The Daughters moved out. Soldiers lay in pools of blood. Burned chunks of flesh were scattered over the floor. A piece of glass fell from the control room and shattered. When Sarah ran toward where it had dropped, a burned corpse fell from the room.

"Looks like we cleaned up nicely." Hurley Girly whistled in appreciation of the carnage.

"Let's get the cyclones out," Lena said.

Dipity scratched her head. "You sure it wouldn't be better to go on foot."

"We need to be fast," Lena said. "And I trust those wheels more than my own two legs."

CHAPTER 55

While the rest of the Daughters were killing soldiers and freeing shippees, Lena's secondincommand had taken the airship on a joyride to rid them of the tanks outside. Outside, Lena kicked the side of one tank, now a burned-out shell that looked like a smashed marshmallow after sitting in the fire too long. The other tanks looked the same. Some of the newly freed shippees stood on top of the metallic corpses. One swung from a barrel, before the heat forced her to drop to the ground.

Just like Ava to take away all my damn fun, Lena thought.

A chirping buzz came from around the shipping port, as the airship hovered in. All of the shippees quickly hid behind the tanks.

"It's OK," Lena shouted. "It's ours."

The airship settled and Dolfuse got out, holding Rory.

Lena squeezed her hands into fists and stomped toward the senator. Dolfuse had had her fucking chance, and Lena had been the only one of them to fight to protect Rory. Lena held out her hands. "Thanks for keeping her safe."

Dolfuse hesitated, long enough for Lena to consider punching her between the eyes, but with a frown she placed the baby in Lena's arms.

Ava stepped from the airship as the engines faded to a stop. "Damn. It's good to stretch my legs."

"You couldn't have waited a little bit longer?" Lena playfully punched Ava in the arm. "Or at least saved one these tanks for us?"

Taylor and the other dwellers trickled out of the airship.

Ava shrugged. "There has to be other transport around here. It was her idea anyway." She pointed to Dolfuse.

"Did you find the girl I told you about?" Dolfuse shivered against the wind.

Lena still couldn't figure the senator out. Was she with them or against them, temporarily or for good? Dolfuse probably didn't even know herself. Well, she was necessary for the moment, and that was enough for Lena. "You never told me her name."

"Rebecca," Dolfuse said. "Red hair. Freckles."

Lena gestured for a shippee to come to her. "You know a Rebecca? Ginger?"

"I've seen her a few times," the shippee said.

"She still alive?"

The shippee nodded.

"Go get her for me."

"Thank you." Dolfuse said it to Lena, but her eyes were back on Rory.

Damn it, woman. Let it go.

Something beeped inside Dolfuse's pocket. She swallowed and tried to look casual while she dug out her phone and read whatever popped on her screen.

Lena watched her with squinted eyes.

What a dumb fucking move, Horror. She should have taken away all the senator's chances of communication. Dolfuse could inform the government about the Daughters' little invasion with a quick text, and have them all blown to hell before they knew what happened. "Give me that."

"It's just my phone. A message from my husband. He's coming back from the war on a temporary visit."

She's fucking lying. Lena grinned and held out a hand. "Then let me share in your joy."

"Why don't you trust me?"

"You're a politician," Ava said. "Give her your phone."

Glancing between the two of them, and seeing she had no choice, Dolfuse slapped the phone into Lena's hand.

Lena hadn't held a cell phone in years. Technology had sped along while she wasted away on Oubliette, and the thin glass of the device felt like holding a puff of air. "Special session of Congress," Lena read. "President to address. Three hours. Mandatory." She glared at the senator, raised her rang. "I can't stand liars. Why shouldn't I just blast you dead right now?"

"I'm not going." Dolfuse shook her head as she shrank into a crouch. "I just didn't want you to get upset. That's why I lied."

"'Cause the result now is so much different?" Lena dropped her arm and again looked over the phone message. She rubbed her chin. "You know, it would be very rude and detrimental to your career not to show up for a mandatory speech. From the president no less."

Ava combed her hair behind her ears. "I've always wanted to meet the president."

"I've always wanted to fire a rang shot up her ass." Lena tossed the phone back to Dolfuse. "Well, aren't you going to ask us to tag along?"

"This isn't a plus-one kind of meeting. There'll be Secret Service crawling all over the Hill. What's the point?"

Lena placed her hands on the senator's shoulders. "I want to give the continent a message. And I want to ensure that those who've been keeping us forgotten on Oubliette get what's coming to them." She stood and looked over all the sheilas looking to her for direction –Daughters, dwellers, shippees. "And it won't be a plus one," Lena said, with her back to Dolfuse. "I'm thinking more like plus a few hundred."

CHAPTER 56

"My fellow North Americans, continental representatives. I've asked to address you about an important day in our nation's history."

Vice President Martin craved a nap like nobody's business, and President Griffin's droning voice only made the desire worse. But where Martin sat, just over Griffin's left shoulder and directly in view of the cameras and countless continental viewers, made that impossible. Still, the president spoke profoundly. It was an important day.

"Today is that day," the president continued. "I've executed my duty as your commanderinchief to end a coup concocted by the shipping port's warden, and seen fit to end the shipping program altogether." Griffin cleared her throat and sipped water from a glass. The wrinkles in her neck stretched.

Martin turned her eyes to the den of snakes watching from the congressional chamber. Some of them had their eyes closed. The more inventive ones held a finger and lowered their heads to make it look like they were reading or in deep thought. Lucky bastards.

"Evidence has also arisen that Oubliette has become a dangerous place. Given no other option, I signed an order to use appropriate force to clear the city of its refuse. Now Oubliette is ready for upstanding citizens to fill its streets, to thrive and prosper. With the support of your elected officials," Griffin smiled and waved a demonstrating hand across Congress, "we have put together a plan to begin a lottery for free passage to Oubliette."

Good job, Griff, Martin thought. The president was following her script to the letter.

Griffin had asked her why they shouldn't keep it secret. "Won't it be obvious all the people selected are… us?"

"By that time, it won't matter what they think," Martin had said.

Griffin pounded the podium for her next remark, waking a few of the sleeping congressionals from their naps. "But we will continue to fight those who would see us dead. We will never quit…"

…*until the ice has passed us over,* Martin followed along in her head.

Movement stirred on the floor. Not the head bobbing of a senator or the calm walk of a congressional page. A Secret Service woman jogged over to one of her fellow agents. They both tilted their heads like curious dogs, fingers at their earpieces. Widening their eyes as obvious concern washed across their faces, they turned and ran for the podium. Other agents joined them from dark corridors at the sides of the chamber. The president shut her mouth, taking a few steps back.

The doors at the back of the room flew open. Motorcycles riding on wheels of blazing blue light flew into the chamber, carrying women with roaring mouths and flapping hair. The carpet caught fire under the wheels, in blazing skidmarks.

No, it couldn't be. Martin dropped onto her hands and knees, crawling for cover. *They were all killed. They had no way of getting here.*

Balls of light and lasers flew throughout the room, tearing into the president and the Secret Service agents who rushed toward her. Martin kept crawling, focusing on the carpet at the edge of her fingers and not the screams and buzzing hums and laser fire filling the chamber.

"Get back to your seats, please," someone yelled, then laughed like mad.

Martin wanted to throw up, but found enough resolve until she came to two pairs of feet, one wearing dirty tennis shoes, and the other slick, black boots.

"That's her." Dolfuse, the crazy bitch. She pointed at Martin's face.

The biker psycho next to her raised a laser rifle that fired a red blast. It was the last thing Martin saw.

CHAPTER 57

Lena brushed away the brain matter that had slapped against her jacket. She had really wanted to be the one who put the president down, but she figured a vice president was good enough.

She nodded at Dolfuse. "Get out of here and take care of Rory for me. Tell Taylor I said Grindy would have been cool with it."

Dolfuse caught her breath, joy trying to bubble up.

"But I'll be back to claim her after," Lena said. "Don't think I won't."

Dolfuse ran along the side wall, away from where the Daughters of Forgotten Light were breaking a senator's neck or where Pao dispersed her berserker rang shots into a fleeing group of congresspeople. Shippees poured in and shot their rifles at anyone not wearing black jackets or white uniforms.

It was glorious.

Lena pointed to two camera operators attempting to crawl away. "Get back on those cameras if you want to live."

They jumped to their feet and ran.

Lena sighed and yelled to Hurley Girly and Sarah. "Let them go. You two think you can work a camera?"

"Yep," they said in unison.

Lena stepped over the dead as she made her way to the podium. The president's body lay sprawled atop it, so Lena tossed the corpse out of the way. The noise inside the chamber faded to whispers and the creaking of old wood. Sarah and Hurley Girly trained the cameras on Lena at the podium.

"My name is Lena Horowitz," she said into the microphone. "Some people call me Horror. What you've just seen from the comfort of your couches might indicate that's a fair nickname. But I'm standing here, telling you that I'm a product of this government's laws and hypocritical beliefs. I've lived on Oubliette for almost a decade, and I used to think I wanted to come back home. Back to Earth. I used to think I wanted a normal life." Lena swallowed. The pitcher of water to her side invited a drink, but she refused to touch anything meant for the president. "But I've changed my mind."

Sarah leaned out from behind the camera. Dipity sat on her cyclone with a confused look. The shippees glanced at each other.

"We've taken the shipping port," Lena said. "We have plenty of firepower and people to use it. We're not interested in taking over the continent or any of that bullshit. From what I gather, there won't be a continent after the ice gets past your enviroshields anyway. So, what's this all about?"

She leaned over the podium. "I'm inviting any man or woman under eighteen years of age to come along with us back to Oubliette. You have three days. We're shipping the manna equipment back to Oubliette and will be just fine for the foreseeable future. When we leave, we'll be destroying the shipping port, just so none of you get the bright idea to come after us.

"Now, to the mothers and fathers out there, those who thought they could give up their sons and daughters to fight in a losing war, to be sent away to Oubliette to be forgotten." She stared into the black pit of the camera lens, seeing her own mother behind the glass. "When the cold freezes your bones and steals your last breath, when you resort to eating each other just to stay alive one more day, when the darkness swallows all of you – we'll be there."

She pointed up. "We'll be able to come back when the ice thaws. We'll be the ones left to write the future and remember the past, but you, for what you did, to the children you didn't want, you will only be one thing: forgotten."

ACKNOWLEDGMENTS

This book is my soul baby. That might sound a little strange, so let me clarify. I think in every author's career, they write *that* book. There may, hopefully, be more of *those* books, but as of writing this, *Daughters of Forgotten Light* is that book for me. I have carried a torch for this thing in your hands for longer than some might have thought was healthy.

I'm so thankful to Angry Robot for publishing this grindhousey slab of sci-fi pulp. I couldn't think of a better place for it to be.

Thanks to Michael Underwood, who remains a big supporter of my work. He not only helped acquire *DoFL*, but he also introduced me to the comic, *Bitch Planet*, which is one of the best comparable pieces of media for it.

Marc Gascoigne, as always, has been wonderful to work with. He runs a brilliant publishing company, and his art direction is spot on. He picked the fabulously talented John Coulthart to create the cover, and I couldn't be more thrilled with the final product.

Penny Reeve is a master of publicity and always a pleasure to speak with. Plus, she deserves major points for understanding how impatient I am. Phil Jourdan is the best editor a writer could hope for. He has yet to give me a note I disagree with, and he knows just what will make a good book great.

To marvelous mustachioed robot, Nick Tyler, I give my sincerest thanks for working the proofs and being so fantastic in online promotion. If he's able to create a Transformers photo for *DoFL*, I'll be most impressed.

I want to thank my agent, Paul Stevens, from the bottom of my heart. He took a chance and signed me as his first client after reading *Daughters of Forgotten Light*. It took some time, Paul, but we did it!

Special thanks goes to Rena Rossner. *DoFL* blossomed after a short Twitter conversation with her. You never know where your ideas will come from. Laura Adams has been a huge fan of this book since reading the first draft a few years ago. She is officially a member of DOFL, and dubbed "Triple L". Michael Mammay was also an awesome beta reader, even though I started sending the manuscript out to agents before I even read his notes.

Last, but definitely not least, I want to thank you. Readers like you are why I write. What did you think of that ending!? Please contact me at my various internet locations and tell me what you thought. I love interacting with anyone who enjoys my wild imagination. Now, let's hop onto a cyclone and ride off into the starlight, along that wide open street of glass.

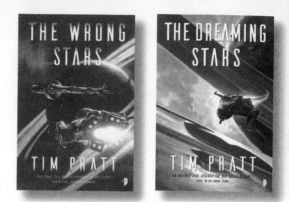

A part of the family.

twitter.com/angryrobotbooks

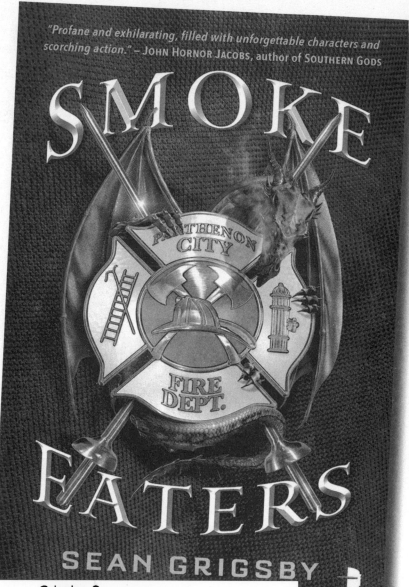

"Profane and exhilarating, filled with unforgettable characters and scorching action." – JOHN HORNOR JACOBS, author of SOUTHERN GODS

SMOKE

PANTHENON CITY

FIRE DEPT.

EATERS

SEAN GRIGSBY